AF435066

A NOVEL OF SUSPENSE AND ROMANCE

BECKY BOHAN

The Santorini Setup: A Novel of Suspense and Romance, 2022
ISBN 9798750126934

Cover, book design & author photo by Sara Yager
Edited by Cheyenne Blue

nanbec.com
E-book, 2022, available on Amazon.com

OTHER BOOKS BY BECKY BOHAN

FICTION

Sinister Paradise (1993)
Fertile Betrayal (1995)
A Light on Altered Land (2020)

NONFICTION

Living Consciously, Dying Gracefully:
A Journey with Cancer and Beyond
(co-author Nancy Manahan, 2007)

To my wife Nancy—
Master of grammar and my heart

Santorini
Oía
Therian Harbor
Thera
Airport
Anthinios Harbor
Fira Winery
Kamari
Old Quarry
Mesa Vouno
Classical Ruins
Akrotiri
Excavation Site
Perissa Beach
Blycháda Marina
0 1,5 2 3 4 km

TABLE OF CONTENTS

AUTHOR'S NOTE

The *Santorini Setup* is a re-imagining of *Sinister Paradise*, published in 1993 by Madwoman Press. In preparing that novel for an eBook edition, I realized that although the plot's skeleton was strong, the muscles could be rejuvenated, organs transplanted, and the hormones jolted. I rewrote the entire novel, transforming it into a romance/suspense blend. I added scenes, deleted others, and romanced up the relationship between Britt and Cassie. I also substantially altered some characters and added new ones, hammered out multiple plot hiccups, and set the action in current times.

Stepping once again into the Mediterranean world of Britt, Cassie, and Nicki—and this time finding the enigmatic Susan Marcello there—has been a pleasure. I hope you enjoy their company as much as I have.

PROLOGUE

"The gods will drink your blood!" Paulos Bountourakis spat.

Two thickset men, bracing against the wind, tightened their grip on his thin arms. They stood at the edge of Santorini's cliffs where the nine-kilometer-wide caldera gaped behind them. Its three volcanic islands glowed like phosphorous in the moonlight.

"Last chance, Bounty!" the interrogator shouted. "Who do you work for?"

"Myself!" Bountourakis lifted his eyes to Orion, cinching the night sky, and envisioned his soul flying toward the stars. He sought courage from his Greek birth line spanning back to the naming of the constellations themselves.

"Who knows you went to Mesa Vouno?"

"No one." Bountourakis closed his eyes. Earlier that night he had hiked up the limestone mountain on the island's eastern side to the stone carvings of a lion, dolphin, and eagle. These men had caught him photographing the airport.

The interrogator shook his head. "We saw what you were doing." He brandished Bountourakis's camera.

"I take only pictures of my village. Kamari Beach is beautiful at night, sparkling with the lights of the tavernas."

"You're lying. You were shooting our Cessna."

Bountourakis stared at the incriminating evidence. *Why didn't I listen to my wife?* Maria had said to avoid Athens and its officials with agendas and expensive suits. "What happens if you get in trouble?" she had asked. "You are an artist, not a spy." *But I left something for you. On Mesa Vouno. Between the rocks.*

"A smoke, please?" Bountourakis asked, seizing at seconds to prolong his life, grasping at the last pleasures of the world—the star-speckled sky, a jolt of nicotine.

The interrogator nodded to his companions.

The howl of the wind caught his scream as Bountourakis plummeted past the 400-meter cliffs toward the old pumice ash quarry. Behind him, moonlight glittered on the indifferent waters of the volcanic crater.

1

May

Britt Evans squeezed her wiry frame between the clutter of furniture in Athens's Syntagma Square and settled into a chair of an open-air restaurant. A waiter appeared and took her order for an Amstel beer.

Britt leaned back to examine the sights of the famous block. Amidst the noisy, relentless traffic, the leaves of the oak and ash trees shimmered in the spring breeze. Water from the fountain in the middle of the square spurted in an arc, and pockets of people gathered around small tables under green and blue canopies.

For the first time in weeks, Britt could savor a stress-free day. She was at the start of the fun part of her time away from her post in the Classics Department at the University of Minnesota. Her lectures at the American School of Classical Studies, based on her book, *The Flora and Fauna of Ancient Greece,* had gone well. Now she looked forward to an extended stay at Santorini where she would continue the research she had begun in the museums of Crete. As she stretched in contentment, the rays of the mid-afternoon sun struck her shaggy black hair and drew a fleeting halo of navy blue on her crown.

As the waiter delivered an icy beer, Britt glanced at her phone. Nicostrata Lampas, her habitually early friend, was late. *Is it because of the surprise Nicki said she's bringing?*

The women had met during Britt's graduate years at Berkeley when she was a teaching assistant in Ancient Greek Culture. Nicki, then a senior architecture student, had been waiting outside the classroom one day for her younger brother. Soon, she was waiting for Britt with a crush as big as her investment portfolio.

Britt surveyed the pedestrians, looking for Nicki. Her eyes briefly met those of a man with a closely cropped beard standing in the shade of a nearby tree. He turned to his phone with a slow, graceful motion, as though he had just glanced up from reading a text.

A familiar voice called above the traffic. Nicki approached her table, looking chic. She wore black gabardine slacks and a white linen blouse with a kerchief as black and glossy as her short hair. Tortoiseshell glasses made her appear older than her twenty-eight years.

"You look divine!" Nicki cried and kissed Britt's cheek.

The smell of a spicy perfume wafted over Britt.

Nicki stood back. "Welcome to Athens," she said. A short man in his sixties appeared by her outstretched arm. Nicki clasped his shoulder fondly. "My godfather, Mikos Zerakis."

So, this is the legendary Mikos Zerakis. Britt examined the stocky man. His gold front tooth winked in the sunlight as they took their seats. She recalled that the long-time politician and current member of the Greek Parliament had been Nicki's advocate, persuading a reluctant father to send his only daughter to America for an education.

Zerakis, dressed in a gray linen suit that perfectly matched the shading of his hair, gave Britt a penetrating look. His eyes lingered on the slight bump on Britt's nose, the remnant of an old break, then locked onto her black, intelligent eyes. "Such a beauty!" he exclaimed. He grinned at Nicki in an approval not wholly affected.

Britt accepted the compliment without comment, knowing it was untrue and only meant to flatter. She was attractive in her own way but preferred her comfortable blue capris and a white cotton top to Nicki's designer clothes.

"Are you enjoying your time in our glorious country?" he asked.

"Yes. It's wonderful to be back. But I've spent way too much time buried in classrooms and museums—although I love the Acropolis Museum."

"It is beautiful, yes?" Zerakis said with pride.

"Absolutely. But I'm looking forward to some island time and getting a nice tan." Britt patted her pale cheeks.

The three exchanged pleasantries for several minutes as they waited for the server.

"What's the issue of the day in Parliament, Mr. Zerakis?" Britt asked after he had placed an order for chilled wine.

"Terrorism." He frowned. "It is a bad situation with no solution, no end." He paused as if unsure whether to go on and risk boring this woman who meant so much to Nicki. But the politician in him prevailed. "Your president thinks we are too easy on terrorists. But this is the irony," he said, holding up a finger. "We open our doors to refugees, then we are blamed if a few smelly goats sneak through! Perhaps we close the American naval base next!" Zerakis slapped the table for emphasis. Britt's beer bottle rocked. "How would your president like that!"

"He'll have to speak for himself," Britt said, steadying the green bottle. "But military cutbacks may close it before you do."

Zerakis kept silent while the waiter set two glasses of wine on the table, then continued. "Those decisions are for the politicians, and this I will tell you," Zerakis said, "we are all a bad lot." He took a taste of the wine. "You know, our relationship with America is complex. You save us in the world war, then support the monarchy, then the junta." Zerakis shook his head. "Greece is the home of democracy. How can America support autocrats?"

As Britt poured the rest of the Amstel into her glass, she noticed the bearded man still on his phone. But this time, he was holding it at a different angle. Was he taking a picture of Britt? No, just making a call, she thought as he lifted the device to his ear. She brushed away a flash of uneasiness as he sauntered down the street, conversing.

"Listen to this," Zerakis continued. "Our governments may quibble, but this is always true: The *people* of Greece love the *people* of America." He raised his glass in a salute.

Zerakis observed Nicki's beaming face, then grinned. "But why do we go on so? The world is not all politics. There are places to see, people to love." He began to recount the strong bloodline of Nicki's family, a clan of wealthy Corinthian landowners and businessmen.

"You fly to Santorini next Tuesday?" Nicki asked Britt. Her light olive cheeks had darkened with her godfather's praise of her family.

"Yes. Bill and Anne, my hosts, are having a send-off party Monday night. Why don't you come? You, too, Mr. Zerakis."

"Santorini, eh?" Zerakis raised an eyebrow. "A man died there recently. A photographer. Part of the Akrotiri crew, I believe."

"I heard."

"Did you know him?" Zerakis asked, his eyes slicing into Britt.

"No."

"Ah," said the politician. "It is a bad business, such an accident."

"True," Britt said. Was Zerakis implying something more?

"You must be careful there. Do not tempt the fates by dancing at the edge," he said darkly.

"The edge of the cliffs?" Britt asked.

Zerakis pasted on the thin, knowing smile of an insider. "Yes, the edge of the cliffs." He shifted his sights to the gleaming white chapel on top of Mount Lycabettus in the distance. "Or perhaps of life."

2

After Zerakis departed for his parliament office, Britt and Nicki strolled through the nearby streets. They caught an occasional glimpse of the mammoth retaining walls of the Acropolis and the blue-and-white Greek flag, fluttering high above the ruins.

As they walked past the Agora, Britt asked, "How is it being back in Greece?" Nicki's face looked thinner than it had been in college, and the passing years seemed to have tempered her exuberant nature.

"Mixed. I like to be near my family, but there's much to miss about America."

"Such as?"

"Organic produce. Good hamburgers. Not having to explain why I'm not married."

"That's a question you wouldn't escape even if you were in the U.S. My mother still has hopes for me."

Nicki laughed. "I tell my mother I am married to my profession. When she sees my creations, I think she understands a little."

"I'd love to see one of your buildings."

"I have several projects now," Nicki said. "A small one near Sounion, a smaller one at Nauplion. A big one outside Milan where I've been for the past month. I'm glad I made it back to see you before you left for Santorini."

"Me, too," Britt said, giving her a smile. "I didn't realize your architectural firm was international."

"Yes. A very prestigious one. I think Mikos twisted some ears to get me hired—there's still much discrimination against women here. But it improves a little each year."

"I'm proud of you, Nicki," Britt said. "You're a great role model for young women."

"Yes, I suppose." Nicki adjusted her glasses. "In Italy, I work on eco-friendly housing with solar power. I want to do that here. Most Greek homes are the same—inefficient sugar cubes. I hope to build affordable carbon-neutral models with government backing—but the current economic crisis makes it impossible for now."

As they turned northward, Britt caught sight of a man standing under a bakery awning. His hand cupped his phone as he talked. Was that the same man she had seen in Syntagma Square? Britt couldn't be sure.

"Do you know that guy?" Britt asked, subtly pointing out the man to Nicki.

"No. Should I?"

"I think he's been watching me."

"Can you blame him? I've been watching you for years."

Britt smiled weakly. Nicki tended to tread dangerously close to old wounds. From the beginning, their friendship had been unsettled, split between the shared joy of the classics and the misery of unrequited attraction. On one hand, they had been united in appreciation of a temple's entablature, but on the other, divided by Nicki's refusal to accept that Britt could prefer another woman—or no one at all—to her. Nicki had developed an annoying habit of reminding Britt of her devotion.

"You are single now?"

"Yes. I plan to stay that way, Nicki." Britt turned away from her hopeful eyes, wishing to close that subject, as well as any thought of her being followed.

▣ ▣ ▣ ▣

Britt and Nicki continued through the narrow, winding streets of the old part of Athens, the Plaka, filled with the aroma of feta cheese, cooked lamb, and sewage. They turned onto the cobbled street of Adrianou and walked in the direction of Saint Catherine's church.

Suddenly Britt heard a strange rattling and the gunning of an engine behind them. Surprised at hearing a vehicle on a pedestrian street, Britt glanced behind her. A battered Renault pickup careened toward them.

The delivery truck's green paint had faded to olive in spots, and the bumper sloped in front of a dented chrome grill. Behind the wheel, someone with a keffiyeh wrapped around their head gripped the steering wheel with a gloved hand. The Arab headgear covered all but the eyes, which were hidden behind wraparound sunglasses.

The Renault's gears shifted. Several large cans toppled from the rear of the pickup and crashed onto the pavement.

"Jump!" Britt shouted to Nicki, tugging her up off the street. The truck's tires thudded against the curb, then gained the sidewalk. The side mirror snapped off when it hit a window ledge.

The pigeons strutting along a red tiled roof squawked at the commotion and flapped into the hazy sky. Tourists outside a souvenir shop across the way spun around to find the source of the uproar.

Britt grabbed Nicki and pushed her into a recessed doorway, flattening herself against her back. The truck whooshed past, the door handle scraping across her leather bag.

The truck sped away, showing its rear gate that fenced in a substantial payload of olive oil tins and mesh bags filled with oranges, and disappeared around the corner by the Arch of Hadrian. The street suddenly went quiet, with only the toots of distant traffic.

"Nicki!" Britt cried, as she stepped out from the doorway. "Are you okay?"

"Fine," Nicki said, tucking in her blouse, and adjusting the silver buckle on her belt. "And you?"

Britt touched the scrape on her leather bag. "All considered, fine." She swallowed hard, her throat dry. "He nearly ran us over!"

Nicki, pale and shaky, managed a tiny smile. "I got the license plate number."

"Good for you!" Britt cried, giving Nicki a pat on the shoulder. "Let's give it to the police."

"No," Nicki said. "Do nothing, say nothing, for now."

"Listen, that guy almost killed us—"

"I know." Her face hardened. "It will be taken care of. By my godfather."

3

On Monday evening, Bill and Anne MacKenzie hosted a small send-off party for Britt. Their two-bedroom apartment, nestled in the upscale Kolonaki district and decorated with Middle Eastern art and Scandinavian furniture, held a mild sprinkling of guests.

While the conversations focused primarily on departmental gossip and the growing turmoil in the Middle East, the Santorini incident threaded its disconcerting way through the evening. The few people who had attended the funeral of Paulos Bountourakis reported the Akrotiri crew had resumed its work.

Britt knew most of the people at the party, if not by name, then by sight. Judy, an art history instructor and Bill's colleague at the American School, sat in the corner. She coolly observed Britt, sitting across from her, and fiddled with a large hoop earring hanging under a sheath of purple-streaked hair. "How long will you be in Santorini?" she asked, her languid voice confirming the boredom in her expression.

Britt's eyes widened. Judy had never initiated a conversation before. "Five to six weeks," she replied.

"Good god," Judy said, without changing her tired pitch, "two days is enough to drive me insane, staring out at those black islands reeking of sulfur."

"I find it has a haunting beauty," challenged Bob Collins, a graduate student in his early thirties sitting next to Judy. He ran his hand over his brown beard and leaned forward, resting his arms on his knees. His legs spread across the width of a couch section. "Actually, it's quite an interesting place if you poke around. Lots of good folklore, like vampire bats and ghosts, things that have been overlooked because of the excavations, and, of course, the inane theory of Santorini being the lost Atlantis."

"Ghosts. Now that's appropriate," Judy said, "since the place is about as close to hell on earth as you're likely to come. Hell must suit you, though, Robert, seeing how often you visit that inferno."

Bob pointed the neck of his Beck's bottle toward Judy, then poured half its contents down his throat.

Judy clicked her tongue in disapproval.

A sudden movement across the room drew Britt's attention. She turned and saw an attractive woman in a cream-colored pantsuit coming directly toward her. A necklace of hematite beads looped down over her light-blue shell. Matching earrings dangled under shoulder-length straight black hair parted on the side and swept back.

"Hello, Professor Evans. I'm Susan Marcello—an acquaintance of Bill's." She clasped Britt's hand in a firm, authoritative shake. "May I join you?"

Without waiting for a response, Susan settled in the chair next to Britt and, in turning toward her, excluded all others from the conversation.

"Unfortunately, Bill's been too busy to introduce me," she said.

Britt cast an eye toward the host, who was entertaining a small knot of friends with a play-by-play of the discovery of Bountourakis's shattered body. A pink flush of excitement had spread across the art professor's scalp, visible through thinning reddish-blond hair.

"I've been eager to meet you, but I couldn't make any of your lectures," she continued, "so I took the liberty of asking Bill for an invitation."

"My pleasure, Ms. Marcello."

"Susan, please."

Britt examined the newcomer with the dark, intelligent eyes. She appeared to be in her late thirties or early forties given the smoothness of her glowing light-brown skin. Her no-nonsense demeanor and erect posture indicated a possible military background, or at least one of significant authority. A gold wedding band signaled her unavailable status.

"I read some of your book," she said, swooping a glass of wine from a silver tray. "Very interesting." She glanced at the doors leading to a small balcony as she took a sip. Her lipstick left a crimson smudge on the glass. "Mmm. Nice wine."

"A cabernet sauvignon from Bill's favorite winery on Crete." Britt caught a *who-is-this-outsider* look from Bob.

"There certainly were a number of plants and animals you mentioned that aren't around today," Susan said in a low, resonant voice.

"It's due primarily to deforestation," Britt explained, flipping her hair over the collar of her red silk blouse. "Crete, for instance, used to be covered with cedar forests. But over the centuries, the trees were cut. The animals were either hunted to extinction or died due to loss of their natural habitat."

Susan cleared her throat. "Would you mind if we continued this conversation outside? This air-conditioning is frigid."

"It is chilly in here." Britt glanced at Bob and Judy who sat quietly, straining to hear the conversation.

Susan rose without joggling the wine in her glass. She undid the sticky latch as easily as blinking and slid the door aside. Like a traffic cop, she crooked an arm to motion Britt along. Susan shut the door firmly behind them.

Although the balcony held a small round table and two wrought iron chairs, Britt stayed on her feet, as did Susan, who set her glass down and propped herself against the marble balustrade. Britt held onto her wine glass and leaned against the wall across from her. She glanced at the door to her right and saw Bob holding up a bottle. Britt shook her head at the offer of a refill and turned her attention to Susan.

"After what happened with deforestation," Susan said, "you'd think the Greek government would jump on the environmental bandwagon."

"Well, it has gotten serious about reducing the sulfuric acid dissolving the national monuments. No more brown clouds of pollution hanging over Athens. But, as far as I know, Greece doesn't have any coherent land-or water-use policies." A small frown tugged Britt's mouth. "I hope they don't wait until their natural resources are as eroded as their temples."

"How about appealing to the government to take better care of the country?"

"It's never crossed my mind, Susan. I'm a scholar, not a politician."

"Oh?" Susan reached for her wine glass. "I would think Mikos Zerakis would lend a friendly ear." She took a sip, her eyes fixed on Britt.

"Mikos Zerakis," Britt repeated, suddenly aware that the appearance of this woman, and her leading her to the privacy of the balcony, implied an agenda. An uneasy vibration ran up her spine.

"I understand you know him." Susan carefully returned her glass to the table.

"How on earth do you know that?" Britt demanded, then spotted her host through the windows. "Oh, Bill must have mentioned it."

"Something like that." Susan leaned forward and lightly touched her forearm. "Forgive me, Britt. I didn't mean to alarm you."

Britt withdrew her arm. "I'm annoyed, not alarmed. When it comes to privacy, the American community here is like a small town."

An easy, vibrant laugh escaped Susan.

"If you want to know something about me, ask." Britt's firmly set mouth drew her strong cheekbones into tight angles.

"Fair enough." Susan folded her arms across her chest and settled back comfortably against the balustrade. "Tell me, how do you know Zerakis?"

"First tell me who you are and what you want. I have a feeling you're here for purposes other than reader appreciation."

"Expecting reciprocity, eh?" Susan said, with a slanted smile. "I work for the U.S. Embassy."

"Are you a diplomat?"

The partial smile bloomed into a full one showing straight, even teeth. "I'm part of the diplomatic corps. A bureaucrat of the State Department would be a more accurate description."

"Is your job title 'Bureaucrat,' or do you have one that's a little more descriptive?"

"I'm a Senior Foreign Service Officer. I directly assist the Ambassador."

"How do you assist him?"

"Quite well, if my job reviews are any indication," Susan said, giving Britt a hundred watt smile now. "Actually, my specialty is government policy. For the past three months, I've been working on some environmental initiatives, none of which I'm free to discuss right now. But, as you might imagine, I found your study relevant."

"Really? In what way?" Britt took a sip of wine.

"Mainly by showing me how much this country has lost." Susan lifted her glass slowly to her mouth and enjoyed another taste of the cabernet. "Enough about me. Tell me how you came to write your book."

Britt explained how the idea had come to her while writing her dissertation when she could find so little data about plant and animal life during ancient times. Then she summarized her doctoral studies at the University of California.

A knock rattled the doors. Britt turned to see Bob Collins standing on the other side of the glass once again with a bottle of wine hoisted aloft. She slid open the door, wondering how long he had been standing there. Both she and Susan held out their glasses to be topped off. After Bob had closed the door and retreated, Susan settled against the balustrade once again. "Now, tell me more about Zerakis."

"Why do you want to know about him?"

"I'm curious."

Britt shook back her tangle of hair and breathed in the evening air. It had a touch of coolness and the scent of grilled lamb from a nearby apartment. "I met Zerakis last Friday for the first time. He's the godfather of a college friend."

"Godfather?" Susan chuckled sarcastically. "Zerakis is godfather to half the population. Some say it's the only way the old goat can get elected. The loyalty of five million godchildren is better than a vault full of PAC money." Tiny muscles on Susan's face played tug of war for a moment. "No, I shouldn't diminish the man. He's a populist, a folk hero. The Greeks love him. He must spend a small fortune on christening gifts, though."

"Maybe he buys wholesale."

"Or owns a toy store. Which godchild do you know?"

"Nicostrata Lampas."

Susan shook her head. "The name's not familiar."

"You can meet her if you like. She should be stopping by in an hour or two."

Susan glanced at her watch. "Can't stay that long. I'm pressed for time as it is."

"Tell me, what's wrong with my meeting the godfather of an old friend?"

"Nothing, if you like a beehive with a very cranky queen. Zerakis's loyalists scurry all over town like a thousand Baker Street Irregulars. They'll untie every bundle of laundry to scrape up the tiniest detail about anybody they choose."

"You mean he's into extortion?" She pictured the gray-haired man. He was a powerful, somewhat arrogant person, but a crime king?

"Not in the conventional sense. As far as I know, he doesn't squeeze people for money." Susan rolled the wine glass between her palms and studied the motion of the liquid. "But that's his genius. The nobodies he chums up with somehow blossom into somebodies after five, ten years. Middle-managers, bankers, shippers, corporate VPs—people who can feed him a steady stream of information. He's like a base-ball scout, always looking for the potential ace who can shut down the game in the ninth."

"He sounds like the consummate politician."

"You could say that. He has friends everywhere, at every level of society. He knows everything that happens in this country."

"Have you tangled with him?"

"Not personally. He's end-run some of my colleagues, though. A staffer had his marriage break up and his career nearly ruined. His wife conveniently found out he had a Greek mistress—a goddaughter, no doubt—thanks to one of Zerakis's men." Susan slid her eyes toward Britt. "Not that I approve of that sort of behavior. Anyway, just be careful of him."

"Don't worry," Britt said, finishing the last of her wine. "I don't trust Greek men much."

"What about women?"

"I'm a little better there. But just a little." Britt set her glass on the table.

"For some reason, I'm not surprised," Susan said, her eyes brightening. "Listen, Britt, I've stayed longer than I should. I'd like to see you again. What time does your plane leave tomorrow?"

"Ten-thirty."

"How about if I pick you up at seven and take you to breakfast at the embassy? I'll have you to the airport in plenty of time."

"Why do you want to meet again?"

"I have some information about Santorini you might find interesting—it could affect your stay. I prefer not to discuss it here, though."

Britt studied Susan for a moment. "I've made arrangements for a ride to the airport, but I'll see what I can do."

"I'll give you my card," Susan said, reaching into her jacket. Holding the card in her palm, she scribbled on the back. "My personal cell number," she explained as she held it out. "Until tomorrow morning?"

"I'll plan to see you then," Britt said, pocketing the card, "but don't bother to pick me up. I'll meet you at the embassy at seven."

◙ ◙ ◙ ◙

From the balcony, Britt watched Susan stride down the street, the heels of her shoes clicking against the pavement. *Attractive woman.* Britt found herself susceptible to, but wary of, Susan's charm. And, of course, that wedding band glittered on her finger. No more married women for me, Britt thought. No more *straight* women, for that matter, married or not!

"You're still here. Is everything okay?" Bob Collins stood in the doorway, trapping Britt on the balcony.

"I'm fine, thanks."

Bob toed one of the chairs with a scuffed Nike high-top, its tongue running up his shin and the shoestrings trailing to the floor. "I've been waiting all evening to get you alone." He edged his eyes up to meet Britt's gaze. "I have an enormous favor to ask." His brown eyes gleamed with what seemed like a mix of excitement and trepidation.

"Yes?"

"Since you're going down to Santorini tomorrow, I thought maybe you'd take a letter to a friend of mine. She's at the excavation."

"Can't you email her?"

"I have. But she's not answering. Or returning my calls or texts."

"Hmmm." Britt was loathe to get caught up in a lover's quarrel but found herself reaching for the letter when Bob held it out for her. She fingered the sealed envelope, white with the name "Cassie Burkhardt" scrawled in big, loose letters across the front and underlined.

"Sure," she said, cutting past Bob and making her way into the living room. "I'll deliver it."

Bob sighed, although it seemed more in sadness than relief. "Thanks a million."

As Britt looped through the guests on her way to the kitchen, she caught Bill by the sleeve and pulled him aside. "Why didn't you tell me about your friend Susan Marcello from the embassy?"

Bill's golden eyebrows jumped toward his receding hairline. "Susan Marcello?" he said, chomping an ice cube. "Never heard of her."

4

Susan Marcello settled her chin on her fists and pondered the closed Santorini folder from the Greek Criminal Investigative Services. It defied her, glaring from the center of her mahogany desk like the Middle Eastern insurrectionists she had once interrogated. A softly closing door down the hall broke the stillness of her darkened office. A corner lamp and low-intensity lights above two abstract prints provided the only illumination.

The party had been the perfect place to size up Britt Evans. She liked what she had seen: an earnest do-gooder. Intelligent and shrewd.

A faint knock sounded, followed by a deep voice saying, "Praying or thinking?"

The furrows on Susan's brow evaporated as she broke into a grin. "Neither."

Alexander Stamos from the CIS swung into a straight-backed chair directly across from her. "How did it go, my friend?" He spoke with a thick Greek accent.

"I can't say I've enchanted her," Susan said, adjusting her necklace, "but I believe I made headway. I had to talk about pollution and endangered species to do it."

Stamos roared. "A tree lover, eh?"

"I expected as much, and I'm not totally unsympathetic," Susan said. "In fact, I found her rather engaging."

Stamos fished a packet of Cleopatras from his jacket and shook out a cigarette. He caught Susan's stern look and, with a heavy breath, put it away. "You read the report, eh?" he asked.

"I did. Thanks for the translation. Not that it helped much." Susan drummed her fingers on the folder. "The police report is so cursory we can only guess what went down that night." She sighed. "I agree with you, Alex. Santorini could use an agent. We don't know what Bountourakis was doing. What a worthless message he sent you: 'Something happening here. Will check it out.'"

"One of the many problems in dealing with amateurs. They substitute melodrama for thoroughness." Stamos ran a hand over his dark glossy hair. His yellow shirt, open at the collar, revealed tufts of chest hair. Only in his middle forties, Stamos's face carried the imprint of too much smoke, sun, and worry. "He worked as a part-time photographer at the Akrotiri excavation. I suspect something is happening there."

Susan picked at the corner of the folder but didn't open it. "All right. Your people are stretched to the limit. Your art theft investigations are confined to the glamour rip-offs."

"Bah!" Stamos got up and poured himself a cup of coffee from a cart. "If it is not Van Gogh, who cares? Even Interpol is a dry teat these days. If some fool wants to stuff a Minoan crock in his shorts, take it, I say. Of course, the Ministry of Culture would say otherwise." Stamos settled back into his chair and took a fortifying sip of the strong brew. "But if that crock is full of poppy powder…then you have my interest, you see?"

"Yes, from the moment you suggested our finding another asset."

"If you can set up this girl on Santorini, we might learn what is happening without the commitment of funds or internal resources."

Susan clicked her tongue. "But another amateur."

"It is the best we can do," Stamos said. "Christ, Santorini is less than thirty square kilometers. A CIS agent mixing with the locals and Akrotiri crew, asking questions…" He drew a finger across his throat. "These crooks—if they exist—are not stupid."

"So, we're left with Britt Evans." Susan Marcello tapped a finger on the folder and pushed it aside. "The one person with a perfect—and legitimate—reason for being on the island longer than a tourist, for poking into corners, and observing the crew at the archaeological site."

"She is perfect," Stamos said.

Susan stared out the window. The murky gray night sky reflected the lights of the city. A timid whir sounded from the ventilation system. "What if she ends up like Bountourakis?"

Stamos shrugged. "If the second canary dies, our suspicions are confirmed."

"That's harsh, Alex," Susan said. "I don't want anything to happen to Britt. I like her. And besides, if she gets hurt, the State Department would have to open an official investigation. That could get awkward."

Stamos regarded his friend as he took another hit of caffeine. They had met three years ago when Susan came to Athens after spending several years in the Middle East. Liaison to the CIS was only one of her many tasks. She was bright, a clear thinker, and attractive. Probably CIA, but it was no use asking. They had liked each other immediately. "You will tell her there may be danger?"

"I'll be candid."

"If she says no to your proposition, she will keep quiet?" Stamos's thick eyebrows squeezed together.

"You saw the report on her. Integrity is her middle name."

"And the Zerakis connection?"

"At this point, I'm calling it a coincidence. He's the godfather of an old college friend. She met him for the first time the other day. If there were more to it, she wouldn't have talked to some of her colleagues at the school about meeting him."

Stamos snorted. "I wonder if anything concerning Zerakis is a coincidence. Perhaps he has already recruited her to be one of *his* informants."

Susan shook her head. "Her connection is strictly personal."

"So they all are, at the beginning. Do not be overconfident."

"I'm not. I don't have the usual screws to turn," Susan said. "She doesn't receive any government grants we could threaten to cut. She doesn't hide her sexuality, so no leverage there."

"Perhaps she would be interested in your charms?"

"Not in my job description," Susan said tersely. "And I'm sure my husband would have something to say about it."

"He might want to join in." Stamos chuckled and glanced at a framed picture of Susan and her elusive husband on the sideboard.

Susan gave a tight smile. Putting up with sexism wasn't in her job description, either. But in her position, she had to choose which hills to die on. Feminism wasn't one of them. Nor was racism, for that matter.

"Perhaps you have a more challenging sales job than you led me to believe."

"On the contrary," Susan said solemnly, yet with a sparkle in her eye. "With scholars, their passion is their greatest strength *and* their greatest weakness."

5

"The truck was stolen from a merchant in Omonia Square," Nicki reported when she had Britt alone.

The *William Tell Overture* galloped through the MacKenzie apartment, Bill's cue to his company that the party should end. A dozen hangers-on paid no attention.

"Lucky for him, he reported it stolen before someone used it to run us down," Nicki said.

"Damn." Britt set her glass on a bookshelf. A small circle of wine sloshed from side to side.

"The keffiyeh was probably stolen, too. Police found it in the truck abandoned by the Olympic Stadium."

"What does your godfather think about this incident?"

"He says Greece is a land of mysteries." Nicki shrugged. "We did talk to the police."

"Their response?"

"They said people are careless behind the wheel, especially when they drive a stolen vehicle. I'm sorry we could not do more." Rossini's music jumped several decibels. Nicki smiled knowingly at Britt. "Listen, I should go."

"We haven't had much time together," Britt said. "I'm sorry our schedules haven't synced better.

"Maybe I can visit you on Santorini?"

"I'd like that. Meanwhile, I'll walk you to your car."

"I had to park several blocks away."

"Good." Britt tracked down Anne MacKenzie, rinsing glasses in the kitchen sink, to tell her she was stepping outside for a few minutes.

"Are you still living with your brothers?" Britt asked as she and Nicki walked down the curved marble stairway to the ground floor.

"Only two. The baby moved back to Corinth to be with Mama. Papa is teaching him to be a lord of land and commerce."

"Is Mikos a godfather to your brothers, too?"

"Yes. All six."

"Is he a relative?"

"Not by blood, but my father and he are like fingers on a hand. Very close."

As the women passed through the stuffy lobby, the concierge, perched behind a marble-topped counter, nodded as the women passed.

Britt shoved open the large glass doors against the heavy Athens air. "You lead," she said.

As they headed toward the church across the way, Nicki hooked elbows with Britt.

"Now, then," Britt said. "Mikos and your family?"

Nicki waited as a bakery van rumbled by. "Mikos and my father go back many years. During the junta, they were student leaders in the opposition. In '74, they were arrested and nearly executed, but the junta was overthrown before that could happen."

"Mikos must have been a hero," Britt said as they angled down a street leading to Syntagma Square.

"A big hero. He worked hard in forming the democratic government and after a few years was elected to parliament. But he bears the scars of those days."

"Literally?"

"I assume there are physical scars like my father's." Nicki adjusted her glasses. "But I speak of ones of the spirit. To this day, Mikos cannot stand the sound of metal worry beads clinking. It reminds him of a particularly cruel prison guard."

"No steel worry beads for him?"

"Wood only." Nicki smiled. "But of the finest cedar."

Their footsteps echoed loudly on the dark sidewalk. On a balcony ahead of them, an elderly couple sipped drinks from tall glasses as they took in the night sounds of the quiet neighborhood.

"So, are you meeting any women? Making friends? I got the impression from your last emails that you've been busy—and feeling isolated," Britt said.

"Mostly true. I belong to a feminist group, and one of the men's bars has a women's night. But that's all. It's hard for us here. You are so lucky in America." Nicki stopped in front of a cream-colored Mercedes. "Are we still on for breakfast?"

"I'm sorry, I can't make it," Britt said. "I need to stop by the Embassy. Maybe when I come back in a few weeks for the symposium?"

Nicki masked her disappointment as she unlocked the car and climbed in. "Get in. I'll give you a ride back."

"Thanks. I'd rather walk."

Nicki started the car and lowered the window. "You're too independent."

"We all are. Consider it a strength, not a flaw." Britt leaned down to peck her on the cheek. Instead, Nicki turned her face toward Britt and caught her full on the mouth.

"Lampas, you're as incorrigible as ever," Britt said.

"Just lonely."

Britt's reserve melted. She kissed her again, soft and steady, tasting the champagne Nicki had been drinking. When she pulled back, she brushed Nicki's bangs to the side. "Maybe you should move back to America. I'll help you get a green card and find a job."

"I think about it sometimes."

"Nicki, I want you to find someone and fall so hard in love—"

"That I forget about you? That would be nice." Nicki showed a row of perfect teeth. "I know, Britt, that you're not my destiny. But I still like your kisses."

Britt laughed and gave her a final quick kiss. Although she waved cheerfully as Nicki squealed away from the curb, when she turned back toward the MacKenzies', she felt a sudden stab of loneliness.

I'm okay, she told herself. But as she passed a jewelry store, its brightly lit window lined with gold rings and bracelets, a lump rose to the top of her throat. What wonderful gifts, she thought, but I have no one to give them to.

She fixated on a gold and lapis necklace. *I've been single for over a year. Will I ever find someone?* Britt stared at her reflection. Her last relationship, Wendy, had lasted only six months. The few prior relationships had left her in tears and confusion. *Why can't I pick the right person?*

She remembered the gentle warnings of her friends: Be careful. Take things slowly. We don't want to see you hurt. But she had a penchant for falling fast and hard, letting her heart careen down the agonizing slope of unequal love.

Actually, being single for so long has been good. I've become self-reliant. Britt now prided herself in being able to admire a woman's attractiveness but hold off on desire—like with Susan Marcello. When a flint did strike her heart, she could smother the spark before it had a chance to ignite.

Britt turned from the window to the outside world. As she passed a colorfully lit kiosk, the headline of the *Herald Tribune* caught her attention: *U.S. Sailors Injured in Piraeus Bar Fight.* More fuel for Mikos Zerakis's mistrust of America, she thought. On impulse, she whirled around to read the opening paragraph of the story. A man a short distance behind her froze. Britt recognized him immediately—the man who had followed Nicki and her from Syntagma Square to the Plaka.

Well, old friend, it's time we met.

Britt strode toward the man. He turned and ran, weaving in and out of a smattering of pedestrians like a football player. Britt dashed after him, mimicking his twists and turns, but lost ground with every step.

"Wait!" she called out. "Wait! I want to talk!"

But the man pressed on. The gap widened to thirty meters. As Britt's breathing deepened, the odor of tar and car fumes became nauseating. Suddenly his steps shortened.

He's slowing, Britt thought. I've got him.

But just at that moment, he whipped around a corner into an alley. When Britt reached the narrow opening, the dim, dirty lane seemed deserted. Britt edged quietly along the brick building for a few meters and stopped.

Against the blare of horns and rumble of engines in the distance, the alley vibrated with a dangerous calm. Britt crept forward, eyes on three trash cans at the dead end of the alley. They provided the only hiding place. A discarded newspaper lifted in the night breeze and settled on the pavement.

As Britt cautiously stepped ahead, she slightly curled the ends of her fingers, forming the straight outer edge she'd learned years ago in a self-defense class. *I shouldn't have had that last glass of wine.*

She consciously inhaled the smells of urine and rotting food so she'd have air to scream for help. Still no movement, no sounds except the distant traffic and the strains of bouzouki music floating from an apartment overhead.

Halfway down the alley, Britt stopped to consider the wisdom of being in a dark passageway, each step bringing her closer to possible harm.

Suddenly, behind her, a door swung open. Britt spun around. A backlit figure filled the frame, then stepped into the alley to face her. Britt locked on his face, the right side aglow from light streaming out the open door. He was an old man with a grizzled gray beard. A flurry of Greek exploded from him.

Shaking her head, Britt pointed toward the end of the alley. "I look for my dog," she said, about three times louder than her normal speaking voice. She ventured half a dozen variations of what she thought would pass for *dog* in modern Greek.

The old man seemed to understand, but he turned his head slowly from side to side. He lifted a broad, twisted hand in the direction of the trash cans and made a motion to the left. Britt, glad for the witness, continued down the alley. When she reached the row of garbage cans, she discovered what the old Greek had been trying to communicate.

The alley was not a dead end. A meter-wide opening appeared on the left, leading behind the brick structure and on to a maze of small paths connecting the apartment buildings in the area.

"American?" the old man said, as Britt made her way back to the street. She nodded at him and noted the look of disdain in his eyes. He knew she had been lying about the dog.

Flushed with adrenaline and embarrassment, Britt regained the street and turned toward the MacKenzie apartment, glad to be leaving Athens the next day.

6

A security guard ushered Britt into Susan Marcello's office and pulled the heavy oak door shut as he left. Britt paused a moment to take in the beige walls and furniture, the colorful pastel prints, and the almost total absence of knickknacks and other clues about its occupant. Only one framed photograph sat on a sideboard, a posed picture of Susan on the arm of a handsome man with a short Afro and trim mustache.

Moving from behind her desk, Susan noticed Britt's eyes linger momentarily on the picture. "Party last long?" she asked.

"Long enough." Britt passed a hand across her eyes. "I need three more hours of sleep to feel human."

Susan motioned Britt toward a leather sofa. She mentally reviewed her strategy as Britt settled on a cushion. "How about some caffeine to brighten you up?" Susan nodded to a silver service of coffee and a tray of pastries on a kidney-shaped coffee table.

"Please. Make it black."

Susan eased her athletic frame into a chair next to Britt. She poured a hot stream into a cup, then held out the china with a steady hand.

"You know, Susan," Britt said after a fortifying swallow, "I don't know what to make of you, and I suspect that pleases you."

Susan poured a second cup of coffee for herself and let Britt continue.

"Why the lies?"

"Lies?" Susan echoed, delighted to see Britt taking the offensive.

"You lied about knowing Bill. He'd never heard of you. You bluffed about reading my book. As a teacher, my b.s. antennae are pretty sensitive."

Smooth as ever, Susan repositioned a few blocks of her strategy as she held out the tray. Britt plucked up a tiropita and centered it on a small plate.

"Would you believe I was testing you? I wanted to see if you could see through me." Susan smiled. "You did. Congratulations."

"Wait, what?" Britt shook her head. "I don't get it."

"You're a private citizen, Britt," Susan said, returning the server to the table after selecting a sweet roll for herself. "If Uncle Sam signed your paychecks and you had security clearance, I could have pulled you into my office and given you an assignment. As it stands, I've had to run a security check on you, have one of my staff interview folks at the American School, and scope you out personally."

Britt bit off a small piece of her cheese-filled pastry and chewed warily as if it were as untrustworthy as this embassy official. "What do you want of me?"

"It has to do with Santorini." Susan broke off a piece of the roll and slipped it into her mouth.

"I'm listening."

"Nuh-uh," Susan said, chewing methodically and swallowing. "Not so fast. I need a promise from you. You have to trust me, and I have to trust you."

Susan stayed silent, while Britt studied her.

"I can't trust you, Susan, at least not yet, but that doesn't mean I'll betray you. I'll hold everything you say in confidence."

"I like your honesty." Susan leaned forward, her eyes narrowing with intensity, letting Britt nibble at her hook. "This information is to be held airtight, okay? No leaks."

"You have my word."

"Good." Susan paused. "I assume you've heard of Paulos Bountourakis—the man who recently died in Santorini."

"Of course. He's been the talk of the school. I never knew him."

"Mr. Bountourakis played the dilettante in the art circles of Europe, flitting around wherever the creative types gathered. If he picked up bits about theft or trafficking rings, he'd notify his contact in the Criminal Investigative Services here in Athens, which is tied into Interpol. In five years, he produced three leads. All duds."

Susan ate another piece of roll then continued. "A few weeks ago, his contact—Alexander Stamos—got a message from him saying he needed to check out something on Santorini. Before he could report, he went over the edge of the caldera."

"Are you implying murder?" Britt asked, surprised at how easily the question popped out.

"We don't know what happened. The cliffs on Santorini are treacherous. The strong winds could blow a small man like Mr. Bountourakis halfway to Gibraltar."

Britt nodded. "I'm still listening."

"Now comes the problem. My colleague at CIS—part of my job is liaison with Greek law enforcement, as well as with Interpol—isn't willing to close the file on Mr. Bountourakis's tip. With his death, though, there's no easy way for Mr. Stamos to find out what's happening on the island."

"Why not?"

Susan explained the problems of resources and logistics Stamos had laid out the night before.

"Essentially," Susan concluded, "we want your help. If you observe anything suspicious, I want to know. I'd pass the word to CIS, who would then initiate an official investigation. Your work would be done once they committed resources to the case."

"You want me to look for suspicious things? Like what?"

Susan yanked the hook. "Like missing artifacts at the excavation site or museum." The tactic was elegant: No one knew what Bountourakis had suspected, but the smuggling of antiquities would be the only thing a classics professor would care about.

Britt rose and crossed the sea-blue carpet to the window. In the distance, bright flowers hung in pots on apartment balconies. "I'm not comfortable with that," she said. "I'm a scholar, not a spy."

"We're not asking you to go James Bond. We just want you to keep your eyes open and tell us what you see."

"I don't know what to look for, and I refuse to go around suspecting everyone I meet. I'm out of my league, Susan. I'm—"

"You're observant and resourceful. That puts you ahead of ninety-five percent of the population."

Britt slowly shook her head. "I appreciate your confidence in me—"

"Wouldn't you want to flush out a thief among your peers?"

"But why report it to you? I've known Dr. Gavas, the director of the excavation, for years. I'd tell him first."

"What if the thief is Dr. Gavas himself?"

"That's absurd."

"You mean you'd rather look the other way than finger a corrupt colleague?" Susan's intense eyes followed Britt from the window back to the couch.

"Look, I don't need—I don't want—my life complicated," Britt said, resuming her seat.

"Don't you love the world of antiquities? Won't you try to protect it?"

"Going undercover against my colleagues is not the way I choose to express my passion for my field."

Susan blinked hard at Britt. Her voice dropped. "I have no bargaining chip then. Only a plea for help. We need eyes on Santorini."

"I'm sorry. I can't—I won't—be those eyes, Susan."

"That's not what I wanted to hear." Susan picked up the last of her roll, studying Britt as she did so, circling, trying to find another weakness she could exploit.

Britt regarded Susan. "It's all a game to you, isn't it?"

"It's a serious one, Britt. I've seen the coffins of too many friends carried down cathedral steps to think otherwise."

Britt's lips parted in surprise, then closed. "I'm sorry."

"Thanks," Susan said, the creases in her forehead deepening.

Britt dabbed her lips with a napkin, all the while studying Susan. "I have the feeling the Foreign Service isn't your only employer, that maybe—"

"No, you don't," Susan said, holding up a finger. "You're not interviewing me."

"At least tell me," Britt said, "how I got involved in all this."

"When you arrived in Greece, you registered your stay with the Embassy, including the addresses of your three residences."

"Ah, yes. The guesthouse in Heraklion, the MacKenzies here in Athens, and the bed-and-breakfast on Santorini."

"Right. You seemed the most trustworthy of the people visiting the island. It was simply a matter of running a security check as well as getting a little background information from the American School." Susan smiled. "Your colleagues think highly of you."

"I'm glad to hear it," Britt said. Her eyes wandered back to the picture on the sideboard. "Is that your husband?" she asked, catching Susan's eyes.

Susan held Britt's gaze for a long moment. "Yes," she said at last. Then she glanced at her watch and took a final sip of coffee. "It's getting late. We'd better head for the airport." She retrieved a small leather purse from her desk, as well as a travel mug for a coffee-to-go.

▨ ▨ ▨ ▨

After picking up Britt's luggage at the front desk, the women left the embassy by a side entrance adjacent to the parking lot. Susan opened the door of her silver Saab for Britt. The interior, already broiling in the early morning sun, smelled of leather. Susan slipped into the driver's seat, started the car, and switched on the air conditioning.

As they merged with the traffic on the main thoroughfare looping past the Acropolis, Britt gave the ruins a long, regretful look. "I always find it hard to say goodbye to the Parthenon. It's a bit like leaving home."

"You have a soft spot for Athena?"

"I do."

"The Virgin Goddess. The Warrior." Susan glanced at Britt. "What's the appeal?"

"She's also the Goddess of Wisdom."

"Hmmm." Susan eased the car into the next lane.

Britt watched the city streets fly by. Large apartment buildings had laundry strung on lines high above the alleys. An occasional palm or mulberry tree poked through a sidewalk. All of this, Britt thought wistfully, had once been the Argive plain, where armies carrying swords and shields had clashed in history-changing battles.

Turning to Susan, Britt asked, "How did you wind up in the State Department?"

"I've been interested in world affairs ever since I was a kid thumbing through issues of *National Geographic.* I majored in international studies and minored in French. The State Department recruited me right out of Stanford for an internship. I liked the idea of seeing the world and making a difference, so I entered the Foreign Service. And, after several stops along the way, here I am in Athens."

"How does being posted all over the world work with your marriage?"

Susan smiled inwardly. Was Britt trying to divine if her marriage was a cover? She reached for her coffee. In another place, another time, Susan could see herself opening to this attractive woman. She took a slow sip. *No. Not in the middle of an operation.* "My husband is an international trade consultant. His home base is Geneva. It's worked out well for us." Susan returned the mug to its holder.

Britt watched Susan's graceful hand move back to the steering wheel.

"Tell me," Susan said, "how did a Wisconsin farm girl wind up in a classical studies department?"

"Ah," Britt said, her face lighting with pleasure. "Blame it on my tenth-grade teacher. Ms. Myers assigned us the *Odyssey,* and I began to live in that world."

"What do you mean?"

"I read and reread the classics until I could practically breathe Homeric and Hellenic air." Britt adjusted the AC vent to blow directly on her. "Even though I was young and inexperienced, their passion touched me. The Greeks conveyed the essence of humanity—our frailties, our desires—like no one else."

"Shakespeare?" Susan said, one eyebrow cocked.

Britt laughed. "Yes. Shakespeare. I'll concede you that."

"Well, Shakespeare did pull a lot from the Greeks."

"True," Britt said. "Humanity may be thousands of years older, but we still have the same emotions and behaviors—love, resentment, generosity, arrogance, malice, courage. You name it." Britt paused, a slight blush rising on her cheeks. "Back at your office, you could say I channeled a bit of wise *and* petulant Athena."

Susan nodded thoughtfully. "I can see that. Wise in not getting involved…and a bit testy about it." She gave Britt a winsome smile. "Don't worry, I didn't take it personally."

"Whew." Britt wiped imaginary sweat from her forehead.

Susan turned her attention to the road. She deftly wove through a slowdown in traffic and regained speed. "You're fluent in ancient Greek and Latin, I assume," she said.

"I am."

"What about modern Greek?"

Britt pursed her lips and made a rocking motion with a hand. "Not so much. It sure would have come in handy last night when I chased a guy down an alley."

The Saab decelerated slightly. "What guy?"

"After you left the party last night, I walked Nicki Lampas back to her car. I caught someone following me, a man I'd seen before in Syntagma Square and the Plaka just before someone in a stolen truck almost ran Nicki and me down."

Susan's training kept her expression neutral and her voice calm. "Tell me everything." She listened closely as Britt recounted the episodes concerning the truck and the man in the alley. "Do you think they're connected?" she asked after Britt finished.

"I doubt it. The person who tried to run us down certainly wasn't the man who's been following me. He ran away when I confronted him."

"The tail could be Zerakis's guy," Susan said after a moment of deliberation. "He wants to see who his godchild hangs around with. Zerakis has pinched off more than one bud before it could blossom into scandal. He wouldn't hurt you, though."

Britt remembered with chagrin the kisses she had exchanged with Nicki. Had the tail witnessed it…and would he report it?

"If Zerakis thought Nicki's seeing you might be an embarrassment, he'd probably pack her off to Britain or Asia for a month or two. I wouldn't worry about it. The attempted run-down, though…that is troublesome. Let me know if you get any more information about it. I'll check things out through my channels, too."

Susan parked in the lot of the domestic airport. After Britt checked in and put her luggage in the baggage drop, she escorted Britt to the security checkpoint. Leaning close, she whispered, "I hope you'll help us out. You have my number. Call me if you need anything."

"Maybe." Britt held Susan's gaze.

Susan was pleased to see a blush spreading across Britt's cheeks. It wasn't the first time she'd flirted in her work…*but Mr. Alexander Stamos, I decide how far to take it.*

Susan lingered at a window until she spotted Britt running up the stairs into the belly of the plane. She let out an airy whistle as she marked the turning of another citizen into an intelligence source. Britt Evans would help her. The hook had snagged her, and she wouldn't be able to shake free.

But the occasion did not call for self-congratulation. Susan was alarmed by what Britt had told her. Being followed? Nearly run down in the Plaka? She didn't like the implications. Had someone on the embassy staff leaked their interest in Britt? Had someone at the American School set off the alarms when her staff did a background check? Had Mikos Zerakis put his web of underworld actors into play? And what scenarios had she not yet thought of?

Most importantly, if the incident with the truck had indeed been an attempt to eliminate Britt before she reached Santorini, would those actors finish the job once she landed on the island?

On the upside, they might reveal themselves, providing the opportunity for breaking open the case. On the downside, Britt Evans could lose her life.

Susan stopped short. *No, I won't let that happen.* She stepped closer to the window overlooking the airfield. The plane bound for Santorini readied itself to taxi to the runway with Britt aboard, alone. She was vulnerable, and hard experience had taught Susan that promises, no matter how well intentioned, often proved flimsy against powerful and determined forces.

7

Britt spent the forty-five-minute flight from Athens to Santorini contemplating her conversation with Susan Marcello. She didn't like being asked to spy on her colleagues. On the other hand, if someone were stealing from this precious Minoan site, she would gladly report it—with or without Susan's request. But would she go around Dr. Gavas, the director and her friend?

Another aspect of the conversation plagued her. "Is that your husband?" It had been an intrusive question. Britt warmed with embarrassment at the memory of her curious glance at the picture on the sideboard. The answer, though, was as intriguing as the question was inappropriate.

Why the eye lock and long pause before answering a simple yes? Perhaps the answer wasn't so simple. Did it involve a separation? An impending divorce? A sham marriage?

Or was she being played? Britt shifted in her window seat. Had it been a purposeful tease? One that said *I might be available, you sexy professor, if you spy for me?* Dream on, Britt told herself, half amused, half horrified that she had spent so many minutes obsessing about the seductive Susan Marcello. I am so done with married women, Britt reminded herself. They're heartbreakers. I'm demanding lesbian bona fides for my next relationship.

Britt pressed her face to the window as the plane dipped. The island of Santorini appeared below, shaped like a croissant, its ends bending to the west. Steep cliffs loomed on the inside edge, remnants of the volcanic mountain that had exploded three millennia ago, destroying its Minoan settlements. Now black lava islands slowly grew within the vast circle of water partially ringed by cliffs.

The plane banked to the right, bringing into clear view the abandoned quarry where Bountourakis had fallen. Britt stared at the open pit with its twenty meters of volcanic ash and pumice resting atop a layer of basalt. What a ghastly place to die, she thought.

Britt followed the curve of the caldera and spotted the main town of Thera embedded in the rim of the cliffs, its whitewashed buildings incandescent in the late morning sun. Steps zigzagged up the cliffs from the cruise ship harbor to the town, with a cable car system spanning the same distance. This, too, passed from sight as the plane swooped to the east, then south over dry grape fields and descended to the airstrip on the flat lowlands on the island's eastern side. Britt craned to see the black sand of Kamari Beach, south of the airport, her home for the coming weeks. It remained out of sight.

Britt looked back to the rising land that ended in the drop-offs. *What had happened at the cliff's edge? What if someone had pushed the photographer over the edge? What had he stumbled on, and would she trip over it, too?*

◙ ◙ ◙ ◙

Theodopolis Alevras swung open the wooden gate at the main entrance of the Fira Winery. Just a few kilometers outside Kamari, the winery sat in a barren patch of ash, surrounded by fields of grapes and barley. A solitary sycamore tree at the side of the building provided scant shade. A guard, slouching in a chair by the door, let his jaws work a freshly lit cigarette as the owner passed.

Alevras ended his phone call and yanked open the front door. "Damn!" he yelled. They were supposed to take care of Britt Evans on the mainland. Now she was on the island. They couldn't risk another death. It would be too suspicious.

His eyes adjusted to the dark interior of the winery. Good thing they had been watching her ever since the U.S. Embassy had made inquiries at the American School. Now they knew she had ties to Mikos Zerakis. An M.P. for Christsake! They would have to be very careful.

Yet accidents happened all the time. Alevras tossed the phone on the desk and approached a rotund café owner talking to a clerk behind the counter. "Your offer is an insult," Alevras declared, muscling the clerk to the side.

"You don't know what it is!" the buyer cried.

"I know you, you cheap rooster. We sell you two cases of wine, and you think you deserve bulk rates."

"Where is your head! It's twenty cases a month. You are lucky for that—tourists have one glass and never ask for another. What happened? Your wine used to be premium. Now, it is nothing!"

"What is this? What is this?" Sophia Delopsos jerked open a yellow-and-burgundy painted door behind the counter that partitioned off her small living space. "Look at you," Alevras's aunt cried, spitting out the Greek words like a curse. "Hung-over and unshaven. Move aside."

"You should be out here in the first place," Alevras growled at Mrs. Delopsos. He perched on the clerk's desk and began playing with a sharp spindle as his aunt concluded the deal.

As soon as the customer left, Mrs. Delopsos said, "Your father should see you." The thin woman patted her black hair, swept back severely and clipped at the rear with a silver barrette. A few strands of gray were visible. "You are a disgrace to our family."

"What are you?" Alevras said, jabbing the spindle toward the disapproving face of his mother's sister. "A beggar to the family."

"I take what life gives me, and I am thankful to God for it. But you…"

"But youuu-uuu," Alevras mocked. He'd spent his childhood listening to his faults. "I have more important business than this…" He eyed the bare walls, the one sign written in Greek, German, and English saying *NO WINE TASTING* and the bars on the dust-covered windows. "…this godforsaken hell-hole."

The ceiling fan slowly churned the thick air. Mrs. Delopsos frowned as she studied her nephew. "I don't know what you are doing, but it is not right. All these men coming and going. The Fira Winery now a shadow of its glory. You tempt fate, Theo, at your own peril." Mrs. Delopsos wagged her head in disgust and retreated to her private quarters.

Alevras turned to the sallow clerk, an old lackey of his father's. "My father, is he still in Athens?"

"No, Colonel Alevras is in Crete."

"Good." Alevras picked up his phone and called the Seaside B&B.

"Hello, my sweetheart," he chirped. "Tell me about the guests you checked in today." He listened intently. "This last one, where is she now?" Alevras grinned. "Take a break. Meet me at the beach and point her out."

The clerk looked blankly at his employer.

"We have a new player on Santorini, an American professor. You see," Alevras said, resting the tip of the spindle on a button of the clerk's shirt, "she is the mouse, and I am the cat. We have a little game to play, and then dinner time."

8

After checking in at the Seaside, two blocks inland from Kamari's beach, Britt changed into swimwear and headed for the sea. She claimed a coffin-sized rectangle on a patch of black sand in front of the Pelican, a taverna of weathered wood. A canopy of vines wrapped around bamboo poles shaded its veranda from the white-hot sun.

Small shops lined the stretch of sand with the expensive hotels marking the end of the well-used portion of the beach. Farther north, a narrowing shoreline curved into low, rocky hills. A plane, lifting off from the airport, glinted in the sun.

Heat rose off the beach in searing waves. A hot breeze stirred Britt's black hair and reddened her cheeks. She slipped out of her white cotton cover-up, already damp with perspiration.

At last, she propped herself on her elbows so she could examine the heights of Mesa Vouno, the mountain rising at the southern end of the beach. Great slabs of rock lay exposed, and tufts of shrubs and burnt grass dotted the shimmering surface. It was hell to climb, but Britt knew she'd make at least one trip to the classical ruins clinging to its top.

She surveyed the swell of the waves and the half dozen windsurfers cutting through the sea. One with a sail of bright orange and yellow spun around at the southern promontory formed by the base of Mesa Vouno, which separated Kamari Beach from its sister black-sand beach at Perissa. The rider flew over deep troughs and landed on opposite walls of water with a force that would have knocked most surfers into the sea.

The rider, bearing in toward shore, suddenly swung the sail around. The board bit into the water and made a 120 degree turn. A woman,

Britt thought, registering the fullness of the hips encased in a black full-body wetsuit. The stiff wind blew back the blond hair not caught under her white goggles.

As the sun beat into her, Britt lowered her head to her towel. "Goodbye, Athens," she said under her breath, letting the swirl of the city flow out of her pores. The smell of salt and coconut oil replaced the odor of diesel and urban waste. The cries of gulls and the slap of the surf supplanted the roar of traffic. Nearby, a small boy squawked in pain as he hopped from foot to foot across the burning sand. Reaching his parents' blanket, the boy rubbed away his tears, gave Britt a trembling smile, and began to dig a trench.

Time to cool down, Britt thought. At the water's edge, she toed the cold surf, waded out, then plunged into deeper water. As she stroked through the sea in a slow crawl, her arms cycling through the water like lazy turbines, her goosebumps disappeared.

Theo Alevras, watching from shore, plotted his strategy.

ꙍ ꙍ ꙍ ꙍ

Eighty meters offshore, Britt dove straight down, twisted around, and pointed herself toward the beach. As she broke the surface, she heard a yelp, then caught a flash of orange as a sail slapped into the water.

The blond windsurfer sputtered to the surface. "Fuck!" she cried. "Where did you come from? I could've cut you in two."

Britt blew out a spout of sea water and took a jagged breath. "I'm in one piece. How about you?"

The young woman adjusted her goggles. "I'm okay."

Britt grabbed the back edge of the yellow board as the other woman reached for the long side opposite the sail now floating on the surface. Peering at each other across the board, the two treaded water. Britt could discern large eyes the color of storm clouds behind the goggles.

"You're out quite far," the woman said. "Would you like a tow in?"

"No, thanks," Britt said. "I want to get my swimming muscles back in shape."

"Do you windsurf?" the woman said as she repositioned the board so the breeze was to her back.

"Not like you."

The windsurfer hoisted herself up and sat with her feet in the water. "You can rent one of these babies on the beach. There are several shops."

"Good to know," Britt said, looking up at the woman, now framed against the expanse of a cobalt sky. Reluctantly, she let go of the board.

The woman nodded and scrambled to her feet. "Catch you later," she said as she hauled up the sail and attached her harness. In an instant, the wind caught, and she sped away.

When Britt returned to her blanket, a man in a white polo shirt and shorts was perched on its corner.

"Hello, pretty lady," Theo Alevras said, his eyes hidden behind reflecting sunglasses.

"Get off my blanket," Britt said, reaching for her towel.

He squinted into the sun and pulled a white captain's hat low over his eyes. "You are a good swimmer, Professor Britt Evans."

Britt regarded him for a moment as she dried off her legs. She straightened herself to her full five-and-a-half feet and looped the towel around her neck. "Who are you?" she demanded. She grabbed an end of the towel in each hand and stood like a colossus over the man, leaning back on his hands. He appeared to be in his early thirties.

"Theo Alevras," he said, sitting up and sweeping his cap off his head. "You have been admiring my yacht. Is this not so?" The cap left a circular indentation in his disheveled black hair.

"No, I haven't." Britt had been so intent on the windsurfer she hadn't noticed the motor cruiser anchored up the beach. Now she shifted her gaze to the lounging craft, its upper cabin of warm, glistening wood, the sides an imposing black. A Greek flag fluttered aft.

"The *Praxis*. She's mine. All sixty-two feet of her. She has engines that can take us to the moon."

"Congratulations." Britt slipped her cover-up over her tired shoulders. "How do you know who I am?"

Alevras reached for cigarettes in a pocket. His biceps swelled slightly with the motion, stretching the sleeve bands of his shirt. "I see your picture somewhere."

"You did? Where?"

Alevras shrugged. "Facebook, maybe."

"I don't do social media," Britt said. "And why would you be looking in the first place?"

"I hear about your visit at Akrotiri. You are a star. Maybe I see your picture on your book. Everyone reads it. Not me." Alevras grinned. "Too many words."

"What do you do at the dig?" Britt asked, reassessing the stranger and softening her tone.

Alevras rubbed his hand across the stubble on his chin. "I make special deliveries there sometimes."

A sail slapped the nearby water. Britt glanced over and saw the windsurfer jump off the sleek board and drag it up on the sand. She watched the woman, mesmerized, as she strode up the beach, pulling the goggles from her face.

"Theo," the woman said, "the speed of your pursuit astonishes even me."

"I speak with the professor." Alevras scowled at the interruption.

"You must be Britt Evans," she said.

"I'm beginning to think my name's tattooed on my forehead."

"I thought you looked familiar out there. I'm Cassie Burkhardt." She extended her hand in a firm, wet shake. Her hair was plastered to her head. Small patches of sea foam glimmered at her hairline. "I work in IT at the excavation."

"I've heard your name before. I have a letter from Bob Collins that I'm supposed to give you."

"No hurry." Cassie reached behind her and unzipped her wetsuit. "Whew, this thing is hot in the sun." In moments, she had peeled her arms out of the suit. The top half now hung from her waist, revealing defined arms, toned torso, and a snuggly filled blue and yellow swim bra.

Polaroid sunglasses hid Britt's stare, but not the sudden intake of her breath.

Cassie pointed her strong, tanned face in Theo's direction. "Is he bothering you?"

"Not yet."

"I could tell him to move along." She gave him a stern look.

Alevras yawned. "I must go." He stood and stretched, all the while looking across the water at his yacht. He nodded to Britt. "It is a pleasure. It is always nice to have such a beautiful lady come to this island. Stop by Blycháda marina someday. I take you for a good time in my yacht." He gave the women a lascivious grin as he tipped his hat and sauntered up the beach.

"I'm sorry Theo was your welcoming committee," Cassie said. The wind had already dried a few strands of fine hair to a rich golden color.

"No need to apologize." The women inspected each other for a long moment. Britt noticed Cassie's eyes were a lighter gray than they had been behind her goggles. "Please, join me."

"Can't. I stayed out longer than I planned. I need to get back to work."

"So, you windsurf on your lunch break?" Britt asked.

Cassie's face broke into a brilliant, dimpled smile, her teeth white and even. "I like to get in at least an hour every day, and some days, lunch time is the only opportunity."

A couple of gulls swung low and squawked at the women.

Cassie glanced at her board and sail lying on the beach. "I'd better take care of my equipment." She started walking away, then stopped and turned. "How about dinner tonight?"

"Oh," Britt said, abashed at having Cassie catch her stare. But even more, the unexpected invitation pleased her. "I'd like that."

"I'll bring along my colleague—Jim Larson. He's an okay guy."

"Fine," Britt replied, just as suddenly disappointed. "I'm at the Seaside—"

"I know," Cassie said. "You're right next door to my place—Maria's B&B. My car—a silver Nissan with a roof rack—is in the parking lot. Meet me there at seven, and we'll drive into Thera."

Britt sat down on her towel and tried not to watch Cassie carry her windsurfer across the beach. But as she leaned back on her elbows, her dark eyes tracked every move of the attractive Cassie Burkhardt.

10

"Computers. That's what brought us here." Cassie watched the Aegean Sea extinguish the last orange rays of the sun. The bare light bulbs hanging from the veranda of the restaurant in Thera took on a sudden intensity.

"I like to think of us as refugees from Silicon Valley," Jim Larson said, setting his wine glass carefully between the breadbasket and his plate. In the dim light, his red hair almost matched the color of the wine. "We were once peons in the vast empire of DeLouise-Benson, Inc. Now we're Santorinian royalty performing magical tricks on a screen."

Britt and Cassie exchanged a look.

Jim scowled. "All right, so we're still on the DB payroll."

"And DeLouise-Benson gets a tax deduction for its contribution to world culture." Cassie raised her wine glass in a toast to the invisible corporation.

"But we, my dear Cassie, get the fresh air of Greece and the privilege of contributing to the archaeological canon. Surely, Professor Evans, you can appreciate us."

"I do, indeed." Britt fingered her wine glass. "What exactly is your role at the excavation?"

"Jim's a hotshot programmer, and I'm a computer engineer as well as a programmer."

"Nerd. She's a nerd," Jim whispered loudly to Britt.

Cassie gave Jim a playful punch on his arm.

"Hmmph." Jim feigned seriousness and stared haughtily into the dark caldera.

"Were you two involved in DB's Arizona project?"

"Just me," Cassie said. "I'm impressed you know about it."

"I remember reading a journal article about it some time ago."

"It was fun. My team installed a cutting-edge computer system and integrated their programs for data collection, data integration and analysis, and the cataloging of artifacts. We're doing something similar here."

"She was brilliant, Professor. The star of DB for an entire quarter. Why they even wrote about her in the in-house monthly and gave her a dinner for two."

"At the company cafeteria," Cassie said with an irony-laden pout.

"So, you both pulled up roots for what—a couple of years—to come here?"

"Eighteen months. The locals take over the project at the end of summer." Jim picked up the empty wine bottle and caught the waiter's eye. The waiter nodded and spun on his heels to fetch a new one.

"Dr. Gavas mentioned you're writing an article on the Minoan culture," Cassie said.

"The Minoans and Minoan-influenced cultures. I'm exploring the interpretation of the natural world by prehistoric Mediterranean peoples and how that may have influenced the later archaic and Hellenistic cultures."

"A companion piece to your book?"

"I'm following up on some ideas I had while writing it. My book begins with the Homeric era, but now I'm stepping further back into time. It's a bit of a stretch, but I'm filling a publication void."

"Well, the new databases at the museum and Akrotiri are all set up, thanks to Jim," Cassie said. "Right now, I'm concentrating on upgrading and customizing the stratigraphy programs that allow us to digitally peel away the layers at any given area of the site. We have a powerful new 3-D mapping and imaging program that's awesome both for the in-ground excavation and artifacts."

"What happens to them?" Britt asked.

"The artifacts? Eventually they're sent to the museum here in Thera."

By the time they neared the end of the second bottle of wine, Cassie had zipped up her fuchsia windbreaker, and Britt had pulled on a navy sweater. Jim remained untouched by the chilly evening air and continued to sit in his short-sleeved plaid shirt. He had also imbibed the largest share of the wine as well as two pre-dinner cocktails.

"Friends," he cried, clutching the now empty bottle, "it's time for departure. We have work to do—pots to dig, data to enter, manuscripts to write!" He closed his eyes and swayed.

"Jim, my boy," Cassie said as she rose from her chair and eased him out of his. "You're not going to be fit for any civilization tomorrow—Minoan or modern."

"You two go on ahead," Britt said, motioning to the waiter. "I'll get the bill."

She caught up with Cassie and Jim on a winding whitewashed street. Most shops had closed for the night. A few merchants were sweeping dust from their doorsteps.

As they passed a gift store, Jim yanked the women to a halt. He squinted at a display window where a red velvet cloth concealed valuable items.

"No, you don't," Cassie said.

But Jim lurched through the open door, flinging off Cassie and Britt. He swayed like a willow in the middle of the shop. Distorted reflections of him played on the glass doors of cases lining the walls, their shelves holding delicately painted replicas of Minoan and classic pottery. Jim focused on a woman thumbing through a pile of receipts and punching numbers into a laptop.

"Irene! Sweetheart!" he cried, arms outstretched.

The dark mop of hair snapped up. The young woman's thick fingers froze in the paperwork. "Papa!" she called, her eyes like large drops of unsweetened chocolate.

A plump man with graying hair stepped through an open door at the rear of the shop.

"Good evening, Mr. Kazantas," Jim said, using his arms to balance himself.

"You go home, now," the mustachioed proprietor said. "Come back tomorrow."

"What? You're refusing me?" Jim tipped backward, then steadied himself. "I have never refused you."

Kazantas cast a pleading look at Cassie. "You take your friend home? Come back when he is not so…" The merchant held out his hands and made them tremble.

"Come back, come back." Jim snorted. "Why bother? I can never see her without a…a…a…"

"Chaperone. You need one." Cassie grabbed him by the arm. "Come on, Britt, let's get him out of here."

Britt latched on to his other arm. He seemed pliant now, the moment of confrontation sapping his strength.

"A touching display, Jim," Cassie said as the women steered him down the street toward his apartment. "I'm sure you impressed your future father-in-law."

"He needs me," Jim mumbled. "He needs me."

◙ ◙ ◙ ◙

"If I were Jim, I'd probably go on a few benders myself," Cassie said after she and Britt had walked Jim home and retrieved her car from a cobbled side street. "He's never been lucky with women, then he gets here and every family on this island sees him as their ticket to America. The cruel twist is that he can't have sex with their daughters outside of marriage."

"So, he's engaged?"

"Yep. He has the in-laws but still no sex. Poor guy," Cassie said, laughing softly. "He's a whiz in the programming department, but outside of his computer, he's the master of self-defeating behavior."

Britt shifted in her seat, angling toward Cassie for a better view. "Why are you staying in Kamari instead of here in town or at the Akrotiri dorm?"

"Easy access to the beach."

"Of course."

"I stayed at the dorm when I first arrived," Cassie said, "but I like creature comforts. And the horny college guys were a little much. I figured I make a good salary. No need to live like a student."

"Understandable."

"The Bountourakis hotel—Maria's B&B—has a couple of studio apartments, so I rented one long term. It's small, but comfy, and my DB managers agreed to cover part of the rent."

The reference to Bountourakis cast a pall over the conversation. The silver Nissan skimmed over the narrow road. The landscape, barely visible in the waning moon, appeared jagged and bleak.

"That's where his body was found." Cassie pointed a long finger at the void. "Down below there." The car sped past the site.

Britt craned around, then turned back to face Cassie. Her hair whipped itself into tangles from the open window. "How well did you know him?"

"We were sort of pals. I saw him a lot, living at the B&B. He taught me a good deal about photography. He has—had—his own darkroom and a sophisticated computer for his digital work. It's all been locked up since he died. Maria says no one wants to touch the possessions of a dead man. Poor woman." A pale ray of moonlight turned a few strands of her hair to a subdued gold.

The Nissan veered toward the connecting roads to the eastern side of the island. After a stretch of comfortable silence, Britt said, "What besides computers brought you to Santorini?"

"Truth be told, adventure. A Greek island sounded exciting and romantic. A paradise. It was, for about five months. Then I wondered what the hell I'd gotten myself into." Cassie gripped the steering wheel at the twelve o'clock position. "I love Greece, but who wants to live on an ash pile? Especially in winter when most of the island shuts down. Summer's here at last…but now we have to deal with the crush of tourists." She glanced at Britt. "Anyway, what I had done, I realized, was escape a relationship."

"Ah-hah," Britt said.

"Not very noble, I admit." The car changed course again, past a small, darkened village. Its whitewashed buildings glowed in the moonlight like fluorescent boxes. "He wanted marriage. I didn't. There are just so many ways a person can say no. I think he finally got the message when I left the country."

"Sounds like he had it bad," Britt said, feeling a twinge of empathy for the spurned lover. She could understand why he had been smitten.

"I know. The poor guy showed up at the airport to see me off."

"I hope he's not still pining."

"No, thank heaven. My mom emailed me an engagement announcement. He's getting married in September."

"Speaking of mail," Britt said, reaching into her bag and extracting an envelope. "Here. Bob Collins sent this by special delivery."

"Oh, fuck," Cassie said, taking the letter and flinging it to the back-seat. "Some guys just can't accept *no*."

11

Cassie angled into a parking spot adjacent to Maria's B&B. "How did you decide to stay at the Seaside?" she asked Britt as they got out of the car.

"I've stayed in Akrotiri and Thera on previous trips. I wanted something a little more vacationy this time. A colleague recommended the Seaside because it's close to the beach. I'm renting a scooter to get around."

"You can carpool with me anytime our schedules coincide. I'm at the dig some days, at the museum others."

"Thanks for the offer." Britt's eyes lit up at the thought of carpooling with Cassie. "When we're at different places—or when you need to leave early to windsurf—I'll use the scooter."

Cassie's smile showed her dimples. "It's a plan."

Britt didn't want the evening to end. She sighed and stretched out her arms as a breeze swept through the streets. "I love being here. The sea. The air. The quiet. I think I'll head to the beach to listen to the waves."

Cassie hesitated. "Would you like company or solitude?"

"Your company would be welcome."

Minutes later, they settled on the cooling black sand and faced the rolling waters of the Mediterranean.

"I guess quiet is a relative term," Britt said over the rumble of the surf. "Nature has its own soundtrack, doesn't it? The waves and the wind."

They sat in companionable silence, legs outstretched, arms braced in the coarse sand.

"You were mighty impressive out there on the waves," Britt ventured.

"Thanks. I've been windsurfing since my teens."

"What drew you to it?"

Cassie sat up and scooped up a handful of sand and let it trickle through her fingers. "I started board surfing as a kid—imitating my big brother—but I got intrigued with the windsurfers as I grew older. I loved watching them fly over the waves, racing back and forth, and not having to paddle out after every ride. They could be on the water forever, it seemed."

"Was it an easy step up to windsurfing?" Britt shifted into a sitting position to better see Cassie.

"Yeah. I had the board and balance down. It took more upper body strength, of course, hauling up the sail and maneuvering it."

Impulsively, Britt squeezed Cassie's biceps. "Impressive."

Cassie playfully raised her eyebrows. "The first time I caught the wind I was hooked." Another scoop of sand and a slow release, as though each grain were a memory of being on the water. "I love the interplay of sea and wind, board and sail. It's calculus in motion."

"A subject I avoided," Britt confessed.

"I love the fight for control," Cassie continued, "knowing that control is, of course, an illusion."

"A metaphor for life?"

"I suppose. But when I'm in the zone, flying over the waves, I feel I could sail around the world."

Britt had an image of Cassie racing to the horizon and her sail disappearing from view. A jolt of loss struck her. "It's a solitary sport, isn't it? Out there alone. Kind of like your job."

Cassie paused to consider both the idea and the source of it. Britt's quick intelligence was a bit unnerving. "Yeah. It's me and the machine. Fighting for control. But the engineering part of my job—creating a user-friendly product specific to the Akrotiri site—requires teamwork. I work closely with Dr. Gavas and the field staff. So…I'm not quite as lonely as you may think."

Britt noted Cassie's slight word change. Not solitary. Not alone. But lonely.

The women fell silent once again, the lapping surf and tang of sea air enfolding them in a deepening companionship.

"I'm excited to get out on the water after seeing your virtuoso performance," Britt said. "It'll be more intense than sailboarding on Minnesota lakes."

"Definitely. You have the surf to deal with, but you'll be fine. Any time you want to go out, let me know. I can spot you—"

"And give me tips?"

"Absolutely. I know a place where you can rent a decent board. I store mine alongside the Pelican." Cassie pointed to the taverna a short way up the beach. "I bet Andreas, the owner, would let you store yours there, too."

"I should pick up a wetsuit," Britt said. "I didn't pack with wind-surfing in mind."

"I can lend you one. We're about the same size."

"Oh, I—"

"Don't worry. I have several."

A gaggle of college students with wine bottles and loud voices descended on the beach. One of them plunked a cell phone and Bluetooth speakers on a blanket and swiped through a playlist. A driving funk beat blasted out of the speakers.

"I think that's our cue to leave," Britt said.

"Agreed." Cassie popped to her feet and reached out a hand to help Britt up.

Britt took it and, once on her feet, let it go with reluctance.

"How was your time on Crete?" Cassie asked as they left the beach and made their way up the street.

"Productive. I spent most of my time in the museum. I didn't mind being holed up, though. I find a port town like Heraklion depressing." Britt took a deep breath and exhaled. "God, I love being back on Santorini."

"Dr. Gavas mentioned you spent a summer here a few years back."

"Yes, I got the Minoan dust in my veins on that trip." Britt slowed in front of a closed ice-cream shop to check the store hours. "I'm look-ing forward to seeing Dr. Gavas and the progress at the excavation."

"I think you'll be impressed."

"What do you think of Minoan art," Britt asked, "now that you've been immersed in it for over a year?"

"I like its simplicity and joy."

"Me, too. So much European art is saturated with violence—the crucifixion, the torture of martyrs, the degradation of women. Even classical Greek art is full of war and rape. But the Minoans depicted dolphins, flowers, children playing."

"I know what you mean," Cassie said, catching Britt's dark eyes. "It's jubilant and playful. The women bare-breasted and powerful. Unafraid of snakes!"

"How I wish the Minoans had left behind a body of literature," Britt exclaimed. "What tales a matriarchy could tell!"

"Without war and persecution, what tales would they be left with? Thrilling harvests? Exciting trade deals with the Amazons?"

Britt laughed. "Seafaring adventures. Romance and heartbreak. Moral dilemmas."

"Such as?"

"Perhaps the classical dilemma of two competing ethics. Does one follow divine law or human law? Does Antigone bury her brother or obey the king's decree?

"Minoan art is simple," Cassie said. "Maybe their literature would be, too. How about an animal story? A young girl finds a wild bull and tames it."

"*The Black Stallion* becomes *The Black Bull*?" Britt asked.

"Exactly."

"A tragedy or comedy?"

"Comedy. I choose laughter over heartbreak any day," Cassie said, coming to a stop in front of her B&B. "I've had a lovely evening, Britt. Thanks."

Britt beamed at her. "My pleasure."

"Welcome to Santorini," Cassie said, giving Britt a quick hug. "I think I'm going to like having you here."

◈◈◈◈

"A good night?" Maria Bountourakis asked as Cassie shut the front door of the B&B.

Cassie entered the lounge, where Maria stood in front of a wall rack straightening the colorful brochures. "You're up late."

"I cannot sleep." Maria's eyes were red and teary. A white handkerchief peeked from the sleeve of her black mourning dress.

"It's difficult. I'm sorry." Cassie touched the widow's arm.

"Ah, well." Maria shrugged as though acceding to the Fates. "And how do you find the professor?"

"Nice." *Exotic. Bewitching.*

"That is good. You can use a nice girlfriend."

"I think I could." Cassie smiled. "It's been a long day. I'm off to bed…unless you'd like to sit and talk a bit."

"No, no. I am done here."

Cassie didn't turn on the lights when she entered her apartment. She stepped out of her jeans by the door, sure they had sand in them, and lay down on the bed. She laced her hands under her head and stared at the white-washed ceiling and the blades of the overhead fan lazily slicing through the island air.

Britt Evans was not what she had expected. Not some snooty, hotshot intellectual basking in the glow of her latest book. No. She was fun. Engaging. Easy to be with. Not necessarily a real-world adult—she was, after all, an academic—but what a refreshing change from her usual companions at the dig—college students and relic-obsessed archaeology pros!

A girlfriend. Cassie doubted Maria was aware of the implications of that term with Britt, whose sexuality had fueled the gossip circles at the dig. She didn't have a Facebook page, but an internet search had yielded a number of student references to the "hot" professor.

Cassie appreciated Britt's seriousness, and that Britt could spark a deeper conversation than she was used to. Yet she could be playful. She didn't flirt like guys did. Or get possessive—grabbing her elbow to steer her, grasping her hand to lead her. *But Britt felt my muscles!* Cassie's skin still hummed where Britt had squeezed her.

Perhaps most surprising, Cassie had stepped forward and hugged Britt goodbye. Where did that come from? And what was this sudden longing to see Britt again? To be alone with her. To talk. To touch her and be touched back.

Britt was a rogue wave, Cassie thought: a delightful and powerful force in the calibration of her world.

12

"As before, Britt, you have my trust," Dr. Alfonso Gavas said, concluding their initial meeting, in which he had set the boundaries for her research. Gavas, who'd overseen Akrotiri for years, was a popular man. His main concern centered on the excavation itself and its family of diggers, not on creating an academic empire.

"Come," he said, rising from a well-worn chair in a cluttered office. Stacks of books and papers towered toward the roof. A white handkerchief smudged with dried sweat lay on his desk. "I show you how our work has progressed since your last visit. Then I leave you on your own."

They strolled through the dusty streets, deserted except for occasional strings of tourists led by a guide. Off to the side in roped-off areas, workers knelt over artifacts protruding from the tawny-colored soil.

"What's new since I saw you?" Britt asked.

"These last years have been busy. You may know that the Minoan Exhibition from the National Museum in Athens transfers more artifacts to our museum."

"Yes. That's one of the reasons I'm spending several weeks on Santorini."

"I hope things are not in too much disarray for you. We have been integrating those artifacts with our collection as well as with newly uncovered ones from here."

"Sounds like a lot of cataloging work."

"Thank goodness for computers—and the DB programmers." The director patted his midriff, which had expanded a few inches over the years. "Computers give me a stomach ache, but they are crucial to our operation. Jim works mainly at the museum. Cassie spends more of her time here."

Shoot. Most of Britt's research would be at the museum. But maybe that was for the better, she conceded. She might be too distracted having such an attractive woman close at hand every day.

They shuffled along like tourists through the winding streets. When they reached the room containing the grave of Dr. Marinatos, they stopped. Their feet pointed at the mound of earth holding the man who had spearheaded the excavation back in the days when the site was just another field of grapevines at the southern bend of Santorini. An accident at the dig had taken his life in 1974. This grave brought to mind another death.

"I was sorry to hear about your wife," Britt said. "You must miss her terribly."

"Yes." Gavas stared at the grave. "Three years now. Every year is harder. Britt remained silent.

"But I have my work." Gavas rubbed his hands together. "And my daughters. One in Athens, the other here on the island. Both are married."

"Grandchildren?"

Gavas broke into a smile. "Yes. Not enough. Never enough." He took a step back and glanced at Britt. "You have heard about our recent loss, I am sure?"

"Bountourakis. Yes. What exactly happened?" Britt turned from the grave, where fresh daisies, poppies, daffodils, and sprigs of ever-green blanketed the ground. Her gaze rested for one intense moment on Gavas, then lifted as he stood silently in thought. Above them, an expansive roof protected the ruins from the elements. A sturdy network of Dexion pillars supported the entire structure.

With thick fingers, Gavas removed black-framed glasses and rubbed his eyes. "Only Paulos could say. We know only that he fell from the cliffs. We think he photographs the caldera in moonlight. Maybe the windmill against the moon—that would make a pretty picture, eh? But who knows?"

They ambled on, taking small, slow steps, and entered the roped-off administration section with its rows of file cabinets and desks. Britt spied Cassie at a computer in a far corner, typing like a madwoman. She allowed herself to think briefly of the previous night and of how much she had enjoyed Cassie's company.

"Ah," Gavas said, as he passed a row of vertical files. He picked up a heavy folder resting on top of the end unit. "Here, Britt, the first batch of extracts. I will have Cassie set you up with a computer or tie yours into our system. Whatever works."

"Excellent. These should help me get my bearings."

"It is good to see you again," Gavas said. His kind smile reached his dark eyes. "You have blossomed since you were here. A Ph.D. A book. A post at a university. Congratulations."

"Thank you. It's good to be back."

"The crew is excited to have you here. I wonder if you would be open to a little party at my house Friday night. To welcome you."

"I'd love it," Britt said.

"Maybe you could tell us about your book and your research."

"Of course."

"And encourage everyone to work and study hard." Gavas let out a wheezy laugh.

"I'll do my best." Britt excused herself and settled at a corner work-table to examine the documents.

Dr. Gavas, Britt thought, was his usual affable self. How absurd to think he'd have anything to do with the theft of artifacts. The only one sleazy enough to do it, she thought, was Theo Alevras. She'd keep an eye on him. She'd…Britt paused. *Damn you, Susan Marcello. You're like some god up on Mount Olympus, pulling my strings. I'm doing exactly what you wanted me to do!*

To spite the embassy official, Britt opened the thick folder and willed herself to forget Athens, the strange man in the street, the speeding truck that had almost run down Nicki and her, and the compelling embassy official who had so expertly maneuvered herself into Britt's life.

13

"Why is a classics scholar studying Minoan culture?" a thin-faced undergraduate asked. A navy bandanna, tied pirate-like, kept his long auburn hair off his face. "Aren't you a little out of your century?"

"Good question," Britt said. She puffed out a bit of air, a subtle ceding to her growing exasperation. Her informal presentation to sixteen students and staff from Akrotiri and the Thera museum in the modest home of Dr. Gavas had been chatty and fun, but after an hour of being "on," she wanted to be off. The emerging testiness of this young man indicated a need to wrap things up. "As I mentioned briefly, some of my current research focuses on what, if anything, seeped into Greek art and mythology from the Minoans."

"Nowhere in the Greek pantheon is there a bare-breasted Snake Goddess," the student said, crossing his arms. "Even the Mycenaeans didn't have her, and they wiped out the Minoans. If there was an entry point into Greek mythology, certainly it would have come through the conquerors. But there's not a glimpse of Snake Goddess titties anywhere."

A few chuckles sounded. In the dining room, where Britt stood at the head of a long table, some of the more mature staff shook their heads in distaste.

"But did the Snake Goddess morph into Medusa and her headful of serpents?" Britt asked. "And what about Clytemnestra, Queen of the Mycenaeans, who in Aeschylus's *The Libation Bearers,* dreams of birthing a snake? In tales such as these, men not only take power from snake-linked women, who could represent an earlier religion—the Minoan religion—they kill them, which…"

"Yeah, like the total crushing of the Matriarchy," cried Ruby, a freckled-faced student who sat at the end of the table. "Don't forget Circe—I mean, like, her snake-entwined goblet and bracelet?"

"Right," Britt said. "Are any of you familiar with the classic study *When God Was a Woman* by Merlin Stone?"

Ruby raised her hand, the only one to do so. "Well, bone up, dude," she said to the cantankerous student. "I mean, really, it's like a feminist must-read."

Randy rolled his eyes.

"The book is controversial in academic circles," Britt said, "but it raises important questions." She swept the array of students and staff with a penetrating gaze. "Now, let me end on a challenge to all of you. We need to decode Minoan hieroglyphics. I know there aren't many samples to work with. Yet."

"But we work with what we have," Dr. Gavas chimed in, rising from his seat.

"Exactly. Maybe one of you could find another Rosetta Stone or develop a computer program to decipher the language." Britt rested her eyes on Cassie for a moment, then focused on the defiant undergrad. "You could be a modern-day Jean-François Champollion."

The undergrad stared blankly at Britt.

"The Frenchman who deciphered Egyptian hieroglyphics," Ruby said, her tone implying *you dummy*.

Gavas, his face flushed a darker olive from the wine, laughed heartily and stepped to Britt's side. "Yes! You leave us with a wonderful challenge. Thank you, Britt."

"You're very welcome, Dr. Gavas. And thank you for your lovely welcome to Santorini."

"The night is young," Gavas said in his most affable tone, "and Mrs. Delopsos has kindly provided wine for our event." He beamed at the former proprietor of the Fira Winery standing in the archway leading to the living room.

Sophia Delopsos, with a tight smile, nodded to Gavas in acknowledgment.

"Please. Enjoy." Gavas patted Britt on her shoulder and motioned to the spread of food. He squeezed past the ornately carved dining room table to the matching buffet, where he pondered the array of appetizers. A Greek Orthodox painting of a stern Jesus hung above the buffet. Next to it were several pictures of his late wife. Britt studied a triptych of striking village photographs to the far right.

"Beautiful, eh?" Gavas said as he piled dolmades on his plate. "Gifts from Paulos. Such a talent."

"Yes," Britt said. "Cassie showed me some of his photos hanging at Maria's B&B."

"Ah. Sad. Very sad to be widowed so young." Gavas plucked a skewer of lamb from a serving dish. Looking over, he observed Britt's empty plate. "Come, you must eat!"

"I'm not hungry," Britt said, taking some hummus and pita bread to be polite. The bantering and teasing rose in volume from the living room, where a motley group sprawled on colorful cushions atop the heavy wooden furniture.

Britt conversed for a while with students as she stood, plate in hand, near the doorway to the kitchen. Ruby had wormed her way to the front of the cluster and was peppering Britt with questions, her cheeks red and eyes large in unblinking adoration. A hand on Britt's forearm made her turn. It was Cassie.

Cassie leaned close to whisper, "Do you need saving?"

"Please."

"Let's go outside," Cassie said aloud, taking Britt by the arm.

With a nod to Ruby, Britt let Cassie lead her through the kitchen, where they deposited their plates on the tile counter. Patio doors led to a covered outdoor space where two students were making out on a settee.

"Oh," Britt said. "Sorry to disturb you."

The students glanced her way, then rejoined in a lip lock.

"Come on," Cassie said, her hand sliding into Britt's. "This way."

Cassie pulled Britt across the scrubby yard to a stand of lemon trees, where Gavas had erected a swing set for his grandchildren.

Cassie sat on a wooden slat, shuffled her feet backwards, and launched into a smooth forward glide.

Britt took the swing next to Cassie. "Whew, it's nice to get some fresh air." She planted a sandal in the dirt and pushed off.

The women silently etched gentle, synchronous arcs in the night.

Throughout her presentation, Britt had been conscious of Cassie's presence. She had tried to avoid eye contact, yet found her gaze often sliding in her direction. Every time those cool gray eyes met hers, her stomach hollowed out. Britt worked to suppress the physical stirrings that signaled attraction. Cassie was straight, and now that she was single, having shed the hapless Bob Collins, the flirtatious young men at the party were obviously vying with each other to be her next consort.

"I enjoyed your talk," Cassie said. "It was like being back in college."

"Is that a good thing or bad?"

"Definitely good." Cassie shifted her grip on the chain. "You handled Randy well. He can be such a pompous ass."

"There's one in every class."

"I bet you're a great teacher," Cassie said.

"I don't know about that. I just try to inspire my students to love the subject as much as I do."

"I'd say that's the epitome of a great teacher."

They swung quietly for a while, listening to the laughter and buzz of conversation coming from the house. Even with the light shining into the backyard from the kitchen, a thousand stars were still visible. The fresh night air smelled of blossoms. The world seemed impossibly large and wonderful.

Britt closed her eyes to absorb this perfect moment that she knew would be fixed in her mind forever. Was it special because of some existential connection to the universe? Or because she was sharing the moment with someone who stirred her hopes, unattainable as they were?

"Look at Orion up there," Britt said, pointing to the constellation overhead. "The great hunter put in the sky by Artemis, who accidentally killed him."

"That's one way to rectify a mistake," Cassie said.

Britt laughed. "He was a Minoan, you know. Grandson of Minos of Crete. Ah, what the stars could tell us, observing us humans!"

"They could solve a lot of mysteries."

Even how Paulos Bountourakis died. Another minute passed. "Tell me," Britt said, "how has living on Santorini changed you?"

"Oh, golly, let me think," Cassie said. She waited a beat before replying. "For one thing, I've become more extroverted. If I hear an American in a café, half the time I'll strike up a conversation. I never would have done that before."

"So, you're seeking more connection?"

"I guess so." Cassie nodded toward the patio where the couple, backlit by the light from the kitchen, had added petting to their kissing. "Though not necessarily that kind."

Britt laughed. She looked sideways at Cassie and noted a stillness about her she had not seen before. This was not only the woman on the waves, hauling sail and skimming over the sea, nor just a computer whiz intent on commands and data flows. This was someone with depth and humor. Someone who resonated with Britt. She liked her. A lot. More than was safe.

"Do you want to hobnob with your colleagues a while longer?" Cassie asked. "If not, I'm ready to head back home."

Britt pictured the drive through the dark in Cassie's small car. The two of them. Alone together. Could anything be more enticing? Britt jumped off the swing. "I'm ready, too," she said. "But as the guest of honor, I'd better 'hobnob' a while longer."

"Take your time." Cassie gave Britt a conspiratorial smile. "Just signal if you need saving again."

14

At lunchtime in Thera the following Monday, Britt sat alone at an outdoor café up the street from the museum. She scrolled through recent pictures searching for a few to send to her family and friends. She selected one showing a brilliantly white monastery against a cobalt sky that she knew her religious aunt would appreciate. Holding up her phone, Britt compared the real sky to the picture; the true stretch of heaven matched the image, deep and cloudless. A small tour boat carrying sightseers made its way toward the cluster of black islands in the distance.

A couple of flies jigged around crumbs from a delicately crusted spanakopita. Britt slid the plate to the side and a waiter cleared it. Only a sweating glass of lemonade stayed on the gingham tablecloth, and a wine bottle with its neck plugged by a well-dripped candle.

Britt read an email from her mother. What should I tell her? she wondered. Britt ran through some thoughts: *Don't worry, Mom. I'm not lonely here. I'm finding friends. A friend, actually. Her name is Cassie. I like her a lot. She windsurfs. She has nicely defined muscles and a slow, but purposeful gait. Maybe it comes from island living. She's intelligent and self-assured and knows all about computers. No, I'm not interested. She's straight, and I bet has never lacked a boyfriend. She's strictly off-limits on that count alone. Then there's the fact that at the end of summer, she's going back to California. And she seems pretty techy for me. I can't see spending my life with someone talking about bits or bytes or whatever they are. So, there's nothing to worry about!*

"Good god," Britt muttered to herself, wondering if she should thump her head on the table a few times. How amusing and horrifying that she had so easily envisioned a future with Cassie. She spoke into the microphone: *Research is going well—I dedicate my mornings to that. I'm spending most afternoons at the beach, but instead of being under an umbrella with a book in hand as I had intended, I'm on the water—windsurfing! I'm in heaven. Oh, and the food! Beyond delicious!*

As Britt corrected the text, someone bumped against the table. The metal legs scratched on the stone walk, and Britt's phone clattered, undamaged, onto the table. "Mr. Kazantas!" she cried, recognizing the rotund shopkeeper from her first night on the island. His daughter followed close behind.

Kazantas's black eyes, surrounded by folds of skin, ran over her blankly.

"We met last week in your shop," Britt said.

Irene, who had recognized the American instantly, spoke sharply to her father.

"So my daughter says. My memory," the merchant said, pressing a finger to his temple, "sometimes she is forgetful. You are the new American at Akrotiri."

"That's right," Britt said, holding out her hand and introducing herself. The father's grip snapped like a jaw.

"I'm sorry we had to meet under those circumstances," she continued, flashing her most winsome smile.

"Yes, yes," Mr. Kazantas said, returning the expression. "Such things happen. A boy so far from home. Sometimes very homesick. It is not so good."

"I'm glad he's made friends such as you," Britt said.

"We are lucky for him," Irene replied.

Her father smiled benignly at his daughter, but his eyes were frigid circles.

"When we marry, and I go to America, I set up a shop like my father's. We will be very happy."

"That's quite an enterprise for you and Jim," Britt said.

"Oh, my brothers are to help. They—"

"Come, come," Mr. Kazantas said, "we keep the lady from her phone."

"But Papa—"

"A pleasure," the shopkeeper said as he steered Irene from the table, his fingers digging into his daughter's arm.

▨ ▨ ▨ ▨

Britt tapped her stylus against the edge of her laptop. The last few days of dedicated work had paid off: the end of one phase of her research neared. She just needed to track down a few loose ends in a storage room of the Thera museum. One end refused to be found.

Printouts scattered on the long worktable listed every artifact connected to animals uncovered and cataloged from the Akrotiri excavation. Lines, circles, and jottings trailed by exclamation points or question marks decorated the paper. Britt had entered dozens of pages of comments and sketches on her laptop and downloaded pictures of specific objects. She already had a preliminary outline for an article.

Britt swung around on her stool and rested her back against the table as she surveyed the cabinets. Holding her laptop, she scrolled through her notes: *Monkey motif, ewer: polychrome, breasted.* According to the database, the pitcher should be in the cabinet directly across from her. But she hadn't found it there, nor in any of the other cabinets along the white plaster wall. Britt had checked each carefully.

This could be it, she thought, thinking of Susan's suggestion that Bountourakis had stumbled onto a smuggling ring. Warm drops of sweat trickled down to her waist. *Don't jump to conclusions.* The ewer could be missing for several reasons. *Remember scholarly detachment.* But given the high level of professionalism both here and at the excavation, a mistake seemed unlikely.

"You look puzzled," a deep voice said.

Britt jumped. "Oh, hi, Jim."

"Having trouble?"

Britt set the laptop back on the table. "As a matter of fact, I am," she said. "There's a monkey ewer that seems to be hiding from me."

"The little rascal. Do you have its catalog number?"

"Here." Britt pointed to a line on a printout.

Jim ran his fingers along its edges. "I think I know the one. Where have you looked?"

"Every place I could think of."

Jim tapped the paper. "Some dolt probably took it to another room and forgot to record it. People get careless."

"That surprises me, but Gavas warned me that some parts of the upgrading and integration have been a challenge."

"Big time. And on top of that, everyone is too busy chasing money. Half the workers here have at least two businesses on the side, grubbing after tourist dollars so they can make a pile and move off this godforsaken lava rock. They've got their wives running B&Bs or cleaning them, and their kids working in the fields or waiting tables."

"Jim," Britt said, "the Greek economy has been in shambles for years. You can't blame people for hustling for every Euro they can get. But if you're saying the staff is inattentive because they're exhausted, aren't you striking a bit close to home?"

Jim's freckled face compressed with confusion.

"I hear you and Irene plan to open a branch of Mr. Kazantas's store in the U.S."

"Where did you hear that?" he said sharply.

"Irene. She and her father bumped into me at lunch yesterday. Literally. Was it a secret?"

"No. It's a fantasy. The dream of idiots."

"Not enamored of the in-laws?"

"The old man is an authority on the world, and he's never been off this stinking island. He has no idea of commerce in the Bay area. Of course, he's got Irene starry-eyed about the scheme."

"Do I still hear wedding bells?"

"Sometimes they sound pretty tinny." Jim fingered the printout on the table. "How soon do you need to see this ewer?"

"Soon." Noticing Jim's eyes widen, she retreated. "I can wait a bit, though."

"I'll check it out. It's bound to turn up. Listen, I need to finish debugging some code. I'll track this down later. Don't worry about it."

"Okay," Britt said, giving Jim an appreciative look. If the piece had disappeared, should she keep the information within the archaeology family or tell authorities in Athens?

15

Shifting on her knees in a corner of the Akrotiri site, Britt carefully brushed off the soil from an emerging wall. Dust hung heavily in the hot, still air. It seeped into Britt's khaki shorts and clung to her hair and skin. She started in surprise at a sudden, warm pressure on her shoulder.

"Sorry. I didn't mean to scare you." Cassie squatted next to her.

Britt rolled back and collapsed in the dirt. She wiped her sweaty forehead with a row of smudged knuckles and laughed. "That's okay. I needed a good jolt—I was beginning to feel hypnotized. If only I could concentrate this hard on the dust in my house."

"You and me both." Cassie's dimples dug into her cheeks. "Couldn't stay away from the trowels, huh?"

"No. I like physical labor. It helps my thoughts percolate."

"And what have you been thinking about?"

"This stone right here." Britt gave the dusty wall a pat. "Someone set this rock into place over 3,600 years ago. Just think of that. It would be over 300 years before King Tut was laid in his tomb." Britt put a hand to her heart. "And the Trojan war was 400 years in the future—Achilles, Hector, Helen, Hecuba...Cassandra..." Britt gave Cassie a significant look, "had yet to be born."

Cassie lifted her eyebrows.

"And it would take another four centuries after that before Homer sang out his stories in the *Iliad*. It truly boggles my mind."

"It's a long sweep of history, isn't it?" Cassie said softly.

"It makes our lives seem very small."

Cassie turned her gaze to the dust-covered pathways, narrow and barren, remnants of a society long gone. "You know what I think when I look over these streets?"

Britt shook her head, her eyes wide with curiosity.

"I think of refugees."

Britt's face softened with empathy. "All the people who had to abandon their homes when the volcano came alive?"

"Exactly," Cassie said. "Families uprooted, fleeing to Crete or one of the other islands. Having to start again."

"It's a major theme of humanity, isn't it? The migration of people. War. Famine." Britt surveyed the remains of Akrotiri. "Natural disaster," she added, the weight of history reflected in her eyes.

"I wonder how those refugees were treated."

"Better than what's happening now, I hope." Britt registered the appraisal in Cassie's look. "You came over for a reason, I take it."

Cassie cleared her throat and rose. "Athinios port called. A dozen new tablets and a printer we've been waiting for have just been unloaded. They're sitting on the dock. I could send one of the guys to pick it up, but I'd like to get away. Interested in coming along?"

"Love to," Britt said, brushing dust from her hands. "Time to rejoin the modern world. Let me wash up."

Cassie reached out a hand to help Britt to her feet.

"Oh, thanks," Britt said. They clasped each other's wrists. Cassie's pull was strong and steady. Britt popped upright, but instead of letting go, their fingers slid from their wrists and into a handhold. Their eyes locked. Their lips curved into shy smiles.

Britt squeezed Cassie's hand, then let go. "Give me five."

"Make it ten. I'm in no hurry."

▣ ▣ ▣ ▣

They sped along the Akrotiri road lined with fields of grapevines. Hazy wisps of moisture churned over the cold waters of the caldera, shaded by its own cliffs. Drawn by the warm air overhead, clouds of water vapor twisted upwards from the sea. A fine mist moved inland

and crept down the eastern slope onto the plains below Thera. From this distance, the town's white-washed buildings seemed wrapped in a heavy, somber sleep.

The breeze coming through the open windows provided faint relief from the pressing humidity. Even the notes from an Adele song seemed to clog in the speakers.

"You know," Cassie said, sweeping the hair off her forehead, "despite my complaints, I'm going to miss this island. There's nowhere else like it. I love the town embedded in the cliffs. Even those black volcanic islands—they're in a sea as lovely as any on earth."

"True." Britt smiled.

"I feel totally spoiled by being able to windsurf so easily. All I do is walk out the door. It's starting to hit me that I'll be leaving in three months."

"Are you anxious to get back to California to see friends and family?"

"Actually, I'm not sure where I'll be." Cassie glanced at Britt, then locked her eyes back on the road as a green-and-yellow tour bus approached them on the narrow lane. "DB eliminated my old department about six months ago—part of a five percent downsizing. I'm on a nationwide list for internal DB job openings. I could wind up cranking code in Chicago or doing graphics in Buffalo...if I even stay with the company."

"That doesn't sound very secure."

Cassie let out a playful cackle. "I prefer to think of it as having a flexible future."

A few miles up the road, they veered left and began a descent along the switchbacks leading down to the harbor of Athinios.

The weathered dock had two ships moored. One, a shiny blue and white commercial ferry from Athens, had already disgorged its tourists. The other, a cargo ferry with peeling red paint, had its wooden gangplank down. Dozens of small trucks lined the cargo bay, but only a handful near the opening had drivers, a few of whom were coaxing their engines to life.

Two boxes with the electronics had been unloaded and stood to one side of the docking area. Cassie went into the small administrative office to sign for the delivery. Britt waited outside, leaning against the car, watching the activity at the cargo ship. Gulls circled overhead, examining the scene for edible scraps. One landed on a post, squawked some complaints, then dropped a white glob on the dock.

A refrigerated trailer truck rolled slowly down the plank from the freighter, maneuvering with care over the raised horizontal boards. On the door of the truck the words *Crescent Vineyard* were painted in bold letters above a waning moon and bunches of purple grapes.

A Mercedes screeched to a halt next to Cassie's car. A lanky man with a two-day growth of beard and a week's accumulation of dirt on his clothes, jumped out and yelled a greeting to the dock hands standing at the mouth of the boat's opening. He glanced at Britt, then at the silver Nissan.

"Cassie's car? She is here?"

"Inside." Britt pointed to the dock office.

"Ah. You friends? I am Raffa."

Britt introduced herself. "Is this your shipment?"

Another truck began descending the plank.

"Yes. It is for the winery."

"The Fira Winery?"

"Ah, you know it. Do you know Theo?"

"We've met." Britt pointed at the trucks. "More supplies for the winery?"

"Grapes."

"Grapes? Don't they grow them here?"

"Some. Not enough. We must ship some in."

"So, they come from the Crescent Vineyard? Where's that?"

"It is on Crete. Outside Heraklion."

"Hmmm. Surely the grapes haven't ripened in Crete already?"

Raffa studied Britt carefully. "These are from last year's crop. Already dried and processed into a concentrate for mixing with our grapes here." He adjusted his navy fisherman's cap. "You ask many questions."

"A problem here?" Theo Alevras asked. He stepped between Britt and Raffa.

Britt hadn't seen the captain since their encounter on the beach the day of her arrival. His face had retained its sneer, and he reeked of a spicy aftershave.

"So, professor, again we meet. I do not see you for a long time."

"I've been busy."

"Busy! You are in the land of the sun! You must enjoy yourself!"

"Don't worry about it, Theo."

He attempted a smile. "Does my worker bother you? I pay him to work not gossip." He turned to Raffa and regaled him in a torrent of Greek.

"Oh my, Britt," Cassie said in a teasing voice as she sidled up to Britt, "I leave you alone for three minutes and look what happens. Come on. You load the printer. I'll take care of the other box."

"Come! Come! Come!" Raffa shouted at them. He and Alevras scrambled to help, but Cassie cut them off. She winked at Britt as they hoisted the boxes into the hatchback without a grunt. "Thanks anyway, guys," she said. "I think we're all set." Cassie rifled through a thick packet of papers. She paused. "Hold on. I'm missing the last page. I'll be right back."

Britt slammed the hatch door down and decided to stroll the length of the small dock while waiting. Before she had taken five steps, Raffa joined her.

They stopped in front of the ship that had brought the supplies from Crete. A few cars bumped down the steep plank. High above, a crane was unloading crates of produce. A piercing whistle came from a stevedore standing at the top of the plank to guide the payload.

"You watch for the operator," Raffa said, pointing to the crane. "He is young—very new. He comes from the shops in Thera, but thinks he knows everything. Sometimes he swings wild."

"Thanks." Britt took in the operator, perched in a tiny open-air cab, working a series of levers. He wore a headband of striped cloth. A round, babyish face looked somewhat familiar.

"All done!" Cassie shouted, waving a sheet of paper as she headed for the car. Britt turned, and at that moment, the crane jerked dangerously. Its payload, a crate the size of a refrigerator, swung out in a wide arc over the side of the ferry. The boom snapped sideways, and the cargo accelerated directly toward Britt.

"Look out!" Cassie cried, knocking Britt to the side. Britt went down on one knee just as the crate swooshed by her head, its breeze stirring her hair.

"Are you okay?" Cassie asked. She bent down and put an arm around Britt's shoulder to help her up. The operator jerked the boom up, and with a terrible grinding of gears, the crate rose skyward and swung overhead like a pendulum.

Britt bent over to dust herself and stabilize her trembling legs. "Thanks. That was close."

Cassie turned from Britt toward the operator. "What the hell are you doing?" she yelled.

Alevras thundered toward the gathering. He shook his fists at the young man behind the controls. The crane operator scrambled down from the machine and ran, leaving the crate continuing its precarious swing. Alevras gave chase.

"Come on," Cassie said, wheeling Britt around by her shoulders, "let's leave. This could get ugly."

As they drove along the harbor road, Britt inspected her knee under Cassie's watchful eye.

"Sorry to push you like that," Cassie said. "Sure you're okay?"

"A bit traumatized, but I'll be fine. I just need to wipe a little cut." Britt tugged a tissue from her bag. She dabbed at the blood seeping from her knee.

"Why don't you wash it." Cassie held out her water bottle.

"Thanks." As she cleaned her wound, Britt thought of Cassie's arm around her at the dock and of how wonderful it had felt—even in the circumstances. Or maybe the circumstances had made it feel wonderful—as if she were protected and cared for. That sensation had been worth the injury. And just now, as their fingers had brushed together on the bottle of Perrier, the electricity had hummed. Or was Britt imagining it?

"I saw you talking with Raffa," Cassie said.

"Yes. He told me the trucks had concentrate for the Fira Winery to supplement their grapes. I didn't realize it was such a big operation."

"It's not, according to Napa Valley standards. Still, it's the biggest one on the island. It used to be the best—the volcanic soil is perfect for grapes, so Santorini makes top-notch wine. But the quality of its wine has slipped, much to the disappointment of Mrs. Delopsos."

"I wonder why they feel they need to blend it with grapes from other islands."

"I never thought of that." Cassie tapped a playlist on her phone. Eurotech music began to thump through the speakers. "The blends are new, according to Mrs. Delopsos. She thinks that's the source of poor ratings these days."

"You seem to know a lot about the winery."

"I'm quite fond of Mrs. Delopsos. Sophia's had a lot of challenges, but she's tough. She visits the excavation occasionally. In fact, there's been some speculation that she has her eye on Dr. Gavas, although I didn't notice any sparks the night of your party." Cassie smiled. "I think it would be a delightful match."

Britt took another look at her injury and wiped a bead of blood from the cut.

"I didn't realize any of the Kazantas boys were working the docks. That was Georgios on the crane."

Cassie slowed the car as she met a bus bulging with tourists and a roof luggage rack piled high with backpacks and suitcases.

"Kazantas? He's Irene's brother?"

"Right. Soon to be Jim's brother-in-law." Cassie gunned the engine. "Love these Santorini roads!" she shouted, roaring to the top of the cliffs.

16

A few days later, Cassie had her windsurfing kit spread out on the empty lot next to the Pelican. The cleats and pulleys, freshly washed with soap and water, were on a cloth drying in the afternoon sun. Cassie had inspected all lines for fraying and replaced two. After swapping out a standing batten, she noticed the fin showing some wear.

As she sat cross-legged in a shaded spot gently sanding the fin's edge, she thought about the question Britt had asked at the party. How had living on Santorini changed her? The more immediate question—how had meeting Britt Evans changed her?

An inexplicable loneliness permeated her usually bright disposition. Cassie knew its source. She was used to having Britt close at hand—at Akrotiri, at meals, or out on the water, where Britt was quickly advancing in the art of windsurfing. She could not get enough of her. Of her laugh. Her thoughts. Her stories. The way her dark eyes seemed to read her as no one else's ever had.

Now, Britt was gone for the day, having lunch with Dr. Gavas and the curator of the museum. Cassie missed her. In fact, she could admit to a bit of jealousy of those lucky enough to be with Britt this very moment. Wasn't that ridiculous! She, who had always been at peace with solitude. Who never needed emotional ties. Who could brush off boyfriends like sand. But Britt she could not shake.

What was happening?

She thought back to Gavas's party, where she had found herself tracking Britt. First during Britt's presentation, when she had an excuse to stare. Every time Britt's eyes met hers, a warmth washed through her body. Then when Britt stood eating, a cluster of students peppering her with questions, she still could hardly look away. How calm, how patient Britt was. How closely she listened to students. And when they burbled with laughter, Cassie had wanted to know what clever thing Britt had said.

And Britt was clever. It had been fun to see her in her element—lecturing, the give-and-take with students—and to have a glimpse into the world Britt had devoted her life to—the culture of ancient Greece. That's it, Cassie thought: Britt's passion for her subject was an aphrodisiac.

Cassie had tried to be cool. Some guys had been flirting with her, but her eyeballs had gone rogue and insisted on swiveling in Britt's direction. If only…

"There you are! Maria told me I might find you here."

Cassie started and looked up to see Britt. "Well, hi! I thought you were going to be gone all day." An uncontrollable grin popped out, and Cassie wondered if it would ever leave.

"My butt can sit in a chair only so long. Being on the waves this afternoon was much more appealing."

"I know the feeling."

"I really want to work on tacking," Britt said. She surveyed Cassie's disassembled windsurfer. "But it looks like you're dealing with some major work here."

"No, just routine maintenance. I'm almost done smoothing out the fin." Cassie ran her fingers along the edge. "I'd say it's in perfect hydrofoil shape."

"You'd be up for a few runs then?"

"More than a few!"

"Are you sure?" Britt squatted next to Cassie so they were at face level. "You weren't thinking, oh, thank heavens that newbie is off today. I can finally get some world-class surfing in."

"First, you're not a newbie. And second, I can break away any time and do my thing. I'd love to work with you on your form."

"That's kind of you. Thanks." Britt considered the array of equipment spread in the sand. "Anything I can help you with here?"

"My last chore is to check the sail for splits. Maybe you could be my sous inspector?"

"Sure."

They knelt in the sand and began to examine every square centimeter of the sail looking for cracks and small fissures that would require patches. As they leaned over the mylar sheet, Cassie found her attention drifting more toward Britt than the sail. The black wavy hair, the fair skin taking on a bit of tan, the face set in concentration: Britt could have stepped out of a Minoan fresco. Royal. In command.

I'm losing my freaking mind.

Cassie took a deep breath and focused. "Britt?"

"Uh-huh?"

"How is it for you being here in Greece?"

Britt glanced up. "What do you mean?"

Cassie plopped back on the sand. "Given your profession, you spend so much head time in this country. What's it like to actually have your body here?"

Britt unfolded her legs, sat back, and pursed her lips for a moment. "It's like coming home after being away a long, long time…and finding it wrecked. Broken statues. Stubs of temples. Scraps of poetry." Britt turned to the sea. "But do you feel what's in the air?"

Cassie stared at Britt. Wordless.

"Great ideas. Great stories. Great emotions. For me, they permeate this land and enrich everything I see." Britt smiled at Cassie. "Being in Greece is living in the past and present simultaneously. Being here is being enchanted."

Cassie could not break eye contact with Britt. Damn, she thought, I'm enchanted! *Is this what it's like to fall in love with a woman?*

Britt looked down and smoothed out a patch of sand with her palm, letting the dark grains spill over her fingers. "Whenever I teach the *Odyssey*, students get upset at one scene." She brought her eyes to Cassie again. "Can you guess what sets them off?"

Cassie shook her head.

"Argos. Odysseus's feeble old dog is the only one who recognizes him on his return home after twenty years. Argos stands up, wags his tail, and drops dead." Britt let out a half chuckle. "You should hear my students howl! For two weeks they read Homer's vivid descriptions of heroism and inhumanity, but it's the dog's staying alive for the last glimpse of his master that gets them…a three-thousand-year-old heartbreak fresh as today."

"Abandoned but as faithful as Penelope." Cassie saw Britt's eyes sparkle with delight at her familiarity with the story. "Do you get emotional when you teach that scene?"

"Occasionally." Britt paused a moment. "But what really chokes me up is in the *Iliad* when Achilles has to choose a short life with eternal fame or a long life with no glory."

"He chooses a short life."

"Yes. And the god Hephestus crafts a shield for Achilles depicting what he will miss—the earth and sky, vineyards and family, the pleasures of a quiet life. That gets me. Knowingly sacrificing all the joys and possibilities of your future." Britt put a hand to her chest. "Oh, god, look at me tearing up."

Cassie touched Britt's arm. "Would you do that?" she asked. "Die for fame?"

"Not for fame." Britt fastened her eyes on Cassie. "But I would," she said slowly, "die for love."

Cassie's insides were caught in an eddy of conflicting emotions: a spurt of warmth at a type of love she was beginning to understand… and a cold, unsettling spray of premonition.

17

June

Jim Larson swung a red Toyota into a dog leg turn and jammed it into the north stall of the excavation parking lot. Britt, wheeling her Vespa from its perch in the building's shade, waited for the roiling clouds of dust to dissipate.

"Hey, are you going to the museum?" Jim yelled, as he jumped from the car and slammed the door shut. *AKROTIRI EXCAVATION* was stenciled in an eye-popping white on the driver's side.

"Wasn't planning to," Britt said, as she mounted her scooter. "Should I?"

Jim hesitated. "It's up to you. I was just there. That ewer turned up this morning—the monkey one you couldn't find the other day."

"Super! Where was it?"

"On a shelf in the back workroom. Some grad student probably left it there."

"Who found it?"

"Dr. Gavas conjured it up. Luck of the Greeks."

"Did he know it was missing?"

"Don't think so. Anyway, it's back in the cabinet where it should be."

"Thanks for letting me know, Jim." Britt pressed the starter. The engine coughed and held on the first try. *I'm relieved the ewer is found…but it's odd how it suddenly appeared.*

Britt purred up the gravel to the main road. Once past the village of Akrotiri, a quaint settlement of white and pale blue houses embedded in a steep hillside, she nudged the scooter into third gear. The wind in her face gave her an exhilarating sense of freedom. She had no plans for the evening…and nothing but a long, lazy weekend ahead. Maybe Cassie would be free to hang out.

To her left lay the great volcanic crater; to the right a spread of grapevines, evenly spaced in the gray fields. Low walls made of black, gray, and iron-red volcanic rock separated the vineyards from small squares of barley fields, the grain already threshed.

Britt impulsively drove to the caldera and pulled off the road. When the Vespa rattled to a stop, she experienced the eerie silence that often accompanies magnificent natural spectacles. Perched on the rim of the giant cliffs streaked with mineral deposits, she observed the navy sea reflecting the descending sun in spangles of flashing light. She peeked over the edge of the gray cliffs to the old quarry. It was a long way down, like looking from the top of a sky-scraper to the street below.

Funny, she thought, stepping back from the cliff's edge, how a spec-tacle like this made her feel such a small part of nature, and that death would be like a tear absorbed into the ocean. The reality, though, would be quite a different thing. What had Paulos Bountourakis thought as he plummeted down the face of this cliff? He probably hadn't mar-veled at the Great Cosmos he was about to smash into. Britt sank to the ground.

Bounty. Britt hadn't thought much about him these last few days. Had she discovered anything suggesting his death was not an accident? No. Had she even seen anything suspicious? Not really. The missing ewer? It hadn't been missing after all.

If Susan Marcello were to call—for Britt certainly would not call her—she'd have nothing to report. Would she be interested in hearing that Theo Alevras, who fancied himself a playboy, seemed a shady soul wandering the seas in his cruiser? And the Kazantas family? Susan would no doubt tell her the ambition of in-laws was not criminal, though god knows it should be.

A car skidded to a stop behind her. As Britt turned, Cassie poked her head out the window. Behind her stood the ghostly carcass of an abandoned windmill, eroding in the element it had been built to harness. "Transport problems?" she asked, pointing to the low-slung Vespa.

"No," Britt shouted into the wind. "I'm here for the view." She patted the ground next to her. "Come on, join me."

Cassie snapped off the engine and made her way to Britt's side. "Ahh," she said, lowering herself to the hard embankment, "I haven't stopped here since Bounty died. It's time I did." She held out a Corkcicle with iced coffee for Britt. "Want some?"

"Thanks." Britt took a swallow and put the cool mug to her forehead.

A mule's plaintive cry rose from somewhere below them. It started like a baby's wail, then broke into breathy sobs. The women fell silent, each hanging her gaze on the horizon, far beyond the brooding black islands.

"Who found Bounty's body?" Britt asked.

"Geology students on a field trip to the quarry."

"Brutal."

"Yeah." Cassie reached out a hand for her mug and took a sip. "I was down there once with Bounty last year. Some professor wanted photos for an article she was writing about the Suez Canal."

"The connection being...?"

"The ash here has a high silica content, which makes it water resistant. Turn it into pozzolanic cement, and you have the perfect building material for a canal."

"Interesting. Do you have a copy of the article? I'd love to see it."

"No," Cassie said, "but Maria may. I'll ask her."

"Thanks." Britt accepted the proffered mug once again. She rattled the ice before drinking. "Have any plans for the weekend?"

"Nope. Now that Bob's out of my life, my weekends are mine." Cassie opened her arms to the distant sea as though embracing liberation. "Not that he bothered me. I could be out on the waves all afternoon, and he'd be absorbed online doing his homework or tracking his investments. Buying and selling. Whatever."

"What happened with you two anyway?"

"I don't have the bandwidth to deal with someone who has the emotional maturity of a toddler."

Britt let out a little chuckle.

"We had some fun at first," Cassie admitted. "But no. He liked me because it gave him an excuse to hang out on Santorini."

"I have to push back on that one," Britt said. "Given the look on his face when he handed me that letter in Athens, I'd say he's still smitten."

"That surprises me," Cassie said, holding Britt's gaze. "We were mainly beach buddies. Maybe he's dealing with some remorse."

"About what? You broke it off."

"Bob was a real shit about Bounty." Cassie picked up a stone and rubbed it between her fingers like a worry bead. "I think he was jealous. He thought Bounty and I were involved."

Britt's eyebrows shot up.

"We weren't, of course. If I had to put money on it, I'd say Bounty walked on the gay side. He sure liked to hang out with the guys."

"That's kind of the Greek way."

"True. He and his wife did seem to have genuine affection for each other, but who knows."

"It wouldn't be the first marriage of facade." Britt flashed to Susan Marcello.

"I think Bob was glad when Bounty died." Cassie caught Britt's penetrating look. "He didn't have anything to do with it if that's what you're thinking. He visited that weekend, but he went back to Athens late Sunday afternoon, long before Bounty had dinner, much less left the B&B to take pictures." She ran a thumbnail along a white swirl on the mug.

Britt noted Cassie's hesitation. "But…?"

Cassie took another nip of coffee. "But I have a feeling there's more to his death than we know. Bob has given me a hard time about my 'woman's intuition.'"

Britt tilted her head in a questioning way.

"You see," Cassie said, setting the mug to the side, "Bounty wasn't even supposed to be here at the caldera. He told me after dinner that night he planned to go to Kamari Beach to shoot some pictures. In fact, I saw him get in his car and drive down the beach road. He never meant to come to this side of the island."

"Why would Bounty drive? The beach is only a couple of blocks from his place."

"I know. It's never made sense…other than maybe he didn't want to carry his equipment."

"Perhaps," Britt replied, unconvinced. She reached for the coffee and took another sip. "Did you mention your concerns to the police?"

"Sure. They shrugged and said, 'He changed his mind.' So, I've done my civic duty," she said bitterly.

"Like your namesake."

"Let's hope not." Cassie finished the drink and wiped her mouth as though signaling an end to the topic. "Actually, I'm named for my grandmother Cassandra. How about you, Brittany?"

"My mother's totally responsible." Britt slipped her eyes from Cassie's gray gaze.

"She didn't breed spaniels, did she?"

Britt laughed. "No. I was named for Brittany, France. My mom's people are from there."

A car whizzed by, whipping up clouds of dust. "Your parents must be proud of you," Cassie said, waving her arms to clear the air.

"Yes and no. They're proud of my career, but they despair of my being an old maid."

"Old maid!" Cassie hooted. "I thought that term died decades ago. Listen, this will be the one and only prediction I'll ever make—you won't wind up alone. How's that?"

"I don't believe you, Cassandra." Britt laughed. "What about your family?"

"Born and raised in Palo Alto. The folks are still there. Dad works at a small computer firm—he's a hardware guy during the day, jazz musician at night—and my mom's a part-time writing instructor at a community college."

"Miss them?"

"Some. We chat online every couple of weeks. I miss the California beaches more."

"A beach bum, huh?"

"I spent the school summers chasing the waves and the boys."

"I bet you caught them."

"Plenty of both." Cassie's dimples flashed. "I guess I've been pretty cavalier about it all. You screw one up, there's always another rolling in behind."

Cavalier, indeed, Britt thought. Who can resist her? But she plays with hearts. *I can't lose mine to her. I can't. I won't.*

A tourist bus rumbled by, sending another barrage of dust billowing over them.

"Too much," Cassie said, blinking grit from her eyes. "Let's go."

"Where?"

"There's a great place down the road for dinner. Then the beach for a beer? Maybe Club Volcano after?"

Britt broke into a smile. "Sounds fun."

As she made her way to her Vespa, Britt kicked a rock out of her path. *So much for my resolve. Cass asks me out like she would a thousand other people, and I jump. I jump.* Before she could start her engine, two white gulls winged up the rising land and swooped out over the yawning expanse of the caldera. Britt marveled at their soaring grace but could not ignore the terrifying edge of the cliff where a young man had taken his last step.

"Bounty," Britt said under her breath, "What happened to you?"

▣ ▣ ▣ ▣

While the sun made a dazzling descent in the west, edging past the burnt islands in the darkening caldera, at Kamari the light drained simply and without spectacle from the eastern horizon, pulling an ever-darkening canopy in its wake.

Wearing jeans and cotton shirts, Britt and Cassie straddled high wooden stools. The open-air bar stood in the middle of a row of tavernas lining the street parallel to the beach. Lights beamed everywhere, strung along roofs and through trees. Tourists, satiated after a day in the sun, hunched over tables and lounged in chairs. Outside a large, dried starfish hung from a rafter, swinging in the breeze like a horse thief.

The sea performed its mesmerizing show. Small whitecaps sprinted to shore, slapping the beach with a muted splash. For a moment, the entire Mediterranean pulled back for a quick breath, then blew curls of water toward the beach. Sitting there with Cassie, nursing a beer after their burgers, contentment settled on Britt. The gloom by the cliffs now seemed distant and silly. Yes, Cassie was insanely attractive, but it was enough to call her a friend. In fact, it was a privilege.

"Hey," Cassie said, "a yacht."

Britt ran her eyes along the northeast horizon. In the distance, a craft wedged itself through the black waters, its portholes ablaze. It leaned in toward the land, making a sharp turn toward Kamari Beach. The sleek lines looked familiar. "It's the *Praxis.*"

Cassie nodded. "So it is. Theo's probably on his way to make a sperm deposit."

Britt guffawed.

The stars winked above; the wind fell to a soft breeze, then intensified. Several men ran to and fro on the deck of the cruiser as its engines shut down. A couple of sailors tore the tarp off a motorboat secured to the port side.

"Isn't it an unusual time for a visit?" Britt asked.

"Not for Theo. The man has no sense of time or of how the world operates. He believes in partying around the clock."

Britt observed the scurrying crew as they repositioned crates on the deck.

Cassie checked her watch. "Speaking of partying, time to hit the club. The best one is up the beach. Let's take your scooter."

Britt glanced at her, then at the *Praxis.* Fun or duty? *Wait, I have no duty, Susan Marcello. Get out of my head.*

"Unless you want to watch the *Praxis,*" Cassie said. "Boring." She tapped a hand over a pretended yawn.

"No way," Britt said, taking a final swallow. "Let's go."

18

The throbbing beat of dance music sounded at the entrance of Club Volcano, a large stucco building on the north end of town and a block in from the beach. Britt slipped her Vespa into a row of scooters and mopeds at the side of the building, while Cassie dug in her pocket for the cover charge that got them entry and an ink stamp on the back of their hands.

Inside, couples gyrated on the parquet dance floor under flashing lights. Britt surveyed the room, searching for a table. The alcoves, stuffed with revelers, rocked with raucous laughter; college-aged tourists mingled at the long wooden bar or propped themselves against the mirrored walls.

"I think we're too late to find a table," Cassie shouted. "Wait, maybe not," she said, spotting arms flagging them. "Jim's over there. With Irene and one of her brothers. Looks like Raffa is there, too. You remember him from the dock? What do you say?"

"I'm game," said Britt.

The group slid their chairs around a table the size of a bird bath. Raffa stole two chairs from a nearby table, whose owners had temporarily abandoned for the dance floor.

"This is my brother, Georgios," Irene said.

"Hi." Britt extended her hand to the young man. Dark marks streaked the left side of his face, and a swollen eye blinked pathetically at her. "I remember you from Athinios Port. You almost cracked my head open."

"It was accident," he said sullenly.

"Looks like Theo caught up with you," Cassie said, shimmying her chair closer to the table. She handed Britt a beer she had picked up at the bar.

Georgios placed a thick hand on his swollen face and said nothing.

"Hey, this is a good song," Jim said, abruptly pulling Irene from her seat. "Let's dance."

"Did you catch trouble from Theo, too?" Britt asked Raffa loud enough to be heard over the music.

"No, not me. Theo barks, but me he does not bite." Raffa tugged on a set of chains—some gold, some leather—around his neck. His blue shirt, open halfway down his chest, revealed tufts of black hair.

"How long have you worked for Theo?"

"Since four years ago—when Alevras family take over the winery. Theo's papa owns a vineyard on Crete. Theo runs Fira here."

"I think Cassie told me Mrs. Delopsos and her husband owned it for several years." Britt glanced over to Cassie whose eyes had sharpened with interest.

"They own it for thirty years, maybe forty. They bottled a few hundred cases a year. Now we do over two thousand."

"You started to bring in grape concentrate from Crete after the expansion?"

Raffa became still. "Island business is not your business." He turned to Cassie and plucked her sleeve. "Come, beautiful lady, time to dance."

Well, that teat dried up, Britt thought as she watched Raffa and Cassie thread their way to the dance floor, where a mirrored ball spun overhead.

Britt leaned back and took in the scene. *This is so bizarre; all these straight couples and no same-sex dancing.* Her experience was grounded in lesbian bars, although she hadn't been to one since her Berkeley years. *But this is how most of the world is.* Britt turned to Georgios. "What will you do for a job now?" she asked.

Irene's brother narrowed his eyes and reached into his shirt pocket for cigarettes even though smoking was not allowed indoors. Once ignited, the Turkish tobacco burned with a pungent odor that mingled with the larger currents of body odors and beer. Georgios' eyes did not move from his sister, swaying on the dance floor with her husband-to-be.

Annoyed at the rebuff, Britt swiveled around to watch the square packed with beat-driven bodies. She focused on Cassie, bobbing to the music. Her silver bracelets flashed in the lights. Her billowing white shirt, tucked into tight jeans torn at the knees, glowed with a violet hue. She moved as gracefully on the dance floor as she did on the surf.

I'm not having fun. Britt sipped her beer. It tasted bitter. *I'm definitely not having fun.* When the foursome stayed on the floor for another dance, she clicked her tongue in impatience. As she watched Raffa lean toward Cassie, put his hands on her shoulders and bend to her ear, Britt's breathing constricted. *Reality check. The lady doesn't play on my team.* For the first time, Britt found herself longing for Nicki's companionship. *Why can't I just fall in love with Nicki and be done with it?* But there was that inexplicable thing called chemistry. It had never bubbled with Nicki; it ignited with Cassie.

Raffa seemed to be engaged in a playful sort of pleading. He opened his arms to Cassie. He covered his heart with his hands. When at last she held up hers in reproach, he slid a leather necklace with shark's teeth from his neck and dropped it over Cassie's head. She jabbed a finger toward him, as if in rebuke. When the beat bled into a new song, Cassie and Raffa returned to the table. A couple of beeps sounded when Raffa swung past her.

"Sorry to be gone so long," Cassie said, her face glistening with sweat. "I didn't know that last cut would go on forever."

Raffa checked his phone. "I must go," he said. "The boss calls."

"We saw the *Praxis* offshore a little while ago," Britt shouted over the music. "Are you going there?"

"I pick up cargo."

Britt raised an eyebrow.

Raffa shrugged. "We must have bottles to put wine in. Otherwise, we drink from barrels." He snickered at his joke.

When Britt turned to Cassie for her reaction to Raffa's leaving, she found her talking to a young German with a heavy accent. "Come," he said. "Dis is goot song."

Cassie made an apologetic face at Britt as she left for the dance floor.

Relegated once again to the role of watcher, Britt began to lose her enthusiasm for Cassie, who proved annoyingly popular with the men. She eyeballed Alevras's hired hand, Raffa, as he squeezed his way past an entering group—students from the excavation, including Ruby and Randy.

Oh, damn! I've got to get out of here. It was bad enough having to watch Cassie dance with men when Britt wanted to be the one dancing with her. But the thought of dealing with admiring—and not so admiring—students was too much to bear in her sour mood. What a bad idea to come here. But what did she expect?

Taking a round-about way onto the dance floor to avoid the students, Britt tapped Cassie on the shoulder. "I'm stepping outside for a bit," she shouted. "I'll see you later." Before Cassie could respond, Britt turned and slipped through the steaming throng to the exit.

The sea air slapped Britt full in the face as a breeze rushed through the streets of the village. Britt savored its freshness as she stepped off the veranda on to the road. She struggled to put Cassie out of her mind.

In the distance, she spotted Raffa sauntering across the sand to a cement landing where the small motorboat from the *Praxis* was tied up. A dark pickup had backed up to the landing and men were muscling crates into its bed. Britt moved in for a closer view.

When the last of six crates thudded into place and the tailgate secured, Raffa slid into the passenger's seat and motioned the driver to leave. The boat glided from the landing and headed back to the *Praxis*.

The pickup drove straight ahead on the road running past the club. Britt slipped back into the shadows, hoping Raffa had not seen her. Watching the taillights veer toward the Fira Winery, Britt wondered what the crates held. They seemed too heavy to contain empty wine bottles.

Moved by curiosity and a desire to put significant distance between her and the disappointments within the nightclub, Britt decided to follow. A five-minute ride to the winery. A five-minute return. She'd be back before Cassie had left the dance floor.

19

Britt untangled her Vespa from a row of scooters and climbed aboard. On the second try, the engine coughed to life for a moment, then died.

"Damn," she snapped.

"Ditching me?" Cassie suddenly appeared next to Britt, her hands on her hips.

"No," Britt said, fidgeting with the starter.

"Right." Cassie's expression indicated disbelief. "Revenge for my abandoning you at the table?"

"You don't need my permission to dance."

Cassie remained silent. A techno-beat from the Volcano thrummed in the background, and the scent of fried food from the kitchen of a nearby restaurant wafted on the breeze.

Sitting on her Vespa looking up at Cassie, Britt tried to maintain a righteous power, but she knew she had blundered as badly as a misfit teenager. "I did feel pretty damn awkward sitting all alone with Georgios," she confessed.

"Why didn't you get up and dance? Don't you dance?"

"Yes, I dance. But generally with women."

"Of course." Cassie, her face softening, placed a hand on Britt's shoulder. "After the ride, let's go back in. I'll dance with you. Promise."

Britt sighed. "I hope I'm not that pitiful."

"Listen, I'm just trying to make amends," Cassie said. "I should have been more sensitive."

Britt's anger flamed out entirely. "No, you shouldn't have. My own issues are kicking in." Britt huffed out a derisive laugh. "This is so embarrassing, but I felt like I was back in high school at a dance with no date, sitting on a hard metal chair along the gymnasium wall watching everyone else have fun."

"We've all been there."

"Really? I can't believe you ever sat out a dance."

"Well, probably not," Cassie admitted. She pressed her fingers into Britt's shoulder. "Where are you going?"

"Oh, down the road a bit. "Just a little night ride—fresh air, you know. I'll be back."

"A night ride! Sounds like fun. How far are you going?"

"Not far. Probably to the Fira Winery and back. Just enough to blow off my bad mood."

"You're not chasing after Raffa, are you?" Cassie teased. "He's definitely not your type."

Britt squirmed on the scooter. She had never been good at subterfuge, and now Cassie was boxing her in. She knew where this conversation was going.

"Take me with you?"

Britt hesitated at this complication. She didn't want to draw Cassie into her extracurricular activities without levelling about the actual agenda: snooping for Susan Marcello. All right. This would be a night ride. Nothing more. And probably for the better. "Okay," Britt said with a nod. "We go there and back."

"Actually, I'd like to stop in," Cassie said, gathering up her loose hair and binding it into a ponytail. "Raffa gave me one of his necklaces for the night. He forgot to take it when he left. If I keep it, he'll be pestering me for weeks, thinking I owe him a hookup for his 'gift.'"

Go *into* the winery? Britt thought. Oh-oh. That felt a bit dangerous. But now she had the perfect excuse to get a close look at Theo's operation. And there was strength in numbers. Should she warn Cassie? But then she'd have to explain what she was doing.

"Let's go!" Cassie cried as she threw her leg over the seat behind Britt. She put her hands on Britt's hips and snuggled in close.

With Cassie's breasts pressing into her back, Britt's mind shut off debate. "Hang on!" Britt called as the Vespa jumped to life.

The scooter sputtered past a row of barrel-vaulted buildings, then eased into a purr when the gears jumped to third. The small headlight threw a faint beam along the deserted road lined with eucalyptus trees. The cool, pungent breeze slapped the women and made their teeth chatter. When Cassie's grip moved into an embrace, Britt warmed completely.

They tilted into a curve and slowed to make the sharp turn into the Fira Winery.

"The gate's open," Cassie cried.

They puttered up the narrow lane toward yellow lights, glowing like candles in the pitch dark. As they neared the main building, Britt spotted the truck they had seen at Athinios harbor a few days earlier. Raffa's pickup was not in sight.

Britt guided the Vespa over ground baked as hard as concrete. Just as they rounded the corner of the building, two figures emerged from a side door. Britt pressed into the handlebars, flew past them, then angled to the rear of the winery where she spotted Raffa's pickup backed up to the loading dock, its bed empty. Under the yawning hood, a man worked on the engine.

"Where's Raffa?" Britt shouted.

The men they had passed at the side of the building approached them. Both had on thin leather jackets opened enough to reveal gun stocks underneath.

Cassie's grip on Britt tightened.

Britt suppressed the urge to slam into gear and tear out of there. She didn't know if the men had meant to reveal their firearms, though, so she pretended she hadn't seen them. "We're looking for Raffa," she said.

The mechanic, dressed in jeans and a grease-stained T-shirt, broke into a jagged exchange with the men. Britt could pick out the word "American."

"You want Raffa?" he asked.

Britt and Cassie nodded.

He curved a couple of fingers into his mouth and whistled shrilly into the winery. "Raffa! Raffa!" he yelled across the loading dock.

Britt craned her neck to see into the warehouse. In the back a dozen wooden barrels rested on their sides. Wedges of wood, like doorstops, kept the barrels in place. An antique wine press, stained purple with the blood of the trade, stood in a near corner. Next to it were crates with the logo of the Crescent Vineyard. A rich, musty smell permeated the evening air.

Raffa, backlit against the bright interior lights, loped toward the loading dock, wiping his brow with a handkerchief. When he saw Britt and Cassie, he grew livid.

"What are you doing?" he shouted. "You go! You go now!"

"Hey," Cassie said, "you forgot to take your necklace." She pulled it off her neck and tossed it at him. The leather thong snaked lazily through the air.

"I forget. Yes." Raffa snatched the necklace before it hit the floor. "You should not be here. You go. Now."

"All right!" Britt cried as she throttled up. "We're going!" The Vespa lurched forward past the mechanic and the two men with guns.

"See you!" Cassie called as cheerily as possible. She turned back for a last look at the winery and saw a pale Mrs. Delopsos peering from the sales room window.

20

Halfway between the winery and Kamari, Britt geared down and eased the scooter to the side of the road. Placing one foot on the ground, she came to a complete stop and killed the light and engine.

Cassie jumped off the back. "Fuck!" she cried, peering back at the glow from the winery, "what's going on?"

Britt put down the kickstand. "You've lived here for a year and a half. You tell me."

"I'm baffled," Cassie said. Her face appeared ashen in the pale moonlight. "I've never seen guns on Santorini except on the police."

Britt stepped around the scooter, never taking her eyes from the steady glare of lights in the distance. "What are they protecting?"

"Or who? Theo keeps some Neanderthals around him. Bodyguards, I've always assumed."

"Why does he need bodyguards?"

"Rich people seem to like them." Cassie watched Britt pace panther-like through the darkness.

"Hmmm," Britt sounded. "Did you notice something peculiar about those crates sitting along a wall?"

"Not really. I kept my eyes on the guns."

"I think those were the crates we saw at the dock at Athinios. Raffa told me they were bringing in concentrate from the Crescent Vineyard on Crete. Some of the crates stamped with the refrigeration warning were still nailed shut, so they're not being kept cold."

"In other words, their contents are bogus?"

"Apparently."

The night breeze kicked into an unsettling gust. "Let's get back to town," Britt said as she climbed aboard the Vespa.

Cassie made no move to join her on the long black seat. She gripped Britt above her elbow. "I'm not stupid, Britt. Your 'night ride' had a purpose. You were checking out the winery, weren't you? I've noticed your interest in it. What are you playing at?"

Britt sighed in resignation. "It's a long story. How about I tell you over a glass of ouzo once we get back to town. But promise me you won't tell anyone about this evening or what I'm going to say."

Cassie fit herself behind Britt. "I don't know. Those guys at the winery won't forget our visit."

Silently, Britt agreed. They may have stirred up the hive. Susan Marcello should hear about this. To her surprise, Britt found herself anticipating the conversation.

Britt's mind and conscience worked steadily on the ride back to Kamari. She knew Susan would not be pleased that Cassie was now caught up in the machinations. But honesty with Cassie trumped allegiance to Susan.

▣ ▣ ▣ ▣

What just happened back there? Cassie tightened her hands on Britt's hips as the Vespa lurched forward. *More importantly: Who is this woman?*

For all her stay on Santorini, excitement had happened only out on the sea, hauling up her orange-and-yellow sail, skimming the white tops, and launching into the air off a cresting wave with the wind billowing the mylar triangle. Her work had been more fun than most DP projects, and the staff of the museum and excavation were fine colleagues. She loved her job and excelled at it. She enjoyed the guys, but it was all surface play.

And then Britt had come busting into the scene, toppling her off her windsurfer. She had lost more than her center of gravity on the sea. She'd lost it on land, too. Ever since that first night on the beach, just the two of them, hardly a moment had gone by without thinking about this dark-haired woman.

Cassie had read Britt's scholarly book, as had everyone at the project, except Jim, who probably hadn't cracked a book since college. She'd heard the rumors of this hot professor. She just never expected to be so...what? Intrigued? Invested? Turned on?

She had been alarmed at Britt's leaving the nightclub. She didn't mind losing the ride back to her B&B—it was within easy walking distance. She *did* mind losing Britt. It had been rude of her to take her to the club and ignore her. And it had been rude of Britt to run off like that with hardly a word, but that had betrayed her depth of emotion. She had admitted to being insecure. Who shows vulnerability like that? Cassie pressed her hands harder on the slim hips in front of her.

Thankfully, she had caught Britt before she had ventured alone into the night. But this "adventure" blasted past normal. Britt seemed on a mission. Could she be a spy? A CIA agent? Was her Minoan project just a cover?

The Vespa slowed as the lights of Kamari came into view. Cassie slid her arms up to hug Britt's waist. When Britt gave her arm a quick electrifying squeeze, Cassie moaned softly. *Britt is between my legs!* Molten heat flowed through her as she pressed her thighs into Britt.

Britt Evans was more exciting than windsurfing in a hurricane. Cassie wanted this ride to never end, no matter who or what Britt turned out to be.

▣ ▣ ▣ ▣

They rolled through the main drag of Kamari and rounded the road pointed east. As Britt came to a stop in front of Maria's B&B, she regretted the end of the ride and Cassie taking her arms from her waist. And she dreaded the impending confession of her being Susan Marcello's eyes and ears on Santorini. How could she explain *that* without losing Cassie's favor, without dampening the obvious fire between them? But wait, their attraction had nowhere to go...or did it?

"Come to my place for a drink," Cassie said, slipping off the end of the scooter. She trailed a hand along Britt's back. "Maria has ouzo at the bar."

"Boy, do I need one," Britt said, tapping down the kickstand. The place where Cassie had brushed tingled like a ribbon of electrified skin.

"What do you need?" a deep voice asked.

The women spun around. Stepping from the circle of veranda lights was Bob Collins, grinning like a bridegroom.

21

"Where did you come from?" Cassie said sharply.

"Athens," Bob said, crossing the sandy parking lot. "Evening flight."

"How long have you been here?"

"A while. Maria said you were at the beach or the Volcano. I checked both. I found Jim nearly passed out. He said you guys had been there but split."

Cassie stared at him, her face a mixture of distrust and annoyance.

Bob did not break eye contact. "Well, I thought it best to come back and wait. I'm having a robust local red. Want some?"

Cassie turned to Britt. "What do you think?"

Britt tried to mask her disappointment. "I suppose," she said.

"What have you two been up to?" Bob asked, taking in their flushed faces.

"Riding the back roads," Britt said quickly, cueing Cassie to how tightly she wanted to hold the incident at Fira Winery.

A couple of sofas delineated a small square of a lounge area immediately inside the front door. A wineglass with a thin pool of burgundy liquid sat in the middle of a marble coffee table.

"Have a seat," Bob said, plopping on the center cushion of a sofa. Britt placed herself at right angles to him on the other couch, and Cassie dropped into a matching chair.

"So, what are you doing here?" Cassie asked.

"I thought I'd surprise you," Bob said. His hair glowed like maple syrup under the illumination of a floor lamp. He was wearing a white button-down shirt, jeans, and sandals.

"You did."

Maria Bountourakis appeared with two glasses, her black skirt swishing between the furniture. She clinked the stemware on the table.

"Drink?" she asked, reaching for the bottle of wine.

"Thanks, Maria," Britt said after Maria poured the wine. "Would you like to join us?"

"You are good to ask," she replied in a soft voice. "Not tonight, okay? You want another bottle?"

"Yes," Bob said.

"No," Cassie said.

Maria nodded and floated from the circle, empty bottle in hand.

Britt sipped her drink and savored the bite of the wine on the back of her tongue.

"I thought you were going to take school more seriously," Cassie said, her eyebrows scrunched together as she stared at Bob.

"I am. I think about it all the time."

"You said you'd study in earnest. Sounds like you're island hopping again. Why don't you quit pretending you're a scholar?"

"There's nothing wrong with part-time students, is there Professor Evans?" Bob turned his large, deep-set eyes on Britt.

She bent her lips upward in what she hoped looked like a smile, not a grimace. "Full-time is best for a scholar. But few people are the genuine issue."

"I'm strictly a student, thank you. No desire to be single minded." Bob rubbed his short brown beard. "I confess I'm a dilettante."

Cassie's frown bordered on a scowl. "I'd like to see you put that on a resume."

Bob showed a row of even, white teeth. "I don't need a resume. I can be an excavation bum for the rest of my life. A little Akrotiri, a little Corinth, a little Heraklion, a little...."

"Just how do you support yourself, if you don't mind my asking?" Britt said, luring Bob's eyes away from Cassie.

Bob put on an imperious smile. "I live off the fat of the land."

"Meaning the fat of his parent's trust." Cassie set her glass back on the table.

Britt sighed. "I'm finished for the night. Thanks for the drink, Bob." She turned to Cassie. "Thanks for tonight, Cass. I had fun—most of the time." Britt flashed a weak smile, then was gone.

回回回回

"Time to hit the hay," Bob said, once the front door had closed behind Britt.

"Did you get a room here?"

"Uh, no. Maria let me put my stuff in your place."

"Wrong move," Cassie said. A couple of sunburned guests sauntered in and began looking at the bookshelf. Cassie watched them make their selections and move down the hallway. She reached for her wine and took a sip before speaking. "Didn't we agree not to see each other?"

"No, *we* didn't agree," Bob said, wing-spanning his arms across the back of the sofa. "That's what *you* wanted."

Cassie pictured herself alone in her room, staring out the French doors to the lights in Britt's room. How easy it would be to walk through the small grove of pistachio trees. She wanted to be talking with Britt, not sitting here with boring Bob.

"Can't we just have a good time this weekend?" Bob said. "Lie on the beach. Eat. Drink. That's all. Just your company."

"Look," Cassie said firmly, "I didn't invite you."

"It's not fair." Bob ran a finger along his mustache. "I've given you space. I haven't seen you since—"

"—since Bounty's funeral. That wasn't so long ago."

"Well, how much space do you need?" Bob smiled impishly.

Cassie knew Bob's charming ploys all too well. "You're not staying with me," she said.

Bob studied Cassie for a long moment. "A late-night ride with the Professor? Given how you two were looking at each other…kinda suspicious. Word at the school is she likes the ladies. I thought you might need a little support in case you're confused."

"Did you come all this way to save me from some lesbian fantasy you're having?" Cassie laughed derisively. "I don't know you anymore."

Bob's eyes hardened. "Why didn't you answer my letter? You should have called. I got worried. You're not sleeping with her, are you?"

"No. But the idea is starting to sound pretty good."

Bob raised an eyebrow. "Sooner or later, she's gonna come on to you. You're too attractive for her to resist."

"Then I hope it's sooner rather than later," Cassie snapped.

"Be careful what you wish for."

Cassie set her glass on the table and stood. "I'm getting Maria," she said. "She can find a room for you."

◙ ◙ ◙ ◙

"I am sorry," Maria said, as she stepped into Cassie's apartment and closed the door. "Your Bob, he tells me it is okay to stay with you."

"Well, he lied."

"Maybe he lies because he cares for you." Maria shook her head. "Do not take him for granted."

Cassie observed Maria's grief-lined face. "I appreciate what you're going through, losing—"

Maria swiped the air with a broad hand. "I speak of Bob, not Paulos. He would not come to see you if he did not care."

"He doesn't love me. I don't love him. Period." Cassie went into the kitchenette and took a bottle of water from the refrigerator.

"Paulos and I, it was not like love in the movies. We did not have children. But we were good for each in other ways."

Cassie dropped into a chair. "I miss Paulos."

Maria, still standing by the door, plucked lint from her black skirt. "Many people do. I, I just tell myself sometimes he is away on one of his trips. Now, you sleep, and in the morning, things look different."

"Thank you so much, Maria, for putting Bob in his own room."

She gave Cassie a kind smile. "For you, anything."

After Maria left, Cassie thumbed the latest edition of *Newsweek* to the lead story about the failed Middle Eastern peace talks. She read the same paragraph five times, then tossed the weekly aside. She stared at the large, framed photos of Santorini hanging on the walls, calendar-worthy pictures taken by Paulos. A wave of sadness passed through her at the thought of the vibrant friend who had died far too young.

And then there was Britt, whose image permeated her mind like perfume. Bob was spot on. Cassie was confused, but she'd never admit it. Not to him. Not to Britt.

I am enchanted, Cassie realized. That's what infatuation is—enchantment. I've fallen under Britt's spell because I've been a bit lonely.

Stop lying to yourself.

Cassie had heard the chatter about Britt's sexuality months ago and had found herself anticipating Britt's stay on Santorini. She'd never analyzed why, settling instead for the superficial reason of meeting someone new and interesting. But on some deep level, had she been hoping for a lesbian adventure? Is that the reason she had so conveniently cut ties with Bob? Other than her boredom with him?

But Britt would be so much more than a summer fling. Her growing passion for this amazing woman was cupped in something new to Cassie—tenderness. She even felt a bit protective, sensing a vulnerability Britt tried hard to cover. She recalled how Britt had watched her on the dance floor, then willfully ignored her. All the while she was dancing, she had sneaked peeks at Britt, wondering what she was thinking. *Britt got jealous, not of me, but of my dance partners. That's kind of sweet.*

"I've got to stop thinking about her," Cassie said out loud, clicking off the light. As she lay in the dark, though, moments with Britt floated to mind: chatting on Kamari Beach the day she had arrived; swinging under the stars at Dr. Gavas's party; wrapping her arms around her on the Vespa. It was magical. All of it.

But this deal with the winery. With Britt asking questions. Snooping. A lot was simmering beneath the surface of Britt Evans. Cassie knew she should be wary—if not scared—with all the red flags snapping in the island winds. But they only made Britt more intriguing. More alluring.

More irresistible.

22

"This may be the break we need," Susan Marcello said Saturday morning. "Greek wineries don't post guards, and the government isn't keen on an armed citizenry. Those weapons have to be contraband."

Britt took the phone off speaker when she saw the Seaside's cleaning woman outside her French doors, rag and spray bottle in hand, beginning to mist the windows. "So, you'll check into it?"

"Absolutely. I'll put my people on it. The Fira Winery on Santorini and the Crescent Vineyard on Crete."

"Right. Both owned by the Alevras family."

"Excellent," Susan said. "We finally have some threads to follow. But, Britt, don't endanger yourself further. I want you to hang low for a while."

"Think I'm in trouble?"

"Maybe. Theo Alevras will know you've been scouting out his operation. He might not want to risk hurting you, though, if he's connected to the Bountourakis incident. It would be too suspicious."

"I agree. In fact, several days ago, Theo slapped some kid around who almost knocked me over while unloading cargo."

"What do you mean, 'almost knocked you over?'"

Britt recounted the incident of the swinging crate at Athinios harbor. "I'm sure it was an accident," she concluded. "Otherwise, Theo wouldn't have been so angry."

"Or he could have been angry that the attack was blatant instead of a middle-of-the-night 'accident.' Who's the kid?"

"Georgios Kazantas. The younger brother of a woman engaged to one of the Akrotiri crew."

"I don't recall any Kazantas appearing on the police reports. I'll double-check, though."

"Was Theo questioned about Bounty?"

"Yes, just a general inquiry. The police considered him a hanger-on with the Akrotiri crew. I'd say his status just changed." Susan paused. "Anything else?"

"Not now."

"You've given me some good info, Britt."

"Glad I could help."

"You know," Susan said after a pause, "when we last spoke, I thought you'd sooner twist my head off than pass along any dirt you'd dig up. Bad pun intended."

Britt sighed loudly. "I was hoping you wouldn't bring that up. Those weapons at the winery scared me."

"That's why I'm urging caution. According to your schedule, you'll be in Athens this coming weekend. Is that still on?"

"Yes. Attending a symposium."

"How about meeting Sunday morning? By then, I should have some information on these folks."

"Terrific. How about something close to the MacKenzies' apartment? Say Kolonaki Square?"

"Name the spot." Susan paused again. "I look forward to seeing you, Britt."

▣ ▣ ▣ ▣

An hour later, Britt parked her Vespa at the Mesa Vouno cul-de-sac that served as a parking lot. A few scooters, a couple of taxis, and four donkeys with their owners filled the circle of pavement. Britt, playing the role of tourist at this archaeological site, held out a handful of Euros to the attendant at the gate, then proceeded up the winding path toward the classical ruins.

A little over halfway there, she paused at the rock carvings of the lion, the dolphin, and the eagle. Standing by the stone with Zeus's bird, Britt adjusted her daypack and continued her ascent to the ruins.

Once at the site, Britt picked her way along the footpaths snaking through acres of broken stones. Unlike the Minoan ruins at Akrotiri, from the fourteenth century B.C., these Hellenic ruins dated from the third century B.C. Atop the second highest mountain on the island, the site afforded a bird's-eye view of the land and surrounding sea. To the northeast, Britt counted nine small islands, and to the south, Crete appeared as a smudge on the hazy seam of the horizon, more mirage than reality. The highest mountain, Profitis Elias, loomed next door, blocking a view of the western side of the island. A monastery and NATO radar station perched on its summit.

Britt wandered through the ruins of the once men-only city, some parts still decorated with ancient graffiti of male genitals. Black beetles the size of a thumbnail trundled across the paths, and hordes of ants marched in ever-changing directions. The burnt grass and dried thistles along the path rustled with the quick movement of small gray lizards. After an hour in the merciless sun, Britt sought respite from the heat in a cluster of pines northeast of the theater. She pulled out a bottle of water from her daypack, drank, then sat quietly, listening to the furious buzz of huge black flies. Her thoughts bounced between Susan Marcello and Cassie Burkhardt. She didn't know what to make of either one of them, but both spelled danger.

Hot and satisfied, she started back to the parking lot. Just before she reached the stone carvings of the animals, Britt strayed from the beaten path to an outcropping that afforded the most spectacular view of the island. The entire crescent of land lay before her. Small groups of buildings marked the island villages, and a patchwork of odd-shaped fields filled the spaces between the settlements. Tiny white monasteries and shrines popped up everywhere like alabaster mushrooms, their domes painted blue to symbolize the sky.

Britt sat on a rock and concentrated on the stretch of Kamari Beach four hundred meters below. Sunbathers dotted the black surface like grains of tossed rice. Britt picked out the Seaside and Maria's B&B, side-by-side, from the cluster of buildings inland from the beach. She quickly turned her attention back to the strip of sand, shutting out thoughts of Cassie and Bob and what they might be doing. She was surprised at her jealousy and alarmed at the feelings underlying it. That she could allow herself to fall for Cassie was…well, preposterous. She absolutely would not permit it.

To the north, a couple of fishing boats were moored at the concrete landing, where the motorboat had put ashore last night. Britt traced the road Raffa had taken to the Fira Winery, through the northern streets of Kamari, past the disco and private homes, past dusty fields of grapes and tomatoes.

Britt heard a ding. She retrieved her phone from her pack.

Cassie: *Where R U?*

Britt: *Sitting atop Mesa Vouno.*

Cassie: *R U coming to the beach?*

Britt: *Maybe.*

Cassie: *Miss you.*

For real? Britt wondered. She didn't know if that signaled good or bad news. She leaned over to put the phone away and caught a flash of green wedged between two rocks.

"No photos," a voice warned.

Britt swung around to find the source of the command. A guard, his face cracked from years in the sun, pointed at the airport in the distance. "No photos. Military."

Britt swatted at a fly, then focused on the island's only airport, owned by the military but used for commercial flights. It sported the largest flat field on Santorini—the concrete runway.

Britt shook her head at the guard. "No photos," she repeated, and the guard plodded on, clicking his worry beads. Alone once again, Britt bent down and extracted from the small crevice a flattened Fuji film box. No photos? Somebody had been up here shooting— or at least changing film. The box said Fujicolor Pro400H. Who on earth used film anymore? A professional photographer. *Like Paulos Bountourakis.*

Britt's spine stiffened. Bounty had told Cassie he was going to take pictures of Kamari Beach. There it was, stretched like a black ribbon far below, and in the background, the airport. Cassie said he'd taken his car that night. It didn't make sense to drive it two blocks.

Instead of going to the beach, Britt reasoned, had he made the turnoff to Mesa Vouno and come here to this very spot? Was he shooting Kamari not from the beach but from up here on the mountain?

The wind rose to a wail. Britt spun around and stared into the eyes of the stone eagle.

"What did you see?" she demanded. Her flesh rose in goosebumps as the howling continued as though coming from the open beak of the limestone bird. "What did you see?"

Again, Britt looked out across the island, trying to imagine what had transpired that fateful night. Failing in the effort, and eager to leave the dizzying heights and calm her profound alarm, Britt leaned over and tossed the water bottle and film box into her pack. Before she rose, she saw a pair of expensive leather shoes. She looked up. Theo Alevras loomed above her, arms folded across his chest. Britt gasped.

"Why you come to the winery last night?" he hissed. His eyes, hard as onyx, bore into Britt. He had on designer jeans and a polo shirt with a tiny alligator embroidered on its front.

"Cassie needed to return something to Raffa," Britt said, rising to her feet. "I gave her a ride." She angled her body toward Alevras so she could keep sight of the petrifying drop-off less than a meter away.

Alevras waved a hand in the air. "The necklace? That is an excuse, not a reason. I ask you again, why you come to the winery last night?"

Britt regarded the arrogant Greek. Had he seen her put the film box in her pack? Emboldened that he had not glanced at her bag, she decided to be defiant and hoped her voice did not betray her fear. "Call it an excuse if you want. It's my reason. Now let me pass."

Alevras widened his stance to block Britt's escape. "Cassie knows the winery is private. Why you come?"

Why did your men have guns? Britt wanted to ask. Do you have a gun now tucked in the back of your tight jeans? Instead, she said in her most commanding teacher voice, "Theo. Let me pass." She tightened the grip on her pack.

Britt waited, her heart hammering. Alevras studied her, seeming to weigh his options.

"Do not concern yourself with my affairs, Professor Evans," he said at last. "I can make things very bad for you. Foreigners trespassing on my property? It is very serious."

"Would you like to go to the police and straighten this out?"

"You make a mistake this time," Alevras said, his voice low. "Next time, I call the police."

"You do that, Theo. Now, if you don't step out of my way, I'm calling for the guard."

"Be careful, Professor," he snarled, moving off the path. "I watch you."

23

That afternoon, Britt lingered on a veranda stool of the Pelican brooding over her awful day. The encounter with Theo atop Meso Vuono had been terrifying. A cold trickle of fear ran again through her veins: Theo had not only seemed menacing, he had threatened her. Susan Marcello's advice had been good. She needed to back off. She would not put herself, much less Cassie, at risk. And that film box? Could it have been Bounty's?

Then there was Bob Collins. Ugh. Turning up as he did, ruining what could have been a special late night with Cassie. Well, it was for the better. Heartache lay in that direction.

And now her windsurfing skills had gone to hell. She hadn't seemed capable of standing upright for more than two minutes. Today's performance had been humiliating. Bob had seemed to take special delight in her dunks—especially that last graceless catapult into the sea. His disdain had fueled her incompetence. Ugh all around.

"You're not done for the day, are you?" Cassie said, sauntering up to Britt. She stayed in the sand and squinted up at her.

"Yeah, the old mojo is missing today." Britt tightened her grip around an Orangina and raised it to her lips.

"Oh, come on, the wind's great now! The waves are perfect! Just one more run. Just you and me out there."

"What about Bob?"

Cassie flicked a hand at her ex-boyfriend, stretched in the sun like a curing hide, oblivious to the world. "He's had enough for the day. Let's go to Perissa Beach. You've been wanting to do it."

"I don't feel like putting on my—your—wetsuit, again."

"Don't. I'm not. The sun's off-peak and you've got a great base-layer tan. You won't burn."

Reluctantly, Britt rose and slapped some money on the table. The day could only get better. She hoped.

▣ ▣ ▣ ▣

Side by side, they cut through the navy-blue water on a westerly wind, Cassie on her brilliantly colored windsurfer, Britt on her lavender and black rental unit. The wave action was strong, as was the wind, but the women sliced through the rolls cleanly, their boards singing. Two small fins broke the surface of the water as Britt and Cassie reached the tip of the promontory at the south end of Kamari.

"Company!" Cassie cried, gaining a small lead to the inside. A pair of dolphins leapt through the waves as if on cue.

Britt grinned. Life was good again.

She and Cassie angled toward the bulge of land while the dolphins effortlessly dipped in and out of the swelling sea. When they approached the beach of Perissa, the dolphins broke away with a flurry of chirps and raced toward the open waters.

"Quite an escort!" Britt exclaimed as they waded to the beach, windsurfers in tow. Once on the black sand, they shed their harnesses.

"Those two follow me around sometimes," Cassie said. "They must have wanted to check you out." They settled in the shade of a sycamore tree. Cassie peeled an orange she had brought along in a mesh bag tied to her windsurfer. They each took a section and savored the sharp, sweet taste.

"So, what's going on Britt? You're not yourself today."

Britt tsked in disgust. "I was having a lovely morning up on Mesa Vouno, then Theo came along and scared me. He's furious at us, Cass, for going to the winery. I was afraid he was going to push me off the edge."

"No way, Britt! What happened?"

Britt related as much as she could remember, except for the Fuji film box, and found herself trembling.

Cassie laid a hand on Britt's arm. "I'm so sorry."

"Theo is dangerous." Britt's dark eyes skimmed the horizon. "I'm steering clear of him and his crew."

"Absolutely!" Cassie said. "Should we report this to someone? Dr. Gavas? The police?"

Britt shook her head. "There were no witnesses. It'd be my word against his. And he didn't do anything other than be menacing. I want to lie low for now."

"Well, I sure feel like pushing *him* over the edge."

Britt smiled at Cassie's protectiveness. "Thanks. Let's not waste any more time on that thug."

"Agreed. Men can be such assholes. Including Bob. I'm sorry about his showing up last night. I didn't want the evening to end like that."

Britt propped herself on an elbow and faced Cassie. "How did you want it to end?"

"Talking with you, not him." She glanced at Britt, then fixed her eyes on a cruise ship far out at sea. "Although we did talk a bit about you."

"You did?" Britt picked up another section of the orange. "What on earth for?"

"Oh, he's worried you're going to seduce me," Cassie said, side-eyeing Britt.

Britt laughed. "How gallant of him to come to your rescue! What did you do?"

"Challenged his sense of entitlement: I made him take his bag out of my apartment and get a room of his own. It's time Mr. Trust Fund paid for his own lodging. What a jerk."

No need to be jealous. Britt smiled and lay back to savor the embrace of the earth and sky. "Ah, this is bliss," she said, acutely aware of Cassie, who had flopped down next to her.

They stayed that way for long minutes, both quiet, absorbing the sensations of the beach: the sound of the beating surf, the urgent cry of hungry gulls, the fragrance of coconut sunscreen mingling with the smell of hot vegetation. But they were aware of each other, their bodies close and revealing so much skin, and the words *seduce me* now curling overhead like a tantalizing incense.

"Do you have a girlfriend back home?" Cassie asked at last, leaning on an elbow to face Britt.

"No." Britt sat up and fingered an orange peel. She placed it in Cassie's mesh bag.

"Nursing a broken heart?"

"Not anymore."

"Tell me about your last relationship." Cassie bit into the final orange slice.

"There's not much to say. We were together about six months. It ended badly."

"What happened?"

"She was bi. Married, but separated."

Cassie stopped chewing.

"Before the divorce was finalized," Britt continued, digging her heels in the sand and squinting at the cumulus clouds hanging low in the eastern sky, "she went back to her husband. I didn't even know they had started seeing each other again."

"Ouch."

Britt continued to examine the clouds, avoiding eye contact with Cassie. "But that's all behind me. Lesson learned."

"What's the lesson?"

"I need to be smarter about relationships. To have my mind in gear as well as my heart. To sidestep situations where I know I'm going to get hurt. To avoid being someone's sexual adventure."

"That sounds healthy." Cassie paused. "So, do you have any prospects?"

Britt's cheeks reddened. If circumstances had been different—if Cassie had been gay—she might have said 'you.' But what she felt for Cassie could only be the camaraderie of two American women on a far-off Greek island.

"Am I getting too personal?" Cassie asked.

"Oh, no, no. I have no prospects." Britt interlaced her fingers and stretched her arms over her head. When she lowered them and glanced at Cassie, she found her eyes boring into her, their expression open and far too deep.

"So, Bob was wrong?" Cassie said. "You won't try to seduce me?"

Fireworks lit every corner of Britt's body. "No," she said, as coolly as possible. "I will admit, though, the temptation is there."

Cassie's lips parted as though she were about to say something, then they curved into a Mona Lisa smile. A subtle blush spread across her cheeks like an early dawn.

Good god, we're flirting! Unable to trust herself not to lean in for a kiss, Britt popped up and scrambled for her windsurfer. "Race you back!" she cried as she ran toward the water. She quickly pushed her board into the sea, hopped on, and hauled up the sail.

Cassie laughed and darted after Britt. Once on her board, she closed the gap, then passed Britt, her eyes bright with the challenge. As she rounded the tip of the promontory, Britt lagged only a few meters behind.

The piercing whine of an engine broke their concentration. From behind the massive tongue of rock, a jet ski hurtled toward them. The driver, a fisherman's cap pulled low across his forehead, gunned the motor to full power. Before either Cassie or Britt could react, the vehicle, its blade spinning like a fan, ripped the water between them. The women toppled into the sea. As the jet ski disappeared down the coast in a descending drone, Britt surfaced.

Cassie did not.

Britt lunged toward Cassie's board, then dove underwater, twisting in every direction, her eyes wide. Panic seized her. *God no! Please, God, no!*

Suddenly a hand grabbed Britt's leg. Cassie rose beside her, steady as a balloon. Together they broke the surface.

"Fuck!" Cassie sputtered. "What the hell was that?" She held Britt by the waist, peering at her face.

"An idiot on a jet ski." Britt fought to keep her tears from spilling over.

"Scared the hell out of me. Are you okay?"

"Now that I know you are." Britt bobbed in the water. She put her hands on Cassie's arms. "You were down a long time."

"Probably not as long as it seemed." Cassie coughed out some water. "Damn it! My goggles got knocked off."

The women treaded water, holding each other close, as they caught their breath.

"I thought I had lost you." Britt pushed up her goggles and wiped away her tears.

Cassie cupped Britt's cheek with her hand. "I'm here. You're safe. That's all that matters." A wave lifted them.

"I never want to lose you." Britt slicked back a lock that had broken free of Cassie's ponytail.

"I feel the same way," Cassie said, her voice cracking.

They floated in the water, their boards and sails rising and falling on the swells. The two dolphins appeared and circled the scene, chirping and clicking as though signaling encouragement.

"You're shivering," Britt said. "We should head back."

Cassie nodded and flashed a tentative smile. She gave Britt's arm a quick squeeze and broke away. Cassie hoisted herself onto the windsurfer, found her footing, and raised the sail.

▣ ▣ ▣ ▣

"Well, it should be reported to someone," Bob said, toweling himself after a swim off Kamari Beach. "These jet ski people can't be zooming around like maniacs. I think we should tell the police in Thera."

"I agree," Britt said, running a comb through her wet hair. Her black tangles separated into wavy strands. "We were lucky. The next people may not be as fortunate."

"You can report it if you want," Cassie said. "They'll just tell us women shouldn't be windsurfing. Or, if we can't resist, we should stay close to shore. They'll find some way to blame it on us."

"Why don't we stay here," Bob said, "until you two settle down. We can drive into Thera later, talk to the police, have dinner, a few drinks, and come back."

"Sorry, Bob." Britt began to gather her belongings into a Greenpeace tote bag. "I want to go back to my room now. I'll catch you later."

"Fine." Bob grinned at Cassie, then spread out on his towel.

Cassie rolled her eyes at Britt. "I saw Jim at a taverna up the beach earlier. I'll see what he has planned for dinner."

"Don't bother," Bob said. "He's smashed again."

Britt sighed. "We've got to do something about him."

"I'll go check on him," Cassie said. "I'm done here."

Britt's eyes caught and held Cassie's. The harrowing experience with the jet ski had shifted the energy between them. She turned and dashed across the burning black sand to the beach road and jumped up onto the concrete embankment. As she threaded her way among dozens of mopeds and scooters, she resisted the urge to wheel around for one last reassuring glimpse, like Orpheus had turned for Eurydice. That had not ended well.

Instead, she replayed the conversation at Perissa Beach, she and Cassie deliciously alone together. What had happened between them? They had explored boundaries. Flirted. Was Cassie signaling her desire to be seduced?

On the beach, Cassie watched Britt disappear. She fought the impulse to run after her. Instead, she rolled up her towel and stood gazing at the horizon in a futile effort to stop thinking about Britt's dark eyes. Their conversation at Perissa Beach had circled closer to the truth of their feelings for each other. And out there on the water, had Britt said she never wanted to lose her? And had she, Cassie, said the same to Britt?

24

Sunday evening, Britt knocked softly on the French patio doors of Cassie's room.

Cassie, sitting on the bed with her laptop on her lap, broke into a grin and motioned her inside. "Gotta go, Mom," she said. She listened a moment to the reply too faint for Britt to hear. "I will. Thanks for your…okay. Love ya. Say hi to Dad." She shut her computer with a decisive snap and an inscrutable smile.

"Sorry to interrupt," Britt said.

"No problem. We've been chatting for an hour. What are you up to?"

"I need a break. I've been prepping for this week's research at the museum for another paper."

Cassie set the laptop to the side. "So, what's this one on?"

"'Nature as Portrayed in Minoan and Classical Pottery: A Comparative Study.' That's the working title." Britt pulled out the desk chair and straddled it, leaning her arms across the back. "Later, I'll think of an esoteric grabber that'll have journal editors drooling."

"Publish or perish?"

"Exactly. I'm just a lowly assistant prof, so I need all the publishing points I can muster."

"I imagine your book has helped."

"Yes." Britt smiled. "My marketability has increased six-fold."

"What do you mean?"

"I've had half a dozen inquiries from other universities. Nothing serious at this point. I'm biding my time for a California position. I'd love to get back to Berkeley." Britt's eyes swept the small studio. "You put Bob on the plane, I take it."

Cassie nodded. "Dropped him at the airport a couple of hours ago. Good riddance. I decided this weekend I genuinely don't like him. He's lazy, shallow, and rude. Not to be judgmental…" There were those dimples again.

Britt glanced out the window at the light of her room across the way. How easy it would be to come…. She turned back to Cassie. "How are your parents?"

"Fine. Mom has the summer off, so she's busy with projects. She says hello."

Britt raised her eyebrows.

"Umm…I've told her about you. She's…ah…impressed that I'm impressed."

"Oh." Britt digested this nugget and decided to move on. "In that case, I'd like to *press* you for a favor."

"That's so lame." Cassie smiled. "What do you need?"

"Do you think you could get me into Bounty's photo lab?"

Cassie straightened up. "I could probably get *us* in. Why?"

"I want to check his camera equipment."

"Why?"

"I'll tell you when we're in the lab."

"Does this have anything to do with the long story you promised to tell me?"

Britt nodded.

"Wait. I want to hear it. Now."

Britt took a seat, drew in a breath, and began her tale of Susan Marcello's request.

◙◙◙◙

"I do not go in here since…you know," Maria said, turning the key in the lock. The photo lab was at the back of the Bountourakis apartment, a small, separate wing of the B&B. "Everything is here except the film. The police keep two rolls found with him."

"Did they give you prints?" Britt asked.

Maria shook her head. "No. No exposures, they say. Paulos takes no pictures before the accident." She flicked on the lights. The room popped into view, revealing an area the size of a small kitchen with tile counters and enclosed wood cabinets underneath.

"The darkroom is there," Maria said, pointing to a door next to a sink.

"He used film, then? Not digital photography?"

"Both. Film is better, he says. Digital too harsh, but he uses that for his archaeology work." Maria ran a finger along a counter-top. "Dust. I must clean." She sighed and let her eyes wander over the surfaces. "Another time. I leave you girls here, okay?"

"Sure, Maria," Cassie said. "We'll let you know when we're done."

"You disturb nothing?"

"We'll leave everything as we found it," Britt assured her.

"Okay, what's up?" Cassie said as soon as she closed the door behind Maria, leaving the room stuffy with a faint smell of chemicals.

Britt tossed the Fuji film box on a counter. "That. Could it be Bounty's?"

Cassie picked up the box and studied the faded lettering. "It could be. He used this film for his 'fun' photography."

Britt opened the mini refrigerator. The bottom shelf held rows of small green and purple boxes. Fujicolor Pro400H.

"Tourists don't use film anymore," Cassie said. "Most don't even have cameras. They just use their phone."

"Can you even buy film like this on Santorini?"

Cassie shrugged. "I've never looked."

Britt slipped a box from the end of a row and closed the refrigerator door. "Let's compare the cartons."

"What's to compare?"

"See any dates or lot numbers?"

As they held together the two boxes, one empty and weathered, the other bright and containing a canister of film, Britt felt Cassie's hand lightly touch hers. Part of her wanted to pull away, but a greater part couldn't resist the magnetic force.

"Same lot numbers."

"Okay," Cassie said, her eyes boring into Britt, "where'd you find this?"

"On top of Mesa Vouno." Britt leaned back against the counter, breaking contact. She wondered if Cassie's hand was tingling as much as hers.

"Mesa Vouno?"

"What was Bounty doing taking pictures up there? Was he taking them the night he died? You said he was going to Kamari Beach. Could he have gone up the mountain instead?"

"I suppose. But why?"

"That does seem to be the question. As well as a few others. Like, why did a professional photographer have only two rolls of film on him?"

"He always carried at least five or six," Cassie said.

"Then what happened to the others?"

Cassie set the film box on the counter. "I don't like this, Britt."

"Me either, Cass."

"Maybe you should talk to your Susan Marcello when you're there for the symposium."

"Definitely. She'll want to know." Britt hesitated at the edge in Cassie's voice. "You haven't had much of a response to my 'assignment.'"

"No. I'm still digesting it." Cassie did a once over of Britt as though reappraising this woman she had thought she knew. "I'm somewhere between being horrified and thrilled."

"Personally, I'm leaning toward horrified. I never dreamed I'd be in this position."

"As an informant?"

Britt nodded. "It sounds duplicitous. Unethical."

"Because to a certain extent, it is. But that's the nature of the spy business."

"Do you think any less of me?"

Cass shook her head. "Surprisingly, no. It makes you even more intriguing."

Britt made a face.

"Are you sure, though, that this isn't a setup?"

"What do you mean?"

"Susan and her Greek pal could be using you to draw out the bad actors."

"I think you've been reading too many thrillers. Susan clearly said I was to observe only. I've done that. I've reported to her. And now I'm backing off as she suggested."

Cassie smiled. "Snooping here in Bounty's lab isn't exactly backing off."

"Touché." A desktop computer with a large monitor caught Britt's attention. "Is that Bounty's workstation?"

"Yeah." Cassie walked over and flicked on the switch. "I set it up for him. He did his digital work on it, a lot of 3D modeling." The computer whirred to life. "I should take all this equipment back to Akrotiri—it belongs to DB—but I haven't had the heart to mention it to Maria."

Cassie leaned over the keyboard and logged on. "Everything he has on here is backed up on the cloud as well as in my archive at Akrotiri." Cassie turned to Britt. "Anything you'd like to see?"

"I wouldn't know what to look for."

Cassie smiled. "Well, here, let me show you something we were working on together. Bounty wanted to expand his tech skills, and I wanted to expand my artistic ones."

After a few taps, the screen showed the fresco from Akrotiri in which boxing boys in loincloths were punching at each other. But unlike the actual cracked and faded fresco, the picture showed an unmarred surface with vibrant colors.

Britt gasped. "This is gorgeous!"

"Here, you can scroll through more by tapping the arrow." Cassie brought up a picture of a solitary man dangling a line of fish. "Bounty and I were playing around with an upgrade to Photoshop and testing some new functions with the frescoes at Akrotiri."

"You did this?"

"Don't act so surprised. I may be a computer geek, but I do have some artistic sense...though some people might consider this as bad as colorizing *Casablanca*. That's my version of how the frescoes looked after they dried on the wall."

Britt scrolled through more and stopped at a picture of a donkey standing outside a souvenir shop with racks of woven blankets and bright handbags.

"These are just experiments," Cassie said. "I was working with colors and shapes."

The next picture showed a surfer riding inside a huge, curling wave.

"An old shot of me at Big Sur—"

"You!" Britt leaned in to study the form.

"Yeah. I was experimenting with color blends, trying to get the entire spectrum of blue. I blocked out all the glare to give it that continuous coloring. I'm still not satisfied with how the wave tips turned out. They look weird."

"I think they look delicate," Britt said, peering at the cobalt sea curling into a huge tube—the perfect wave—with silver tips scattering into a lacework of white spray. She straightened up and gave Cassie an appreciative smile. "I'm impressed. Is there anything you can't do?"

Cassie continued to stare at the screen. "Get you to make a pass at me, it seems."

Britt froze.

"Did I just say that out loud?" Cassie half-whispered in shock. She turned toward Britt.

The moment hung between them, both women uncertain of whether to pretend it had never happened, shuck it off with an embarrassed titter, or step onto the path opening before them.

Britt studied Cassie's face, giving the conflicting voices inside her head time to come to a decision. One side said, *There's no future here! Stop now! Run!* The other screamed, *Kiss her! Kiss her now!*

"You did say it," Britt said softly, the internal battle still playing out, but the pieces arranging to skew carnal. Her eyes did not leave Cassie's face.

Cassie's eyes had picked up the colors from the screen. They appeared luminous and large with an unmistakable look: desire. The mental barriers Britt had constructed against her attraction clattered down into a heap. She turned to Cassie and leaned into her, pressing her against the counter.

Their mouths met in a detonation of desire, hard and hungry. Cassie clasped Britt in arms as strong as iron bands.

Britt cupped a powerful shoulder with one hand and grasped her waist with the other. Their mouths moved in ever deepening circles, opening with further invitation.

Cassie moaned at the press of Britt's tongue. Her fingers grasped Britt's thick black mane, intensifying the pleasure.

Britt broke the kiss and found Cassie's glazed eyes. "Did that qualify as a pass?"

Cassie paused to catch her breath. "Definitely," she said, her voice husky. She leaned in for another kiss, and Britt obliged. Their mouths fused and moved in ravenous concert. Their legs pressed into each other's warmth.

Britt slid her tongue into Cassie, who drew it further in, sucking it as though it were the juiciest slice of orange in all the world.

The force surprised Britt, and she thought for a moment Cassie would suck her entire being into her and swallow her. That she would be eaten. Gone. Lost. And part of her wanted that.

Britt slipped her mouth from the kiss and laid her cheek against Cassie's.

"Cass," she whispered, remorse swelling in her. "Where can this go?"

Cassie moved Britt back and held her by her arms, searching her eyes. "Wherever we want it to."

Britt leaned in again, forehead to forehead, and whispered, "This has all the earmarks of doom."

"Not from my vantage point." Cassie raked Britt's hair back.

"I don't know. I don't know." Britt sought a reliable prediction in the grey eyes holding her own. But already the armor was snapping into place.

"I care about you. Deeply."

Britt nodded. "Can we take a little time?"

Cassie huffed out a bit of air. "Not too much, Britt. You'll be gone soon."

Britt ran her fingers along Cassie's cheek, then turned and quietly eased herself out of the studio, leaving behind two women, one an image flat and static on a computer screen, the other more real and alarming than she would ever have believed.

25

Cassie stepped outside her B&B into a brilliant day. She noticed immediately the absence of Britt's Vespa. No doubt Britt was on her way to Thera to spend the day at the museum. She, herself, planned to work at the Akrotiri site as usual. A little separation would do them both good after last night's…whatever it was.

Have I been a flaming fool? Cassie hadn't realized how skittish Britt was. And, she had to admit, looking at herself through Britt's eyes, she wasn't at all Princess Charming. Cavalier with relationships—or at least those with men. Unsettled in her job once this gig ended. No wonder Britt had slammed on the brakes—she did not want just a summer fling.

But, boy, could she kiss!

And how thrilling to embrace her, to have their breasts pressing in kisses of their own. To have her hands in that thick mane. To know her heat. Cassie practically panted at the thought. Not only could she not get Britt out of her mind, but, oddly, every thought of her came wrapped with a ribbon of tenderness. Why had she never known this soul-shaking attraction before? Could this be the true love that had always eluded her? That people sang about in love songs—songs she was now hearing with new ears as their emotion resonated deeper than she had ever experienced.

As Cassie approached her Nissan, she noticed a familiar figure trudging up the street. "Why, good morning, Mrs. Delopsos," Cassie said, eying the colorful tote bag of the Fira Winery. "Doing a little shopping?"

"Hello, Cassie," Sophia replied. "I run out of milk for my coffee and must dash to the mart. You go to work?"

"Yes. But on such a beautiful day, I may have to leave early and go windsurfing."

"A usual day for you, I believe." Mrs. Delopsos's worry lines vanished with her smile. "Say hello to Dr. Gavas for me. I do not see him since the party."

"I will." Cassie hesitated. "Do you have a moment to talk?"

Mrs. Delopsos looked up and down the street. "What is on your mind?" She set down her bag.

"I saw you Saturday night at the winery. I went there to return a necklace Raffa gave me at the nightclub."

"So I hear," she said cautiously. "I see you, too. I worry for you… racing around on a scooter on a dark night."

"Um…there was a lot of commotion at the winery. Something didn't feel right. Are things okay? Are you safe?"

"Yes, of course." Mrs. Delopsos's eyes darkened. "Well, I do not know. It is not the same since Colonel Alevras and Theo take over. My husband and I had a good operation, especially the wine tasting. I like to meet people, talk to tourists. And we make good wine. Theo cares nothing about quality. Only money. He tells me I should sit in the corner and be grateful."

"I'm sorry, Sophia. That sounds hard."

Mrs. Delopsos's eyes filled with tears. "It is fate, and I accept it. I have my rooms, enough food, a few friends. Who needs more?" She smiled grimly. "And I can buy a little milk when I run out."

Cassie put a hand on Mrs. Delopsos's arm. "I'll suggest to Dr. Gavas that we have you to lunch. You've been so generous with your gifts to the crew."

"I will like that." Mrs. Delopsos touched Cassie's cheek. "You are a good person." She picked up her tote, and as she stepped toward her dusty little Fiat, she turned back to Cassie. "Please be careful. An evil wind is blowing."

▣ ▣ ▣ ▣

Britt stopped for breakfast at a little five-table café at the edge of Thera. She had eschewed the complimentary meal at her B&B this morning, wanting to leave early enough to miss Cassie. She ordered eggs and orange juice and sat back to savor the coffee the matronly waitress had set in front of her without prompting.

Britt had done exactly what she had not wanted to do with Cassie: light a physical fuse between them. She had acted purely on a hormonal level. Was she so weak she couldn't resist a kiss? Apparently so. But that kiss!

She eased up on herself as she contemplated the situation. Who wouldn't be attracted to the golden Cassie Burkhardt? Her whole being exuded vitality and promise. She embodied the life force of the sea, the wind, the sun. *Listen to me.* Britt took a sip of the strong coffee. It sounded as though she were turning Cassie into a goddess. But isn't that what infatuation does?

All her past loves had inhabited the rarefied universe of academia. But Cassie worked for an international company, a Fortune 500 conglomerate. She was of the real world: the world of computers and coding, of programs that sorted and tracked and made data comprehensible. She could even transform lovely art onto an even higher plane of beauty. And she lived in the elements, riding the wind and surf for pleasure. She was so unlike anyone Britt knew, all academics lost in books and theories. Cassie's mind, brilliant as it was, bent to the practical.

The waitress delivered a plate with two eggs swimming in olive oil and a couple of slices of white bread to sop it all up. Britt tore off a piece. Would a summer fling be so awful? she thought as she dabbed the bread into the oil. Of course not. But a fling denoted something light-hearted, and when it came to Cassie, Britt's heart was anything but light. Besides, did she even know how to do casual?

The freshly squeezed orange juice made Britt pucker. She wouldn't see Cassie today. Maybe not even tomorrow. She dreaded seeing her… yet couldn't wait.

26

*T**hat kiss. That kiss. That kiss.*

Britt wondered why she had stayed so late at the museum. She shut her computer and slipped it into her bag. She had an outline for one article and the opening page for another.

Well, yes, she did know why she lingered. Infatuation equals inefficiency. As much as she had tried to concentrate, her mind kept snapping back to that kiss. She'd had some great kisses in her life, but that one shot to the stars.

Walking down the quiet hallway, Britt passed the small IT room with the lights still on. Jim must be working late, too.

"Hey, Jim," she said, stepping through the doorway.

Jim jerked violently at the surprise. As did Dr. Gavas, who was leaning over Jim's shoulder, studying the screen.

"Oh, sorry," Britt said. "I didn't mean to interrupt. Just wanted to say good-night."

Dr. Gavas stood upright and smiled at Britt. "Come see Jim's latest miracle with the inventory database. A new way to slice the data. A new report to generate."

Britt peeked over Jim's shoulder, noticing that his ears had turned bright red. She saw only a screenful of commands using about every symbol available. "Computer programming is a mystery to me," she said. "It could just as well be hieroglyphics."

"Yep, yep, yep," Jim said. "It's a foreign language."

"That is true." Gavas chuckled. "Well, it is time for me to go. Sophia invited me for dinner, and I cannot be late." As he backed away, his foot touched Jim's green daypack resting against the wall. "Oops, I hope I did not crush anything."

"No. It's fine."

Dr. Gavas hoisted the pack off the floor and placed it on the table next to Jim. "It is safer here from my clumsy feet."

Britt noted the sudden sheen of sweat on Jim's forehead even though the air conditioning was frigid.

Jim swiped the moisture from his brow and turned back to the computer. He began to hammer on the keyboard. Britt and Gavas watched for a few moments at the blaze of characters appearing on the screen.

"Well, I go then and let you work," Gavas said.

"Me, too," Britt echoed, following Gavas toward the door.

"See ya!" Jim called, not looking at his colleagues.

Britt closed the door as she left, reluctant to leave. Something was wrong.

𐄷 𐄷 𐄷 𐄷

"Jim's been positively surly all day," Cassie complained to Britt on Tuesday evening as she examined the stained menu of the Pelican. "You're lucky you were at the museum. We almost threw him into a hole at the site and covered him over. Let the next generation of archaeologists find him."

Jim pretended not to hear.

The three Americans sat at a round table under a low-watt bulb at the back of the taverna. With business light at the early dinner hour, Andreas had time to show them skewers of lamb and beef.

Jim selected souvlaki with pilaf. Britt ordered the day's fresh catch. And after a moment of contemplation, Cassie said, "I'd like the kota riganati."

"Good choice," Andreas said, referring to the chicken flavored with lemon and oregano. He sauntered into the back room, a white towel slung over a shoulder, to pass along the order to the cook.

Britt watched Cassie slip the menu between a candle holder and a rack of napkins. Cassie was the most attractive woman she'd ever met.

Her hair was radiant, like a crown of wheat, and her smile playful. And those eyes! When they held her own in a steady gaze, Britt experienced a sharp, twisting, sexual ache.

But Sunday night had been a mistake, Britt thought. Hadn't it? Cassie would be a big heartache down a short one-way street…wouldn't she?

"Why don't they turn off that tinny noise," Jim complained of the music. "If I wanted wailing, I'd go to that wall in Israel."

"See what I mean?" Cassie said. "He's absolutely impossible."

While Britt struggled to meet Cassie's eyes, Cassie seemed to have no problem searching her face. Britt found herself on the verge of blushing, but Cassie seemed cool and composed. To avoid her look once again, Britt turned to Jim. "Is it true you've been impossible?"

"Quite the contrary. I've been my charming self." Jim frowned and reached for the wine bottle to pour himself another glass. His words were heavy and without the usual trace of mockery.

Britt shot Cassie a quizzical look, but she shrugged her ignorance. Clapping her hand over Jim's glass, Britt said, "You're not going to get drunk, Jim. And you are not going to sit around and be unhappy if there's something we can do to help."

Jim clunked the bottle down. He fingered his knife, then the fork, all the while staring at his glass, still capped by a row of female knuckles. He said nothing.

"Jim?" Britt said, moving her hand to his forearm. Her voice was soft and low but firm.

"Leave me alone."

"Not when I see you constantly drinking yourself into a stupor."

He wagged his head awkwardly as though he had been stunned by a blow to his head.

"Is it Irene?"

He nodded. In the poor light, his red hair had taken on the color of mud.

"What?"

"You don't understand," he said. "Women make me do foolish things."

Britt burst into laughter. "I totally understand. I've done many foolish things for women. But," she continued, "you always have a choice, though your emotions sometimes say you don't. No one *makes* you do anything." She shook his arm gently.

Jim heaved his shoulders, breaking free of contact with Britt. "No more wine for me tonight. That's my choice."

"All right. That's good enough. For now." She glanced at Cassie, who was watching her closely. "Now, let's have some pita," she said, tearing an end off the pocket bread and dipping it in tzatziki sauce.

Later, after Jim had left in a cab back to Thera, the women walked up the road to their rooms. Cassie turned to Britt. "I admire how you handled Jim."

"I'm concerned about him. He's so unhappy."

Cassie nodded. "His relationship with Irene is going badly."

"Has he said anything about it to you?"

"No. He's pretty tight-lipped. I think he has some serious issues. Maybe he thought he could work them out here, away from his family and the American definition of success." Cassie kicked a stone off the road. "Too bad he became entangled in an octopus of a family. There are plenty of good families around. The Kazantas are going to squeeze him for all he's worth."

"Does he realize that?"

"Oh, yeah. He tries not to care."

They passed a two-story B&B under construction. The stark, bright lights in the building's interior revealed the wooden framework amidst swirls of dust. Weary laborers were closing for the night. A man with a red bandanna tied on his head leaned a board across an open stairway.

"I have a question," Cassie said.

"Shoot."

"Your comment tonight at dinner about doing foolish things for women…have there been many?"

"Women? No, not many." Britt laughed. "I won't bother asking you the same question."

"I suppose not." Cassie hesitated. "I've missed you these last two days."

"I've had my nose buried in my research."

"I thought maybe you were avoiding me."

Britt remained silent.

"I have the film box you found. You left it in Bounty's lab." Cassie paused. "Why don't you come in and get it. I'll fix us a drink."

"Just take it to work tomorrow. I'll be at the dig in the afternoon."

"No. Come in now." Cassie grinned mischievously. "It shouldn't be a problem since you're not avoiding me. Besides, I owe you something." She slipped her arm through Britt's and guided her up the walk.

⌑⌑ **27** ⌑⌑

One of Cassie's most admirable traits, Britt thought as Cassie ushered her into the apartment, was precision: on the water, her reading the elements and being able to maneuver a sail exactly to maximize the power of surf and wind; on the job, perfecting computer codes to capture data, parse it, and display it in amazing reports and graphics; in her home, positioning everything to create a calm and comfortable environment. Only one item seemed out of place: the flattened film box on the desk.

Cassie made her way to the refrigerator. She popped miniature ice cubes into a couple of glasses and added a generous splash of Perrier.

"Here you go," she said, handing the fizzing water to Britt, who had taken the padded chair by the French doors.

After closing the drapes, Cassie swung the desk chair around to face Britt and sat, watching the ice cubes floating in her glass for a moment. Finally, she turned her gaze on Britt. "That was the most exciting kiss I've ever had."

"Yeah, it was something," Britt said softly, trying to control the back-flips in her stomach.

"Why did you run away?"

Britt glanced at the green Fuji box on the desk behind Cassie. She could just grab it and flee. But she didn't want to. Her body stayed rooted to the chair. "My feelings for you scare me." Her hand trembled slightly as she took a sip of water.

"Why?" Cassie's eyes had taken on a brightened sheen. "We're so comfortable together—we can talk about anything. And that zing going on between us? Whew."

Cassie placed her drink on the desk near the faded box. To Britt, that flimsy fold of cardboard seemed insignificant now, like a piece in some elaborate boy's game. A smuggling ring on Santorini? It paled next to the passion roiling inside her.

"But you're straight," Britt said.

"Maybe I've just been waiting for…a woman like you."

Britt set her glass on the small side table next to a well-worn Dan Brown paperback. She didn't trust herself to hold it any longer. She leaned forward, elbows on her knees. "What are you saying?"

"What I'm saying is…well, I know neither of us has been able to sustain a relationship. But does that mean we stop trying?"

"No, but…"

"How many tries did it take until you could stand up on a sailboard?"

Britt hmphed. "Too many to count."

"But you kept trying, and once you found your center of gravity, you got it. To your core. For the first time in my life, I feel that steadiness clicking into place. With you."

"Cass, I don't want to be just another wave rolling through your life."

"Another wave!" Cassie hooted. "Britt, you're a fucking tsunami!"

Britt's eyes widened.

"I'm totally smitten," Cassie said, her voice low and intense. "Don't worry about losing your heart. I've already lost mine."

Britt sat stunned.

After several moments, Cassie stretched toward her phone on her desk and fussed a moment with it. "I found the perfect song. Oldie but goodie." She tapped the play button and held out her hand. "I owe you a dance from the other night."

The opening notes from Foreigner's 'Waiting for a Girl Like You' filled the room.

Britt raised an eyebrow at the slow beat. "You could have chosen 'Dancing Queen,' you know."

"Right. But I don't have a mirrored ball to hang from the ceiling." As they stood, Cassie lightly placed her forearms on Britt's shoulders.

Britt automatically put her hands on Cassie's waist, but not around it, leaving a few inches between them.

"I don't want a summer fling," Britt whispered.

"Neither do I," Cassie whispered back.

They moved together, tightening their hold until no space remained between them. Britt broke eye contact to rest her cheek against Cassie's. Their cheeks were warm and as soft as two wisps of clouds.

The stillness of concentration: Britt held its essence in her arms. She could sense in Cassie the same patience she plied on the waves. But here the calculus of love and desire, twined with vulnerability and respect, gathered with an inner force, waiting to seize the perfect moment.

But Britt made the first move, so subtle, so unconscious, that at first, neither woman was sure it had even happened. Britt rolled her head slightly, pressing the edge of her mouth lightly into Cassie's cheek. After a few warm breaths, her lips parted and closed in gentle nibbles. Cassie mimicked the half kisses.

Millimeter by millimeter, their mouths repositioned until finally, they turned into a full, straight-on kiss, but light as though testing the waters before the plunge.

A second kiss. Solid. Solemn.

With the third, their mouths joined in commitment, hungry and wet. Their arms roamed freely now, and one of Cassie's hands pressed Britt's backside. Their pelvic lock tightened, their hips pulsing in unison as heat radiated through their shorts.

Cassie broke the kiss. She peered into Britt's eyes, open portals to destiny. "Stay with me," she whispered.

Britt did not, could not speak.

Cassie smiled at the "yes" in Britt's gaze. And at herself, for this being the first time she had been the one to speak those words: *Stay with me.*

The next kiss, long and deep, ended with Britt tugging on Cassie's T-shirt. Cassie raised her arms and let Britt ease it off. "This, too," she said as she reached around and undid the bra clasp. The bra joined the T-shirt on the chair. In one swift motion, Britt removed her own shirt. No bra.

They paused in admiration.

Cassie reached up and gently took one of Britt's breasts in her hand like a child holding a fragile Christmas ornament.

Britt inhaled deeply. "It won't break," she said after a moment.

"No," Cassie replied. "And I won't break what's under it."

As Britt's soft nipple transformed into a hard bead with her thumb strokes, Cassie's eyes brightened with delight. Britt unsnapped Cassie's shorts, the sharp sound jolting them like a starting pistol.

Cassie drew in a quick breath. "Let's move to the bed."

"Okay." Britt's hand trailed inside the opening she had created and withdrew. They stood shakily, stepped out of their sandals, and dropped their shorts to the floor, undies still inside.

They collapsed onto the bed, clinging to each other: two bodies honed on the waves of Santorini, skin tinted by the Mediterranean sun. After several minutes of bruising kisses, Britt rolled to the side. She ran her fingers along the patterns on Cassie's skin, the lines at the shoulders where the sleeveless wetsuit had ended, the seams between dark and light marking the boundaries of her bikini and one-piece swimsuits.

"My god, you're beautiful," Britt whispered. "And so strong." Her hands stroked the toned torso.

"Comes from pulling a sail up from the water a million times."

Britt pressed herself into Cassie again, found her mouth, and kissed her with a soul-expanding fierceness.

Cassie slid her hands across Britt's back as she accepted her full weight. "Ohhh," she said when they broke for air, "I thought I had a good imagination, but it wasn't even close."

Britt nibbled Cassie's neck and shoulders, kissed her firm breasts and the valley in between. Her palm skimmed along the curve of Cassie's hips as if she were riding the perfect wave. Down, down, her hand cruised near Cassie's knee to the tan line of her shorty wetsuit and pivoted in a 180-degree turn, sliding upwards, stroking the inner thigh. Cassie's cry propelled Britt onward. She slipped her hand between Cassie's legs, seeking the heat of her depths.

Cassie responded to Britt's rhythm with one of her own. They rocked to a shared physical song until Cassie began to pant. She made a final thrust against Britt.

Feeling her orgasm, Britt stilled. "I love you, Cass," she breathed, holding her tightly. She felt a tiny hug in response.

After many moments of silence, Britt asked, "Okay?"

"Definitely." Cassie was so depleted she could barely muster a smile.

They stroked each other silently, their languor only a brief respite. When their eyes caught again, they sought each other's mouth. As their kiss deepened, Cassie playfully rolled Britt over. She cupped a breast, sought its nipple with her mouth, and let her hand slip to the smooth skin below. She took command of Britt's body, as surely as she surfed the swells of the Aegean...but then the wind flagged.

"Is this right?" she asked. "Is the pressure okay?"

"Yes and yes. But here," Britt said, placing her hand over Cassie's and moving it slightly, "a little adjustment."

"This is my first time with a woman, you know."

Britt kissed Cassie's forehead. "I know. You're doing great." Swollen with desire, she opened fully, letting Cassie dive into her. Britt rode a gathering force, like the sea responding to the tug of the moon. The power escalated into a solid wall of blue, rising higher and higher. Then she was atop the crest, with the wave curling over. Britt's muscles exploded into convulsions.

"Yes!" Britt cried. Her long climax finally dissipated into a quiet calm, and she lay still in Cassie's embrace.

"My perpetual wave," Cassie said, smiling with relief and pride. "I'm riding you to the horizon."

After a minute, Britt turned on her side. She touched Cassie's flushed cheeks and ran a finger along the blond eyebrows arcing above the gray eyes. Eyes as placid as a calmed sea, but with life teeming in the depths.

"I've wanted you since the moment we met," Britt said.

"When you knocked me off my windsurfer?"

"No, when you ran me down." Britt put her mouth on Cassie's. Passion lapped at them once again, and they rode their desire well into the night, mounting their curves, cresting and crashing, and rising back to the surface.

At last they lay in each other's arms, exhausted, joyous, wondrously alive—and oblivious to the small green film box across the way belonging to a murdered man.

ロロロロ

Thursday morning in the Thera museum, Britt moved sleepily. Try as she might to stay focused on her task, her mind kept slipping back to the previous thirty-six hours of lovemaking. They had stayed in bed all day yesterday—Cassie had called in a vacation day—and had finally managed about three hours of sleep last night. Even this morning after breakfast, they had made love before Cassie roared off to the Akrotiri excavation, where she would arrange to take a long weekend so she could accompany Britt to Athens for the symposium.

Now Britt labored in the back workroom, tidying up her research and rechecking a few of her references. Nothing, thankfully, that required careful thought or analysis. To her relief, the monkey ewer had not swung to another shelf. It clung to its assigned spot.

But something's wrong. Another ewer, this one with a series of blue dolphins swimming around the circumference, was not in its place, nor anywhere else.

"It's missing," Britt murmured. The second in as many weeks. Had it been mislaid? She could understand a single error, but not two. If this one were missing for real, she'd tell Dr. Gavas. Britt rubbed her bloodshot eyes. Could her exhaustion be playing tricks on her? She could barely find her own hand in front of her face, much less some Minoan pitcher.

Britt glanced at her watch. Too late to worry. She and Cassie had a plane to catch. She'd leave a note for Jim to track down the ewer while she was in Athens. If it were still missing when she returned, she wouldn't stay silent. No more tiptoeing around.

28

Susan Marcello smoothed an edge of the napkin under her Bloody Mary. "The Alevras family is a two-generation conglomerate," she said, "built from scratch by the father, Dimitris."

A Sunday morning breeze swept across the tables lining the sidewalks of Kolonaki Square, full of the scent of cedars mixed with the pungent fumes of diesel engines.

"How did he manage that?" Britt asked. She bit off a corner of her buttery pastry and returned it to its plate.

Britt and Susan sat in a far corner of an outdoor café in the quiet Athens neighborhood, away from the main cluster of diners. Britt had dressed comfortably in capris and a striped sailor's top. Susan presented a more elegant picture in navy blue dress pants and an off-white sleeveless silk top that revealed her toned biceps.

"He was a young go-fer during the dictatorship back in the sixties and early seventies. The higher-ups did time; he evaded responsibility and continued with a career in the Army. He ranked out at colonel and retired with more money than Midas."

Britt smiled at the reference to Greek mythology. "Sounds like corruption."

"It's a familiar story," Susan said. "He's invested in several businesses over the years, including vineyards in Crete and partnerships with army buddies. I'd say the old man is as clean as a Sicilian mobster. Unfortunately, we can't get his bank records—or his son's."

The green canopy overhead flapped in the warm breeze. A stray tabby rubbed against Britt's leg.

Susan took another sip of her Bloody Mary. "They seem to be the upstanding businessmen they claim to be. No dirty noses or clear fingerprints. Interpol doesn't have a thing on them. But I think Bountourakis stumbled onto something. And Theo's threatening you makes me even more suspicious."

Britt nodded. "Finding Bounty's film box on Mesa Vouno clinches it for me."

"Circumstantial evidence. But, again, suspicious."

"Definitely," said Britt. "So, do you have enough to send in an investigator?"

"CIS won't question Alevras based on a Fuji box. The weapons at the winery might be the trip wire, though. My contact is submitting paperwork to open an investigation."

"It can't happen soon enough for me." Britt tasted her delicious screwdriver made from freshly squeezed orange juice. "What should I do now?"

"Keep clear of the winery and Alevras." Susan stirred her drink with its celery stick.

"Don't worry," Britt said. "After what happened on Mesa Vouno, I'm running in the opposite direction if I see him."

"Good."

"What do you think is going on?"

"Definitely not smuggling Minoan artifacts, even given your missing pottery." Susan crunched into the celery. "Too small-time for these guys. Probably drugs or arms."

"Hmmm…" Britt ran a thumb down the side of her sweating glass. She was becoming fond of the cool and competent Susan Marcello. She sensed in Susan a true and undaunted ally. Maybe being in love with Cassie had elevated the whole world.

Susan plunged the ragged end of the celery back into her drink. "So, Britt, what's got your eyes shining so bright?"

Britt's grin stretched to her molars. "I'm having a good time."

"Who is she?"

"Cassie Burkhardt. How did you know?"

"I noticed you being quite tight with a very attractive woman at the symposium."

Britt's stomach fluttered at the thought of being secretly observed by Susan. "You were there? I didn't see you."

"I dropped in for a bit." Susan gave Britt an enigmatic smile.

The waiter approached the table, but Susan waved him off. "What does Cassie think about Mr. Bountourakis's death?"

"She's skeptical about it being an accident." Britt paused. "After our escapade to the winery, I felt I had to tell her about you and my little side project on Santorini."

Susan clucked her tongue. "Well, we have no choice but to trust her now."

"It's *my* choice, Susan. I won't allow my work for you to threaten my relationship with Cassie."

Susan nodded. "I understand."

Britt finished her drink. "What did you find out about the Kazantas family?"

"Zero. I think we can assume they're a harmless clan banking on a ticket to America."

"Anything else, Susan? Otherwise, I'll be off." Britt opened her bag to retrieve her wallet. "Got a busy day ahead of me. Cassie and I are driving down the coast this afternoon. We're seeing Nicki Lampas, then on to Sounion to see the temple of Poseidon."

Susan waved off Britt's cash. "What's Ms. Lampas doing down that way?"

"Working on a housing project."

"Have fun. Stay in touch." Susan got to her feet as Britt stood up. "By the way," she said, "have you seen anything of the man who was following you around Athens?"

"Not since the night I chased him down the alley."

Susan smiled. "I bet that's one experience he didn't share with his boss. Zerakis must have pulled him off once you left for Santorini."

"Are you sure he's working for Zerakis?"

"One of my assistants questioned him. He denied everything, of course. Threw a five-star tantrum. Said he'd never interfere with his godchildren by having their associates followed."

"You don't believe him?"

"Sure," Susan said dryly, "and Elvis is conducting tours of the Acropolis."

𐤘𐤘 **29** 𐤘𐤘

Britt and Cassie took the scenic route south of Athens along the jagged coastline. The road held a few cars throttling to the beaches and some tour buses bound for the tip of the peninsula. As they drove slowly to enjoy the view, every vehicle but one passed Britt's rented Audi A4. The exception hung at a distance and appeared not much more than a wavering heat mirage.

"What's this town we're going to again?" Cassie asked, studying the GPS on her phone.

"Saronida. We should be coming to it soon."

"Found it," Cassie said. She enlarged the map, then reached for Britt's hand. They rode in silence, enjoying the shore views of white sand backed by the cobalt Saronic Gulf. The sea breeze blew through the open windows, and tunes from Britt's love song playlist blotted out the road noise.

Cassie sighed and kissed Britt's middle knuckle. "This is heaven. It feels like summer distilled to perfection."

"I can't believe we didn't bring swimming suits," Britt said. "Seeing these beaches makes me want to jump in. But we're kinda pressed for time as it is. I wouldn't want to keep Nicki waiting."

"She's down here for the weekend, you said?"

"Yeah, a work project had an emergency. The very weekend of our symposium. So this is the only chance we get to see her. You don't mind, do you?"

"No. I want to meet your friends. I'm glad it worked out. Besides, I get to see a part of Greece I've never been to. Boy, I'd love to spend more time here."

"Me, too. It would be a real vacation." Britt slowed to take a left turn into Saronida, leaving behind the view of the sea.

Cassie checked the GPS. "Right turn coming up." Still staring at the screen, she asked, "Were you and Nicki lovers?"

Britt threw a glance and smile in Cassie's direction. "No. Nicki had one of those crushes—cute *and* annoying. Luckily, we were able to maintain a friendship through it. She's totally cool. As loyal as they come."

"Hmmm. Will this be awkward?"

"I hope not. I told her about us when I called her Friday. She seemed okay. Her crush these days is more like playful flirting. It's not serious."

"Still," Cassie said, "we should be sensitive."

"You're amazing. I love you."

Cassie's dimples flashed. "Of course, you do."

"Pretty town," Britt said as they drove down a long row of palm trees. Coffee shops and open-air restaurants lined the sidewalks. Tourists and locals filled the small tables, and clusters of beachgoers threaded their way toward the sea.

Two turns later, Britt and Cassie rolled up to a three-story building a few blocks inland and around the corner from a row of swimwear shops.

Nicki emerged from the construction zone. She waved at them and removed her white hardhat, which had not messed up her stylish short black hair a bit. Cassie hadn't yet closed the car door before Nicki reached out to grasp her hand. "Nice to meet you, Cassie."

"Thanks," Cassie said with a big smile as she acknowledged the special little squeeze of Nicki's handshake. "My pleasure."

Nicki gave Britt a big hug.

Britt gestured at the building. "This is your baby?"

"Yes. Another miracle rising from blueprints into reality," Nicki said as she escorted them into the framework of an eight-unit apartment building. She handed them each a hard hat. "On schedule and on budget."

"That's a miracle in itself," Cassie said. "My company would give you a walnut plaque to hang in your office."

"What about the problems you mentioned?" Britt asked. She sidestepped scrap wood and nails littering the floor. A makeshift table stood in the corner with rolls of blueprints on it.

"Ah, the ones that brought me here for the weekend." Nicki repositioned her glasses and wiped a broad hand across her brow. "The owners decided suddenly they want more closet space. I fixed it by moving some walls. Smaller utility rooms, bigger closets. Everyone is happy. Especially me—since the interior walls are not up yet. But that phase is scheduled to begin next week."

"I can see why it was an emergency," Britt said.

"Yes. It's much easier to change blueprints than solid walls." Nicki winked, an old habit she had no intention of breaking. She noted in her friend a resonance missing since their days at Berkeley. Well, good for Britt. Too bad for her own heart, but her day would come. Soon. She could feel fate's warm fingers. "How did the symposium go yesterday? I'm sorry I could not make it."

"No new ideas," Britt said. "Just venting of emotions—leave burial grounds alone? Or dig 'em up?"

"Did they say anything about the British Museum sending back their plundered goods?"

"You bet. More than a few people got hot about it. But the moderator kept the focus on burial sites." Britt stepped past a workman hauling a bag of plaster on his shoulder. "Well, we should push off, Nicki. The temple is waiting for us at Sounion. Can you still join us?"

"Yes, of course." Nicki retrieved a bag from an on-site locker. "My good camera," she explained. "I'll be the official photographer of this adventure."

"Great!" Britt said. "Better bring a sweater, too. We plan to stay for the sunset."

▣ ▣ ▣ ▣

Britt's car blazed along the two-lane highway toward Sounion. The indigo and navy sea extended to the western horizon, where it brightened under the collapsing light of the sun. Near the rugged shore, the water broke into rolling rows of white capped waves.

As Cassie and Nicki talked about architectural software and computer-aided design programs, Britt withdrew into her own thoughts. She relished the temporary privacy. It seemed as if every moment for the past three days had been spent presenting, listening to speakers, talking with colleagues and students, or exploring a bit with Cassie.

She could hardly believe she was in a relationship again. But her return to the States loomed ahead. She and Cassie hadn't talked about what would happen once she left. Even if she did exchange her ticket for one giving her a couple of extra weeks, the summer would end. What then?

Britt glanced into the rearview mirror. Nicki caught her look, held her eyes for one long moment, and gave her a warm smile with a nod. *She approves of Cassie.* Relieved, Britt slid her eyes to the reflection of the road behind her. Again, one car, tucked safely in the distance, matched her speed. Hugging low to the road, it appeared to be the same car that had followed her earlier.

Steering the Audi around a blind curve, Britt squeezed the brake to slow down.

"What's wrong?" Cassie asked.

"We're being followed," Britt said. "It's the same car that's been behind us all the way from Athens."

Cassie and Nicki turned around in their seats.

"Don't look," Britt said, and they assumed their previous positions just as a green BMW came around the curve. The driver, realizing the Audi had slowed, slammed on his brakes. Too late. Britt had a quick view in her rearview mirror of a man with a dark beard.

30

"Who is it?" Cassie asked.

"I'm not sure, but I think it's the guy who followed us in the Plaka," Britt said. "Remember him, Nicki?" Britt checked the mirror again. "Watch now. He should be passing in a couple of seconds."

As the BMW cruised by Britt, the driver turned his face away.

"Damn, I didn't get a good look," Cassie said.

Spotting a roadside café, Britt swung the Audi into the parking area. A cloud of dust churned around the car, then rolled across the two small iron tables on the veranda. "How about you, Nicki? Did you see him."

"No luck."

Britt studied the squat building, stuck in the middle of nowhere. "Either of you need anything while we're here?"

"Water," Nicki said quickly. She popped open the car door and disappeared into the dark interior of the restaurant.

"Come on, Britt, what's going on?" Cassie said as soon as Nicki was out of sight.

"I wish I knew," Britt replied. "This is the first I've seen him since I've been back. I spotted him in Syntagma Square when I met Nicki and her godfather before I left for Santorini. He followed us as we strolled through the Plaka. And I saw him the night of Anne and Bill's going-away party." Britt let out a derisive chuckle. "I chased him down an alley, but he got away."

"Fuck, Britt, that sounds crazy dangerous."

Britt shrugged. "He ran from me, which I took as a good sign. If he had wanted to hurt me, he had his chances."

"Did you talk to the police?"

"I told Susan Marcello about it," Britt said, smiling with reassurance. "Don't worry."

"Don't worry? Listen," Cassie said, adjusting herself for a fuller view of Britt, "you seem to attract a fair amount of odd stuff and 'accidents.' I see red flags with the word 'DANGER' in big freaking letters on them. Even if you don't."

"I hear you," Britt said. "Minimizing is my way of avoidance." She ran her hands along the top of the steering wheel.

"If Susan Marcello has asked you to 'be her eyes on Santorini,' she'd better protect you." Cassie put a hand on Britt's thigh. "Maybe you should set up another brunch with her. I'll join you and give her a piece of my mind."

"Thanks for your support, Cass." Britt patted Cassie's hand. "Maybe I've been too naive. And I don't want anything to happen to you."

Cassie softened. "I don't want anything to happen to you, either." She glanced toward the restaurant. "I wonder what's keeping Nicki."

"Hmmm. Maybe I should check." Britt reached for the door handle, then stopped. "How do you think she's dealing with our being together?"

"She seems okay to me, but I just met her. She's had a lot of years to get over her crush."

Britt nodded. "Yeah, she seems good. You two have certainly hit it off."

"Oh, you know us techies. Can't stop talking shop."

"I noticed."

"Feel excluded?"

"Not one bit." Britt looked past Cassie. "Oh, here she comes."

Nicki bounced down the steps of the restaurant cradling three bottles of spring water. "He is gone?" Nicki asked, sliding into the backseat. She handed two bottles to the front.

"Thanks," Britt said, opening the bottle and taking a long pull. "I wouldn't be surprised to see him again. But so far, he's been totally harmless. Just annoying."

Indeed, they didn't have long to wait. They spotted the BMW in the Sounion parking lot. Its driver was missing. "If we find him, maybe we should tie him to a pillar until he tells us what he's up to," Cassie suggested. "The tourists would probably think it was part of a show."

"Great idea, Cass." Britt laughed and stopped the car at the entrance.

"Think he's got a gun?" Cassie asked.

Nicki motioned for Britt to drive into the lot. "Go on. We're safe. No guns allowed in this country."

"Yeah," Cassie said, "tell me about it."

"You know, we could shoot him," Britt said, easing her foot off the brake. "Right, Nicki?"

Nicki adjusted her glasses, then caught Britt's meaning. "My camera. Ah, yes. We will capture beauty today. And perhaps a bit of the ugly."

▨ ▨ ▨ ▨

The trio hiked up the hillside to the temple of Poseidon. Its white marble columns gleamed against the brilliant blue of the sea. Britt and Cassie stood at the southwestern tip of the ruins, peering inland, back at Nicki. Positioning herself halfway across the temple, she began snapping pictures.

From their vantage point, Britt and Cassie could see the stranger emerge from a row of foundation stones at the north side of the temple. With his hands cupped over his face, he lit a cigarette while drifting toward the backside of the ruins.

As they explored the site, Nicki took on the role of tour guide. "Notice these columns," she said, her bangs blowing back from her forehead. "They have only sixteen flutes instead of twenty. The fluting is more shallow than usual to give the column a slender look. Now," she continued, her voice dropping, "move to your left so I can take a picture of our friend."

Nicki shot Britt and Cassie framed against a row of huge marble columns where the pediment was still in place. Behind them, the blue sea sparkled, and in the far-right border, the man appeared.

"Wait!" Nicki cried, holding up her hand. "Let me get a couple more." Quickly, she switched to zoom mode. She perched on a column broken near its base and set a steep angle for the shot. Wild crocuses, wilted and dried in the cracks of the stones beneath her feet, jerked stiffly in the wind.

"He plays a poor tourist, doesn't he," Britt said to Cassie. Through her sunglasses, she eyed the stranger, dressed in khaki pants and a dark shirt. "He doesn't even pretend to enjoy the view." By now, the man had made his way to the western edge of the ruins. A family with young children clambered on nearby rocks.

Nicki focused her Nikon. A child's screech turned the stranger's head three-quarters of the way toward Nicki. She clicked the picture. The man's head jerked fully around to Nicki, his mouth twisting in anger. She snapped another shot.

The man scuttled around the edge of the temple. He paused in a cluster of tourists viewing Lord Byron's name scratched into a pillar and glowered at the women who had outwitted him. He scurried to the exit and back to the parking lot. Moments later, his BMW screeched away.

▣ ▣ ▣ ▣

Britt and her companions nursed beers at the open-air tourist pavilion adjacent to the ruins. She watched the sun drip slowly into the horizon. "How many shots did you get of him, Nicki?"

"Three, four not so good ones. Two good zooms of his face. That should be all we need. I can enlarge them."

The table was small, the taverna quiet. Three couples sat at different tables, each with red-and-white gingham cloths. Two English couples enjoyed drinks only. A Swedish pair ordered dinner from square menus written in English and Greek.

"Could you email the pictures?" Britt asked.

Nicki nodded. "Will do. Soon as I get back to Saronida."

An orange smudge on the horizon was all that remained of the day. Britt felt the heat of the earth rise into the cooling air. Above, the stars stared at the darkening land. "Well, it's time to head back to the city," she said, stretching her arms overhead.

"Good. I'm exhausted," Cassie said. "Let's hope that guy is long gone."

Nicki checked her watch and nodded.

31

As they started up the coastal road, the BMW failed to appear. Once past black pools of water used for salt drying, the road straightened for a small stretch. Suddenly distant headlights flashed in the rearview mirror. The circles of light came up quickly and stayed dangerously close. "I believe our friend is back," Britt said. "He must have parked on a side road and waited for us."

"He's probably pissed as hell," Cassie said.

Britt's stomach shrank into a tight, cold sphere. She pushed the accelerator, and the Audi leapt into the night, its headlights stroking the roadside foliage. Britt leaned back in the seat and let the steering wheel become part of her body. The Audi sped around the curves of the snaking road.

When the road straightened for a stretch, the BMW took advantage of it. It moved into the left lane and nosed alongside the Audi. Britt glanced over and saw the bumper, then the door. Through the open passenger window, she could see a gun aimed at her.

"Look out!" Britt cried, leaning over and shoving Cassie down. A shot sailed past the sedan. Britt swerved to the right and onto the shoulder. She popped her head up and saw the car still adjacent to them. Her mind registered something else—a curve in the road, to the right. She pulled back onto the pavement. Another shot rang out. Britt slammed on the brakes. The companion car, its occupant fixed on the Audi, zoomed ahead and missed the curve. Airborne for a moment, the car and its red taillights disappeared into the awful darkness, followed by a terrible crunch of snapping steel and breaking glass.

Britt angled the Audi off on the shoulder and jammed on the parking brake. The three women flung open their doors and dashed across the road to the spot where the BMW had careened over the edge. Fifteen feet below them, it rested, smashed against a boulder twice its size. The driver's door had folded open. The man sprawled half in, half out of the car.

"His legs are pinned," Britt shouted as she charged through the sharp, dry brush with Cassie and Nicki close behind.

As they approached the wreck, Britt slowed, then stopped. *What would Susan Marcello do?* Britt shut her eyes for a moment to focus. *Stay calm. Be cautious.* "Any of you see the gun?" she asked.

Nicki snapped on a miniature flashlight from her camera pack, which she had carried down from the car. The beams played over the injured man. "No gun here," she said kneeling for a closer look. "He's still alive."

Britt tugged on his legs but couldn't budge him. "Can you help me, Cass?"

Cassie shook her head and backed up. "Let's get out of here."

"Who are you?" Nicki said in Greek to the man. His eyelids fluttered, then closed to shut out blood streaming from a gash in his forehead. He worked his jaws, but no sound emerged. "Who sent you?" Nicki placed her ear directly over the man's mouth.

"Christ damn you," the man rasped in Greek.

"Tell me who you are. We will help."

"No." The man's eyes receded in fright.

Cassie stayed in the background, her hand over her mouth, half horrified, half in awe of the cool efficiency displayed by both Britt and Nicki.

Nicki glanced over to Britt. "One more try." She bent down close to the man. "My son, my son," she cooed into his ear, betting on his disorientation. "Tell your mama. Tell your mama what you are doing following these pretty girls."

"Protect...protect..." the man whispered, his breath thin and ragged.

"Nicki," Britt said, putting a hand on her shoulder.

"He's almost dead anyway," Nicki said, turning back to the trapped man. "Tell me again."

The man's head slumped.

"Tell me, you naughty boy!"

The man's jaws ground together painfully, and a surge of blood bubbled through his lips. Nicki leaned closer for the breathy response.

"Hurt the American…hurt…" The man's head fell to the side. He coughed and went still.

"Translate, please?" Britt said.

Nicki rose slowly. "Nothing but prayers. His stupid prayers." She bent over and tapped the man's pockets. "No wallet," she said. "No identification." She pulled out her camera and snapped a couple of photos of his face.

"Come on," Cassie said. "We should go."

They heard crashing through the wild oleanders and scrub oaks and turned to see a middle-aged man bounding down the embankment, yelling at them in Greek.

Nicki matched his tone, word for word.

"Shit," Cassie said, staring at the dead man at her feet. "I don't believe this. What a bloody mess."

Britt put an arm around a trembling Cassie as she turned to Nicki. "What's he saying?"

"He saw the accident. He wants to know what's happening. I told him the man is dead." While Nicki spoke to Britt, the stranger made his way to the body and examined its features. He shook his head sadly at the three.

"Come on," Britt said, tugging Nicki's sleeve. "Let's call the police."

"Right. Let's go now." Nicki spoke again sharply to the newcomer, then searched for footholds in the hillside.

Britt and Cassie scrambled up after her. As they reached the shoulder of the road, Nicki wheeled around. "We didn't check the glove compartment. Maybe his wallet is there. You wait here. I don't want that guy to get it. I'll be back in two minutes."

At the wreckage, Nicki approached the man who was screwing off the rear license plate. "I thought you would not make it," she said softly.

"I drive like a crazy man from Athens after your call to Mr. Zerakis. Your godfather thinks you are touched in the head."

Nicki shrugged. "I had no time to explain. My friends waited for me in the car while I made the call. They thought I was only buying water." She turned her attention back to the car and quickly ran her eyes over the twisted metal. She slipped an arm through the window on the passenger side and flipped open the glove compartment. "Damn," Nicki said. "Nothing here. Did you find his phone?"

"Yes. I have it. It's locked." The man leaned over, and using a Swiss Army knife, deftly sliced off the fleshy portion of the dead man's left index finger, wound a handkerchief around it, and stuffed it in the pocket of his jacket. He recovered the victim's gun and started to put it in his waistband.

"Wait," Nicki said. "Give me the gun."

The man hesitated. "Your godfather…"

"Would be happy if I had it." Nicki held out her hand. "Give it to me."

The man checked the safety and obeyed the goddaughter of Mikos Zerakis.

"Did you find another clip?"

He withdrew it from a pocket.

"Good." Nicki fit the clip and the gun in her bag.

"I am done here. I have everything I need," the man said.

"Not quite." Nicki gestured at the body. "I have pictures of this man. Tell Mikos I will text them tonight." She wanted her godfather to take care of this business and not let Britt get caught up in police matters.

"Done," the man nodded.

Halfway up the embankment, Nicki turned back in time to see the man flip a lighted match into a patch of dry vegetation a short distance from the car.

"Did you find anything," Britt asked Nicki upon her return.

"Nothing," she said. The man from Athens had now reached the road and half trotted to his car.

"We have to call the police," Britt said, turning to face Nicki.

"Not on our phones," Nicki said firmly. "The first public phone we see, we stop and call. But I give them no names."

Britt nodded. "No names."

"I'll stay in Saronida tonight as planned. Maybe I can find out more if I stay close."

"Okay," Britt said. She placed a shaky hand on the parking brake and released it. As she swung the Audi onto the road and gained speed past a stand of cedars, a tremendous explosion from the wrecked car rocked the coastal highway.

32

"Nicki called the police from a phone booth," Britt reported. "Anonymously."

"You did the smart thing." Susan Marcello's voice was calm and reassuring over the phone.

"Are you sure?" Britt gave Cassie a thumbs up.

Cassie leaned against the kitchen counter, across from Britt who sat at a small table in the MacKenzies' apartment.

"Absolutely," Susan continued. "Right now, the last thing any of us wants is the Greek authorities drawing you into an investigation. Nicki handled it like a pro."

"What happens if they do find out?"

"Your defense is airtight. He tried to run you off the road. He just killed himself instead of you."

"Aren't we lucky?" Britt said dryly.

"Do the MacKenzies know what happened?"

"They were in bed by the time we got home."

"Keep them and everyone else out of it. Right now, it's just we four who know."

"Plus that guy who stopped after we did. And Mikos Zerakis. Nicki said she'd call him from Saronida. Family duty."

"And family protection. It's a plus in a way. Zerakis will take care of his godchild. He won't want her name splashed in the news." Susan paused. "When do you two head back to Santorini?"

"Ten tomorrow. Nicki said she'd email the pictures to me. I'll forward them to you as soon as I get them."

"Good I'll run them through Interpol." Susan's voice softened. "Be careful, Britt. Don't take chances. I'll call you when I have more news."

"Good. Thanks for your support, Susan. I feel better having you in my corner."

"Take care."

Britt hung up. "The embassy is handling it. Susan says not to worry."

"Easy for her to say." Cassie scowled as she headed into the bedroom. Britt followed. "She has diplomatic immunity. We don't."

"You know, this isn't exactly the evening I had planned for us," Britt said as she turned down the bed covers and crawled between the sheets.

Cassie scoffed and tossed her phone on the nightstand between the two single beds. "Today we get chased, shot at, and see some guy die. I don't know what we could do for an encore, except maybe chew through the bars of the Athens jail."

Britt adjusted the pillow propped against the headboard. "You're mad at me, aren't you?"

"You bet I am." Cassie sank next to Britt on the narrow mattress. "But I'm more scared. You—and now I—have gotten dragged into something that nearly killed us."

Britt pulled Cassie into her arms. "I know. I'm scared, too." She picked up Cassie's hand. "But we have each other. We have a champion at the American Embassy. We have Mikos Zerakis hovering in the wings."

"Not reassuring, babe."

"It's the best I can do. I'm too tired to think. Can we talk more in the morning?"

Cassie snuggled in close. Her shoulders twitched as she fought a shiver. "I just flashed back to that guy in the wreck. I've never seen anyone die."

"Me either. I've seen several animals die on the farm—never a human, though. It's eerie how the light drained from his eyes."

"Enough about death." Cassie ran a finger across Britt's cheek and over the slight bump on Britt's nose. "This must have hurt."

"Yeah. A softball took a nasty hop. I made the play, though. A blazing throw to first."

"Good arm, huh?"

"Arms," Britt said, bringing them tightly around Cassie and drawing her closer.

𐃩 𐃩 𐃩 𐃩

Mikos Zerakis looked out over his country, shimmering in the white light of a hot morning, and thought of darkness. Not the kind that brings relief to a steaming population at the end of a blistering day, but the kind that coaxes men to evil. There, to the south of him, past the tops of the palm trees dotting the National Gardens, past the vast stretch of apartment buildings and the still wider expanse of dry land and deep sea, men plotted ways to fill their pockets with more gold than a thousand people could spend in a lifetime.

"What is in your thoughts, Mikos?" Nicki asked as she joined her godfather on the balcony.

"Of a bad time many years ago."

"The junta?"

Zerakis dipped his head slightly. "Sometimes I think Greece is a carnival ride spinning around and around. The Nazis come. The monarchy returns. Democracy comes. The dictators come. Democracy returns." He shook his head.

Nicki leaned on the iron railing and breathed the air of freedom. "What do you see now as we spin?"

Zerakis clicked his wooden worry beads, worn from years of anxiety. "I see a clown, Colonel Dimitris Alevras, a bastard from the dark days. He kissed the rump of the junta and, with his lips puckered, funneled millions of drachmas into his pockets."

"Alevras. The name is not familiar."

Zerakis shepherded his favorite goddaughter from the balcony of the government building into the brisk atmosphere of his air-conditioned office.

"The man at Sounion—he worked for the retired Colonel. The photos you took, the print from the finger my aide brought back. They confirm this. Yannis Thadion was his name. The pet of a dog. I am sorry my man did not get to him before he tried to run you off the road."

Nicki picked up a print of the photo she had taken in Sounion and carried it from the desk to the sofa. The eyes of the now dead man burned into her.

"Do you know him?" Zerakis asked as he tapped the computer on his desk.

Nicki shook her head.

Zerakis swiveled the monitor around and swiped through several photos of Britt, Nicki, and him in Syntagma Square. And of Britt and Nicki walking the streets of the Plaka. "From the phone of Thadion. We read emails and texts about your professor friend. Someone has hacked into her accounts."

Nicki blanched. "But why?"

"Santorini," Zerakis said, thinking out loud. "A lackey from the dictatorship has enough money to buy a fine winery there. A small-time informant for the CIS falls off the caldera cliff. Then an American agent appears in the form of a professor—one whose life is threatened on a street in the Plaka and on the road to Sounion."

"Mikos, Britt Evans is a real professor."

"She cannot spy at the same time?"

Nicki rearranged herself on the white leather cushion. "No, not Britt."

"She has met with American intelligence. Susan Marcello from the U.S. Embassy."

"I don't believe it."

Zerakis lifted his heavy eyebrows at Nicki, then continued pacing. "I have my sources at the embassy. I know who comes and goes."

"Then Britt doesn't know what she's doing."

"Perhaps. The innocent make good eyes, sometimes. They see things with fresh sight. Now, the question is, what is there to see on Santorini?"

"You mentioned a winery?"

"It would make a good front, yes? You can have bills of lading, but who can say what is in the crates shipped in and out?" Zerakis clasped his hands behind his back and resumed his stride across the thick carpet. "On an island like Santorini, the police watch the girls and bandage injured tourists for their return flight to Athens. As long as Alevras's men are careful, or pay off the appropriate people, they can do what they want."

Zerakis paced for a few more moments in silence. "Are these Americans back on the island?"

"Yes. They left Athens today. I told Britt I would call her tomorrow with more information," Nicki said. "She is as mad as a scorpion."

"What happened?" Zerakis asked, his eyes brightening.

"I told her I wouldn't send her the pictures. They could cause trouble if the Greek police found them.

Zerakis's rumbling laugh had an edge of sadness. "You acted wisely. It is Greek business, not American."

"Yes. My thought exactly."

Zerakis picked up one of Nicki's photos of Britt and Cassie standing against the white pillars of Poseidon's temple. "American intelligence has blundered into dangerous territory. It crushes the innocent—and not so innocent—beneath its gigantic feet." *Among its victims could be two pretty American girls. A shame.*

"Mikos, why not have Greek intelligence check into the matter? It can't hurt."

"Yes, it can. For the same reason this Marcello and the CIS send an amateur to do the work. An intelligence agent would show like a mole on one's nose. They needed someone with a legitimate reason to be on the island." Zerakis thumbed through his worry beads. "If we are wrong about our suspicions, Greek intelligence—and your god-father—would look very silly. The Conservatives would make much of it in the next election."

"But we're not wrong, Mikos. Britt *is* in danger." Nicki stood up. "I'll go to Santorini to warn her."

"You cannot call her?"

"Her communications are compromised. Who knows who listens?" Nicki's black eyes burned with intensity. "Godfather, I must go. I go with or without your blessing."

He held her eyes and, for once, did not know what to say.

"I do it for love and honor, Mikos. I owe much to you both. Without you, I would not be where I am today. Without Britt, I would not know who I am."

Zerakis was well acquainted with Nicki's fiery spirit, but he had never seen her fierce bravery. He paused as his eyes watered. "You will go, then," he said. "Your father told me once you would make a good freedom fighter. Nicki, use your wits, as you did last night."

"Can you arrange passage for me on a ferry?"

"A ferry?"

"Airport security is too tight. It will be easier to go through at the ferry terminal—especially if you send an escort," Nicki said. "You know I have a gun."

"Yes, the dead man's." Zerakis looked at Nicki with both concern and disapproval. "I can pull you out of legal trouble, but if you get in the way of bullets…"

"I won't."

"You know how to use it?"

Nicki paused. She had played plenty of paintball in her college days. And she had gone once to a firing range with her brothers. "Yes. Remember, I lived in America. Guns are a national sport there."

Zerakis could not hide his shock. "My child, I do not want you to do this thing!"

"I will go, Mikos." Nicki's voice resonated with power. "And you will give me your blessing."

$$\boxed{33}$$

Tuesday morning the sun streamed through the high windows of the Thera museum, flooding the back work area. Britt's long fingers paddled the workbench. The ewer was still missing. After the terror on the road from Sounion, just how important was a 3400-year-old "pot," as Susan had called it?

As Britt unpacked her laptop and printouts from her bag, she noticed how detached she had become from the objects of her study. A week ago, it had taken full discipline to concentrate on her research when fantasies of Cassie fired her mind. Now, she thought only of protecting her. Danger lurked in the ashen hollows of Santorini.

Britt halfheartedly searched the cabinets and cubbyholes for the ewer with the grinning dolphins and rechecked the database. By ten o'clock, she conceded defeat and took a break.

When she returned from the employee lounge after a cup of coffee, she found Jim Larson making a hasty exit from the room. His green nylon daypack swung by a strap over his shoulder. "Just the man I wanted to see!" she exclaimed, mustering up a smile and grabbing his upper arm. "Come in here a second, would you?"

Jim quick-stepped into the workroom, propelled by Britt's grasp.

"I have something to show you," Britt said. "Before I left for Athens, I asked you…Oh!" Britt released his arm and pointed to the shelf where only a few minutes earlier there'd been a space where the ewer should have been. But no. Like a magic rabbit, the ewer had appeared on the second shelf, sitting plump and happy. Pieces of the puzzle tumbled into place as Britt opened the glass door. She slipped on protective gloves and carefully lifted the artifact out.

"Recognize it?" she asked, turning the painted dolphins toward Jim. She noticed the sheen of perspiration on his forehead. His green daypack hung limply from his shoulder. Empty.

Jim shrugged. "Of course."

"It's been missing for days."

"So what?" he said, angling his blue eyes at the floor.

"You just returned this ewer to the cabinet, didn't you? Ten minutes ago, it was missing. You come in and, eureka! Here it is, just where it should be."

"Leave it alone."

"Tell me now, or I get Dr. Gavas on the phone."

"I wouldn't if I were you!" Jim snatched the pitcher from Britt's hands and held it aloft like a football. "You want this?" He feigned a toss against the wall.

"Put it down," Britt said, her voice firm. "Smashing it will only make your problems worse." Her eyes drilled into him. "Jim, help me understand what's going on."

His arm dipped. "Fuck you. I don't want your understanding."

"You'd rather deal with Gavas?

Jim blanched.

"Listen, I want to be on your side."

"Damn you," he said softly.

Britt reached out and took the ewer from his hands. "Sit down," she ordered as she placed the pitcher back in the cabinet and removed her gloves.

Jim slumped on a stool. Britt dragged another seat next to his. She faced him squarely, an elbow resting on the table.

"Are you stealing artifacts?"

Jim shook his head from side to side.

"Borrowing them?"

"Yes," he said, his voice small and fragile.

"Why?"

His shoulders heaved. "Don't," he said, his voice cracking. His large hands flew up to cover his face.

Britt let him weep. She fetched a box of tissues from a counter across the room and handed it to him.

Jim blew his nose loudly; his eyes were wet and pink.

"What's going on?"

"Irene's father is making me do it." Jim wiped his eyes with the second tissue. "After Irene and I first started dating, he asked if he could see a vase, any vase with a pattern that hadn't been put on public display."

"To see it?"

"He wanted to make duplicates so when the original went on exhibit at the museum, he'd have copies ready for sale. He'd be ahead of the other merchants by months. So, I did it, to impress him, and to impress Irene."

"Why on earth do you have to impress them?"

"I want her to be happy, and pleasing her old man always cheers her up. I get scared that he'll take her from me."

"So, how do you do it?" Britt asked softly.

"I sneak a vase out in my daypack. That's how easy it is. After Kazantas finishes sketching the pattern and dimensions, I bring it back."

"For heaven's sake, Jim, why didn't you just take some photographs? You didn't need to remove items. Not only did you risk someone noticing they were gone, you risked damaging them."

"He's an artist. He wants the feel, the weight, the thickness, the *spirit*." Jim blew his nose again. "No one noticed until you came. I knew you'd be looking things up, so whenever I took an object, I temporarily removed all references to it on the database. I stored it in a hold file. Then, when the object was back in place, I'd reinsert the data into the main files."

"You missed a reference on this last one."

"I'm not surprised," he said. "Gavas was buzzing around like a manic bee that night. I got nervous and careless."

Britt pursed her lips. "Yeah, and Gavas practically stepped on your pack that night."

"I know. Listen, I hated doing it. But when I told Kazantas I wouldn't bring him any more pieces, he said he'd go to the police. He'd tell them I was stealing artifacts and trying to sell them."

"You believed him?"

"I didn't see any options." Jim twisted his head, trying to throw off the nightmare. "But the worst part…the worst part…"

Jim reached for another tissue.

"The worst part was that I told Kazantas you had noticed the monkey ewer missing."

Britt frowned.

"I thought that would scare him into stopping. It didn't. Then when I heard…when I heard one of his sons—Georgios—had swung a crate toward your head at Athinios, I knew it hadn't been an accident."

Britt paused to absorb this new information. "Jim, how can you be sure?"

"Wake up, Britt. We're talking about the family's pass to America. Georgios said he did it on impulse—the first time—if that's any consolation."

"The first time?" Britt's frown deepened.

"The jet ski was the second. He stole it and tried to run you over. Georgios was royally skunked. He'd matched me beer for beer at a taverna and told me how he'd aimed that crate at you. He said he needed to get the job done right and ran off." Jim pinched his eyes shut, then sighed. "If you blabbed to Gavas, you'd threaten their dream."

Britt retrieved the ewer from the cabinet again and examined it. "Are you sure he's giving you back the real thing?"

Jim nodded. "I still have a few working brain cells. I put a small chalk mark inside any vase I took."

Britt looked inside the neck of the ewer.

"He'd have to use a flashlight to see it. He gave me back the same vase, I'm sure of it. He wouldn't have had time to make a duplicate."

Britt studied the ewer. The design was clean, the lines incised with precision. She believed she held the original, not an imitation.

Britt turned back to Jim. "How many times have you done this?"

He flinched. "Six."

"Does he have a piece now?" She set the ewer back in the cabinet and scanned Jim's puffy face as she sat down.

"No."

"This is the last time. Right?"

"I promise." Jim drew his palms over his mottled cheeks, rubbing away the tears. "What are you going to do?"

Britt slid off the stool. "I have to think about this. It seems the only casualty in this whole matter is your integrity. And perhaps the pocketbook of competing souvenir merchants."

As Jim crossed the room to throw his tissues away, he passed in front of a row of excavation photos taken by Paulos Bountourakis.

Britt had a sudden idea. "Could Bounty have suspected something?" she asked.

"I doubt it. He didn't spend much time in the museum."

"How about the day he died? Did you see him around here?"

"He was bumming around town that Sunday. He seemed his normal self."

"You didn't see him that evening?"

Jim shook his head. "No. I had dinner with Irene's family here in Thera, then hung around the store. I didn't see anyone associated with the excavation that night. Except Bob. He trotted past the store about eight o'clock."

"Bob Collins? I thought he took a plane back to Athens that afternoon."

Jim shrugged. "It was Bob. I'm sure of it."

⌐⌐ 34 ⌐⌐

"**J**ust checking in," Britt said.

"Where are you calling from?" Susan Marcello asked, her voice warm.

"My B&B." Britt kept her voice low. "I've solved one mystery." She told Susan about her confrontation with Jim over the "borrowed" artifacts and how Georgios Kazantas was the culprit in a couple of recent incidents. "But Theo is a different matter. I'm scared of him."

"You're keeping out of his way?"

"Absolutely." Britt took a shaky breath. "Any news about the dead man?"

"No. All the identification was either burned or stripped from the car. The police are checking dental records, but that could take weeks."

"When CIS did background checks on the Akrotiri crew, did they include Robert Collins?"

"I don't believe so. Let me look at the file." After a stretch of silence, Susan said, "No. Who is he?"

"A grad student at the American School from the University of Pennsylvania. You may remember him from my going away party at the MacKenzies. He kept offering to refill our wine glasses."

"Ah, yes. Do you want me to run a check?"

"If you could. I googled him, but there must be a hundred thousand men with the same name."

"What's your concern?"

"I found out he was here on Santorini the night Bounty died. But Cassie says she took him to the airport earlier that afternoon."

"Hmmm. That doesn't add up, does it? I'll try to get back to you this evening. Anything else?"

Britt paused. "I don't like what I've gotten myself into, Susan. It's too dangerous. Is there any way I could drop out?"

"I'd love it if you could, Britt. But somebody put you on the playing field. You were tailed before we ever met. The one big advantage you have is that I'm in your corner."

Yeah? Where were you on the Sounion road? "You're a long ways away if I need help, Susan."

"I'm a forty-five-minute plane ride away," she said. "I'll be there if you need me."

▣ ▣ ▣ ▣

Sophia Delopsos closed the door to the sitting room of her small apartment at the back of the Fira Winery. Cassie's question had been haunting her for days: *Are you safe?* She sat on a straight back wooden chair.

No, I'm not. Neither are you nor your professor friend. Mrs. Delopsos had tuned into clipped conversations at the winery. For some reason, her nephew wished to harm the Americans. She supposed they had spurned Theo's advances, but plenty of girls did so without arousing his ire. And their late-night visit to the winery? Something was not right.

Mrs. Delopsos fingered the hem of the traditional black dress she often wore. She took a breath to gather her courage and picked up her phone. The call went through immediately.

"Yes, Sophia? What do you want?" The gravelly voice of Colonel Dimitris Alevras rumbled over the line.

Mrs. Delopsos could picture her brother-in-law sitting in his villa outside Heraklion. He would now be pivoting from his desk to the bank of floor-to-ceiling windows to gaze at the gardeners laboring in the beds of azaleas down by the grove of cedars. Or perhaps he was fixing his hard, black eyes on a ship edging toward the harbor.

"Theo is out of control. You must speak to him."

"The less I speak to him, the better," the Colonel said. "He is a lazy fool who squanders the fortune of his father."

Mrs. Delopsos needed to tread carefully. It had been Dimitris's money that had saved the winery after her husband had died. And he allowed her to live in its back rooms.

"Take Theo and his friends from Santorini. I want to run a decent winery as I did when my husband lived. I want Fira to produce a wine worthy of its heritage." Mrs. Delopsos pursed her lips to avoid the threatening tears. "Have you seen the online reviews? One star for our prized Assyrtiko!"

"Yes, yes. There have been a few bad years."

Mrs. Delopsos closed her eyes. She did not like this man, a man her sister had found irresistible. He had paid no attention to his wife when she was alive. He slept with women and took pleasure in telling her of it. Many times her sister had come running to her, her eyes streaming, her heart broken in a hundred pieces. His son had been cut from the same cloth. Selfish and uncaring.

"You know he uses the winery for nasty business?"

"Eh?"

Mrs. Delopsos heard a match being struck. She could imagine the Colonel tilting his head to light a Turkish cigarette.

"The crates of 'grapes' you send. What a joke. People see things."

"What do they see, Sophia?"

Mrs. Delopsos paused. She was not certain, but she could guess. "Smuggling."

"And who sees this?"

"Anyone who has eyes. The workers at Athinios Harbor and the marina, the shop owners at Kamari Beach. Everyone sees crates coming and going, during the day, during the night."

"Even those two American girls, I have heard."

Circles of sweat bloomed under Mrs. Delopsos' arms even as a chill swept through her. She had never stood up to the Colonel before. She knew his power. "What are you planning, Dimitris? Are you putting the winery in jeopardy?"

"No, I only help people realize their dreams. I sell them what they need. It is business. Is it legal?" The Colonel took a pull on his cigarette and exhaled loudly. "With the right connections and enough money, everything can be made legal."

"Please, Dimitris. I am afraid."

"You have nothing to fear, Sophia. Stay in your back room and do the accounting."

Mrs. Delopsos ended the call. She would be extra vigilant. She vowed to protect her winery, her only hold on the earth. And to see that no harm came to the young American windsurfer who bested all the boys and had always been so kind to her.

35

Britt swallowed half a glass of cold Perrier. "Ahhh," she said. "Refreshing! Want some?" She extended the remainder of her drink to Cassie.

"I had my fill out there," Cassie said, pointing to the sea. "I think half a dozen waves swan-dived into my stomach on that last run. Seems like someone has taken me off my game."

"Are you accusing me of distracting you?"

Cassie smiled. "I was focused more on you than on my sailing. You're cutting a fine figure out on those waves, Britt Evans. Your windsurfing has improved one-hundred percent."

"I've had a good tutor. Sailboarding on Minnesota lakes is going to seem pretty tame after this."

A handful of sunbathers ambled up from Kamari Beach as the mid-afternoon sun weakened enough to justify abandoning their lounging plots. A pelican sat contentedly on a post while a sleepy, yellow dog eyed the bird but hadn't the energy to chase it off.

Andreas glided toward the table on the veranda, pen and order pad in hand. "Something for you, Cassie?"

"I'm famished. How about sharing some dolmades? Maybe some bread?"

"What about dinner?" Britt said.

"Right. But I need food now."

Andreas scratched down the appetizer order and sauntered toward the kitchen.

"Cass, what do you know about Bob?" Britt said.

"Still jealous?" Cassie grinned, tousling her wet hair to hasten its drying.

"He seems like a playboy, yet he hangs out in the academic world. What's he about?"

Andreas placed dolmades, pita bread, and complementary tzatziki on the table. He took their orders for dinner and retreated.

"Bob's a dig bum."

"Yes. He mentioned something about dropping in at excavations. Did you ever go with him?"

"Nuh-uh. A couple of times, I wanted to—especially the time he went to Rhodes. He wanted to be off on his own, though. I didn't press him."

"How does he decide where to go?"

"He never says." Cassie tore off a corner of the flatbread and dunked it in the yogurt dip. "He'll just say, 'I'm going to Cyprus on Wednesday,' or more likely, 'Listen, sorry you couldn't reach me. I was at the dig in Rhodes.'"

"How does he manage to get into these sites? A person just can't stroll into an active excavation."

"He always claims to have friends. No one turns down an experienced hand with a trowel. What's this about anyway?" Cassie folded the bread into her mouth.

"It's about his not going back to Athens as early as he said on the Sunday Bounty died."

Cassie stopped chewing. "What do you mean?"

"Jim saw him that night in Thera."

Cassie swallowed hard. "But I dropped him off at the airport."

"Did you watch him board?"

"No. I never do. He always wants to be at the airport hours before departure. I don't stick around."

"Do you think he could have gone back into town?"

"Maybe. But why?"

"That," Britt said, pointing a dolma at Cassie, "is the question."

◙◙◙◙

The power of the mammoth engines reverberated through the steel hull. The ferry rocked to port, then to starboard. Edging off the mattress, Nicki blinked at the bright window as she emerged from a fitful nap. She hated ferries, but at least she had been able to snag a first-class cabin.

She was alone, but aloneness was a suit that had come to fit her well. She retrieved the flask filled with Metaxa from her daypack and poured a modest amount into the plastic cup from the bathroom. The amber liquor—a brandy wine—held the strength of gods and, perhaps, the Black Corinth grapes from her family's estate. She drank it straight up and let out a long, frustrated breath.

"What am I doing?" she said to the wall across from her decorated with pictures of Cycladic islands. She had been so brave in her godfather's office, rallying to be a heroine, to save a woman she had been infatuated with for years. A woman who now had a lover. "I'm a total idiot." *But a good friend, with the bloodline of warriors.*

The engines protested as they clicked into reverse. From the large window, Nicki watched as the ferry edged alongside the dock in Athinios. Buses and taxis lined the port road, ready to take tourists to their destinations.

Nicki slipped her phone into her back pocket and immediately changed her mind: pickpockets. Instead, she slid it into a secure compartment in her pack. With the Metaxa, toiletries, gun, extra ammo rolled into a change of clothes, and her phone and charger, the pack weighed a ton. Nicky looped the strap over her shoulder, slid back the deadbolt, and opened the door.

Two huge, square men stood across the narrow hallway.

"Nicostrata Lampas," the man on the right said, "Mr. Zerakis sent us."

"What? Why?" Nicki stepped back.

"He fears for your safety." The man worked through steel worry beads in one hand. Click. Click. Click. "Come. Anton will help you with your bag."

Before she could react, the second man had snatched the strap from Nicki's shoulder. In a moment, the daypack hung from his meaty hand. He hoisted it onto his own shoulder as though it were filled with air.

Nicki examined the men for a moment. The cuffs of their suit jackets were frayed. One smelled of fish. Such a contrast to the personal security officer Mikos had dispatched to escort her though the checkpoint at the Piraeus port! That solicitous, well-groomed man in a bespoke suit had even given Nicki a few tips on gun handling. These gruff men were not the type of polished professionals Mikos would ever employ, much less send to attend to his goddaughter.

"Come, we leave now," said the man not named Anton. He gripped Nicki's arm and turned her down the narrow hall. Anton began walking away with her pack. Nicki shook off the man's grasp, but she was trapped in between them.

Click. Click. Click. One worry bead after another sounded behind her. Mikos forbade any employee to use metal worry beads. Wood or plastic, okay. Never metal. He could not stand the clicking.

These are not my godfather's men. Nicki's breath quickened with the realization. *But I'll play along. For now.*

Her one chance, she thought as they maneuvered her along the corridor, was to make a break when they went down the steps to the lower decks. The narrow stairways would allow the width of only one person. She'd have to abandon her daypack. And the gun. And phone.

At the first stairwell, Nicki made no move. Seemingly trusting herself to these men, she meekly followed. The man behind her trod on her heels twice he was so close. When they reached the third level and began descending to the deck used to disembark, Nicki hung onto the railings as she took one step after another. Midway down, before the first man had reached the bottom, she knew the moment had come.

In a burst, Nicki swung herself over the railing and landed in a crouch on the deck. She sprang forward, pushing aside the passengers straggling toward the gangplank.

"I get her!" the unnamed man called. "Hold onto the bag!"

Nicki flew off the inclined ramp and wormed her way through the crush of hundreds of tourists waiting for transportation into Thera.

"Excuse, please. Excuse, please. Sorry." She pushed her way through grumbling tourists to the front and slipped into the transport's darkened interior just before the door closed, leaving the crowd to await the next bus. The minutes ticked by as the luggage loaders made final adjustments to the many suitcases and bags in the large storage compartments. Finally, a shout and a thump on the door and the bus was underway.

Nicki caught sight of the two men opening the doors of a black sedan. Each was eyeing the bus and shouting into a phone. They'd tagged her escape and now, and they'd be following her to the station in Thera.

The air-conditioning provided scant relief to Nicki as she hung on to an overhead strap. She had to think her way out of this. The excited chatter of the tourists and the roar of the engine challenged her concentration. She figured she had twenty, thirty minutes at most.

The shuttle labored up the zigzagging road to the rim of the caldera, the driver working the floor shift and clutch with the deftness of a maestro. When the road leveled off, Nicki elbowed her way to the front. She crouched next to the driver.

"Is there a black car behind us?" Nicki asked the woman.

The driver checked the side mirror. "Many cars are behind us. A black one, yes. Directly behind me." She looked as if she had been driving this route for years. Her gray hair testified to the harrowing trip made several times a day.

Nicki noticed the driver's appraising glance and knew that fear played openly on her face. The driver studied the road for a few seconds, then said just loud enough to be heard, "Are you in trouble?"

Nicki stared through the wide front windshield to the neat field of grapevines coiling in the sinking sun and to a small flock of sheep grazing on a ribbon of green grass. Life going on. And it would go on without her.

"Yes," Nicki said, turning back to the older woman. "Can you help me?

36

"What can be taking so long," Susan Marcello complained. "What's so hard about digging up the background of one American student?"

Alexander Stamos cradled a scotch and let his friend spout. "Perhaps it is not so easy. Interpol has nothing."

Susan gazed without appreciation at the subdued blue of an evening sky outside her office window. "What the hell's the problem stateside?"

"That is a question we Greeks ask often."

An email notice popped up on Susan's screen. "About time," she said as she slipped into her desk chair. A few seconds into reading the mail, she groaned.

"What?" Stamos asked.

"Did I know this, or what? It couldn't have been simple." Susan scrolled down the document. Her face turned stony. "Robert Collins died nine years ago in a car accident. In the States."

"Then who—"

Susan held up her hand like a traffic cop and skimmed farther down. Without looking at Stamos, she grabbed her phone. "I've got to warn Britt."

While Susan waited for connection, Stamos sipped his drink. His mind was already racing with half a dozen scenarios.

"Damn!" Susan said when she heard Britt's voice mail answer. She left a quick message warning her of Bob and asking her to call back immediately. Susan leaned back in her chair. "How long do we wait?" She turned to her phone again. "I'll send a text, too."

"It is not an emergency," Stamos said. "Tomorrow we go to the American school and find Collins."

Susan remained still, palms on her desk. Thinking.

The intercom crackled. "Ma'am, there's a call from Mikos Zerakis. Can you take it?"

Susan and Stamos locked eyes.

"Put him through." Susan lifted the receiver and listened for several minutes. Her face was fixed in a neutral expression, but her eyes flicking to Stamos, said *not good*.

"What?" Stamos said when Susan hung up.

"Zerakis says his goddaughter—Nicki—took a ferry to Santorini to warn Britt about the Alevras family. She was supposed to call him as soon as she landed, but she hasn't."

"The ferry?" Stamos said with a chuckle.

"She's got a gun."

"Christ."

Susan punched a button on her console. "Donna, book me a seat on the next flight to Santorini. And reserve a rental car."

Stamos held up two fingers.

"Make that two seats. And, if needed, call airport operations so Alex can hold the plane for us." Susan turned to Stamos. "You can do that, right?"

Stamos nodded.

"Good." Susan opened the bottom drawer of her desk and reached for her firearm, a SIG Sauer compact. She placed the semi-automatic and shoulder holster on the desk.

Stamos started. "You can't take that on a commercial flight," he said.

"I'll put it in a diplomatic pouch," Susan replied, her smile tight. "While you let your people know what's going on, I'll put on more appropriate clothes." She stepped toward the armoire by the small bathroom.

"Should we call the island police?"

Susan stopped and turned. "Can we trust them?"

"No," Stamos admitted. "They may have covered up Bountourakis's death."

"Precisely. Britt and her friends may be resourceful," Susan said with a shake of her head, "but they're facing forces that can crush them."

Stamos pulled out his phone to make a call.

"Damn!" Susan said, yanking open the door of the armoire. "I set Britt up. It's up to me to save her."

🔲 🔲 🔲 🔲

"Damn it, find her!" Robert Collins, his face contorted in anger, pounded a fist on the counter at the Fira Winery.

"We will." Theo Alevras jabbed at his phone. He listened intently for a few moments as his cigarette dangled from his lips. When the call ended, he slipped the phone into his back pocket. "We assume Nicki makes her way to Kamari. Anton has her phone, so she can't warn the girls."

"If she makes it to Kamari, though, Britt can call for help."

"I call my pet at the Seaside. Maybe she can do something."

The air in the small showroom reeked of sweat and cigarette smoke. Five fully armed guards, some in jeans, others in cargo fatigues, milled around. The door to Mrs. Delopsos's apartment remained firmly closed, but a shadow moved closer in the light under it.

A ping sounded. Alevras retrieved his phone and read the message. He nodded to Collins. "The last commercial flight lands now. Our plane is ready."

"Good. As soon as the airport shuts down," Collins said, "take your men there and start loading the cargo."

"What will you do?" Alevras eyed the American suspiciously.

Collins checked the ammunition in his Beretta 92F. "What I should have done weeks ago."

37

The sun had dipped behind the curtain of mountains southwest of Maria's B&B, turning the nearby fields to charcoal gray. Inside, Britt and Cassie drifted from dream to dream, stirring occasionally to physical need, only to be recaptured by the sweet weight of sleep. Doors slammed down the hallway as vacationers sauntered off for a late dinner along the beachfront or to find a dance club. Outside, crickets scraped out their mating tunes.

Someone tapped softly, then more loudly, on the door.

"Let's not answer," Cassie said, tightening an arm around Britt.

"Sounds important," Britt said as she peeled off Cassie's embrace.

"No, stay here."

But Britt, already halfway out of the bed, had a white bathrobe in her grasp. She pulled it on and made her way across the room. She slid back the bolt and opened the door. Nicki stared at her from the hallway, panting, her eyes wild.

"Nicki! My god, what happened!" Britt cried, drawing her banged up friend into the room.

Nicki toppled forward. Britt caught her and helped her to a chair.

"What's going on?" Cassie scooted up to the headboard, drawing the sheet up to her chin.

Nicki's eyes roamed around the room. She didn't seem to understand or care about the scene she had entered. "We're in trouble," she said, trying to catch her breath. "Much trouble."

Britt tossed a robe to Cassie, who slipped it on.

"Calm down, Nicki," Britt said softly. She grabbed a bottle of Scotch from under the night table and dumped a couple of shots into a glass.

"We must be quiet, okay?" Nicki took a large hit of the liquor.

"We'll be quiet," Britt said in a soothing voice. "Now, tell us what's going on." She propped herself at the foot of the bed and bent forward, elbows on her knees.

"I don't know exactly. Two men on the ferry tried to abduct me, but I escaped."

"But why were you on the ferry? Why are you even here?"

"To warn you." Nicki shared what she had learned from her godfather about the man who had crashed his car following them from Sounion."

"So, this Yannis guy works for Theo's father?"

"The Colonel. Yes. The winery is a cover. Mikos thinks they are smugglers. Of what, we don't know." Nicki fortified herself with another swallow of the potent liquor.

Cassie slipped into the bathroom and returned with a wet cloth.

"Thanks," Nicki said. She wiped sweat and grime from her face. "They took my phone on the ferry so I could not call you. I would have borrowed a phone, but…"

"You don't have her number memorized," Cassie said. "One downside of technology."

"Now, listen to me," Nicki said, her voice low. "These men, they planned to kill me, I'm sure."

"Good god," Britt whispered. She and Cassie exchanged a look of horror. "We've got to get out of here. Cass, would any flights to Athens be going out now?"

Cassie glanced at the clock on the nightstand. "Not this late. And surely the Colonel's men would be watching for us there."

"I need to reach Susan," Britt said, pausing to think of where she had left her phone. "My phone's in my room charging. I'd better go get it."

"Maybe we should go into Thera," Cassie said. "Hide out at Jim's apartment."

Britt stared at Cassie for several moments, calculating. "We might have a better chance there."

The three women looked from one to another in silent affirmation. "Let's go," Britt said at last. "All of us. Together."

"My taxi waits outside," Nicki said.

"Excellent." Britt's said. "Cassie, while you dress, I'll run back to my place to get my phone. I'll call Susan."

"Susan, from your embassy?" Nicki asked.

"How did you—"

"Mikos has his sources."

"Better put on some warm clothes while you're there," Cassie advised.

"Can you do this in ten minutes?" Nicki asked.

"Less than that." Britt left through the French doors and dashed through rows of pistachio trees to the Seaside across the way.

Cassie took in the frightened woman in front of her. "You've been very brave, Nicki."

She shrugged. "I bow to the Fates. It is the Greek way."

"How did you get so banged up?"

"The bus driver made a special stop where I would be shielded from the men following me. I stumbled off the steps in my hurry and scraped my knee. I ran through some yards and got cut by branches. Here," she said, sticking a finger through a hole in her black jeans, "my pants caught on a fence."

"Want to put something on those cuts while I dress? I have some first aid cream in the bathroom."

Wincing in pain, Nicki shook her head. Then she realized Cassie might want some privacy to change her clothes. "Yes, I should clean my cuts."

When Nicki returned from the bathroom, Cassie was draping a navy fleece pullover around her shoulders. The evening was warm, but the wind would be cool.

"Hurry, Britt," Nicki said, her fingers tapping on the desk. Suddenly, a loud knock rattled the hallway door. Cassie and Nicki's eyes locked, the thought flashing through each mind that Britt had returned. It couldn't be, though. She would have come back through the patio doors.

The knocks sounded again, this time more urgent. "Britt? Cassie? Are you there?"

"It's Bob!" Cassie cried. "It's okay," she said without thinking, "he's a friend." She pulled open the door.

"Hiya!" Collins said, nonchalantly striding into the room. He stopped to take in the scene before him. "Well, well, well, young lady," he said to Nicki, "has Ms. Burkhardt had her way with you, too?"

"Bob, cut it out," Cassie said. "This is a friend of Britt's from Athens."

"Where's Britt?" he asked Cassie, now ignoring Nicki.

"Why?"

"That's my business," he said with a harshness unfamiliar to Cassie. "Where is she?"

Cassie gripped the cuffs of the sweater hanging around her neck. Britt had suspected Bob of being involved with Bounty's death. It seemed impossible, but could she have been right? Cassie tied the sweater's arms into a thick knot over her chest. "She's in Thera. She's having dinner with Dr. Gavas."

"Now, why don't I believe you? How about you, Nicki, you know where she is?"

"How do you know my name?"

"I know a lot of things. Including that you used your godfather's secretary to buy ferry tickets for you." Collins smirked. "That's misuse of government funds. Now where's Britt?"

"I don't know." Nicki shook her head. "I checked at her room before I came here. The lady at reception said to try here."

"And no Britt. How about that." Collins unzipped his jacket. The handle of his automatic popped out. "Well, ladies, let's go find her."

/ / / **38** / /

Her phone was gone. The charger remained in its usual spot, plugged into the desk outlet.

"I'm sure I left it here," Britt muttered. She searched her room but didn't find it. "I don't have time for this." She fired up her computer thinking to at least email Susan. Britt quickly changed into jeans and a sweater while the computer came online.

But another roadblock: *No internet connection.*

Britt stared at the screen in disbelief. "What the hell!"

She ran back through the pistachio trees to Cassie's apartment. But no Cassie. No Nicki.

"Where the hell are they?" Britt cried as she ran down the corridor to the lobby. Maybe, she thought, they'd decided to wait in the taxi. But there was no taxi. Didn't Nicki say she had one waiting? And Cassie's car was parked alongside the courtyard curb.

Britt turned to the front desk. "Maria, did you see Cassie leave?"

Maria's eyebrows rose in sympathy. "Ah, you just missed her. She left two, three minutes ago with Bob and her friend—the one who is hurt."

"Bob! Are you sure?"

"Why should I mistake such a thing?"

"You wouldn't, Maria," Britt said. Panic rose like heated mercury from her stomach to her throat. "Did they say where they were going?"

Maria shook her head. "No, but I hope they take Cassie's friend to hospital."

"I didn't see the taxi outside. Is that what they took?"

"No. I see Bob pay the driver and send it away. They go in his usual rental—a Mercedes."

"Thanks," Britt cried over her shoulder as she ran back to Cassie's room. Cassie's phone was still on her desk. She would not have left it behind. Britt checked the drawer where Cassie kept her purse. That, too, was still there. "No. No. No. This is all wrong!" Britt dumped the contents on the bed. Her shaky fingers snatched the car remote out of the pile.

"Where am I going?" she said to herself as she started up Cassie's car. To the hospital in Thera? To Jim's? Why couldn't they have waited for her? Cassie would have at least left a note. Obviously, she couldn't.

As she pulled out of the parking lot, a black Nissan rolling by the entrance screeched to a halt and made a U-turn. It quickly closed in behind her, its headlights flashing. When the driver momentarily turned off the headlights and flipped on the interior light, what Britt saw in her rearview mirror nearly made her heart burst: Susan Marcello frantically motioning for her to pull over.

◙ ◙ ◙ ◙

"Cassie's gone!" Britt cried, leaning through the passenger window of Susan's car. She pressed her lips together to keep them from quivering. "She left with Bob Collins and Nicki. What the hell is going on?"

"Slow down and start from the beginning," Susan commanded.

Britt summarized Nicki's story and their plan to hide out at Jim's apartment in Thera. "But I don't know what happened. Bob showed up before I got back, and they left without me."

"Just a sec." Susan picked up her phone lying in the passenger seat. "Alex?" she said.

"Here, my friend," came the reply.

"I have Britt. Collins has Nicki and Cassie. We're going after them now. I'll be in touch."

"Who's that?" Britt asked.

"Alexander Stamos. The investigator from Athens I've told you about. He went to the marina in Blycháda. We want to locate the *Praxis*."

Susan tossed the phone on the passenger seat and stared into the darkness. She turned and caught Britt's gaze and held it. "Robert Collins has been dead for nine years."

Britt's stomach lurched. "If that's not Bob, who is he?" she whispered.

"We don't know. But given the ties to Colonel Alevras and the military, it's a good bet he's an arms smuggler."

"Arms!" Britt gasped. The danger quotient had suddenly quadrupled. "But…but…Bob? Are you sure?"

"Positive. I'm sorry." Susan let Britt absorb the information for a moment, then turned to business. "You know this island. Where do we start looking for them?"

The headlights of an approaching car brushed the road. A dusty Fiat stopped alongside. The driver rolled down the window.

"Professor Evans!" the woman called out in a thick Greek accent.

"Yes." Britt hurried around the front of Susan's car. "What is it?"

"I am Mrs. Delopsos from the Fira Winery."

"Yes, I remember you. I'm sorry. I'm in a—"

"Cassie is in danger. They take her to the airport."

Britt and Susan looked at the woman in amazement.

"Who does?" Susan asked.

"Bob Collins. His men look for you, professor."

Susan checked her watch. "They must be getting the product off the island tonight." *Maybe Cassie and Nicki, too.*

"I drive here to be with Maria. I do not feel safe at the winery."

"Good idea," Britt said. "Maybe you should go to the police."

"Who can I trust? Theo and Bob pay people everywhere to help them. Even the police, I believe." Mrs. Delopsos' eyes darted anxiously between Britt and Susan.

Britt placed a hand on the Nissan to steady herself. "We have to do something, Susan."

"Okay, Mrs. Delopsos," Susan said. "Thank you for your help. We'll find them. It'll be all right."

Mrs. Delopsos looked doubtful. "It is dangerous. They have guns."

"Yes," Susan said. "We'll be careful."

Britt and Susan watched Mrs. Delopsos drive off, giving a little wave.

Susan turned to Britt. "It's the two of us. And Alex. But it's going to be dangerous." She paused. "You can stay here and…"

"Be safe? I doubt it. They're looking for me. And there's no way I'm letting them hurt Cassie and Nicki. I'm in."

Susan nodded. "Okay."

Britt quickly calculated their options. "We have to stop them at the airport. I have an idea. It may sound crazy, but it could work."

Susan listened, her eyes widening in astonishment.

39

Every gambit has risk. Susan Marcello turned up the air conditioning, unneeded in the chill of the island night, but she liked AC in situations like this. It helped cool her brain as she weighed the possibilities.

The lonely road was dark with only the stars and moon for light. Her headlights swept vineyards marked by fences of volcanic stone. She slowed, pulled onto a side road, and killed the lights. She picked up her phone. "Alex, where are you?"

"Still at the marina. I'm walking toward my car."

"What about the *Praxis*?"

"I just miss her. The harbormaster says she put to sea ten minutes ago."

"Any itinerary?"

"No. Bearing east, he says."

Damn. One more piece on the board.

"Okay. Here's what's going down." Susan filled him in on the situation and the plan she and Britt had hatched.

"Britt will never make it to the airport," he said. "We are on our own."

"I have to believe in her," Susan said. She checked her watch. "We need to coordinate timing." More calculations.

"You should wait for me." Stamos cautioned.

"I need to go first. You'll be right behind me. Silence from now on." Susan turned off her phone and stowed it under the seat. She could not risk its light or vibration. She checked her watch again, counting the minutes. She smiled at Stamos's incredulity at their plan.

Never underestimate the ingenious power of women.

Robert Collins adjusted the rearview mirror so he could have a better view of Nicki in the back seat. In the time they had been on the road, no car had approached from behind.

"What about Britt?" Cassie said. "I thought you wanted her."

"I'll leave her for the others. They probably have her by now."

"You bastard!" Cassie cried, lunging at Collins across the front seat.

Collins blocked her punch with his arm, then shoved Cassie into the passenger door. "Stay there, or I'll shoot your friend," he said, withdrawing the gun from under his jacket.

"Fuck you!" Cassie swung a right hook at Collins. Once again, he blocked it with his arm. Collins hit the brakes, sending Cassie into the dashboard. Her forearm scraped along an empty cellphone holder, leaving a jagged tear that quickly swelled with blood.

Nicki, propelled forward, grabbed at Collins' throat. He flicked the barrel against her head. Nicki flopped back into her seat, moaning and clutching the wound.

"Fuck!" Cassie cried, trying to staunch her inch-long cut while twisting in her seat to check on Nicki.

"Dammit!" Collins said, stepping back on the gas. "Stop bleeding on the seat."

The lights of the airport glowed like an internment camp a short way up the road. "You'll never get away with this, Bob," Cassie said. "There are people at the airport who'll help us."

"Not tonight. Let's say it's a private 'rental' for the evening."

Cassie found a square of tissue in her pocket and used it to apply pressure to the wound. "What does that mean?"

"You'll find out." Collins caught Nicki shifting slightly toward the car door. A trickle of blood ran over her ear and branched onto her cheek. "I'm telling you, if one of you escapes, the other dies."

Nicki eased herself back to the middle of the seat. She pressed the sleeve of her sweatshirt against her head but made sure several drops of blood spotted the leather seat. Evidence she had been in the car.

"Britt reminds me of Bounty," Collins said, "playing at being a spy. Snooping around. Being stupid. Know what happened to him?"

Cassie and Nicki were silent.

"I gave him his last ride. Your fate won't be any better. Maybe worse."

For Cassie, all sound faded. Even the engine seemed to quiet. "Did you kill him?" she asked.

Collins' eyes stayed on the road. "I'd say Bounty killed himself. I just helped him along."

"You wouldn't tell us this," Nicki said weakly, "unless you plan to kill us, too."

"You know," Collins said, "none of this would be happening if the embassy had been more careful about making inquiries at the school. It didn't take a genius to figure out they were going to try to rope Britt into something. If she had just let me run her down in the Plaka, she'd be in the hospital, not here."

"You were the one in the truck?" Nicki murmured.

Collins ignored her as he stopped in front of the terminal. "Instead that embassy woman showed up at the party and got the wheels rolling. Always send a woman to recruit a lesbian." He snickered, opened his door, and pointed the gun at Cassie. "Get out," he said, "and help her into the terminal. She seems a little woozy."

◙ ◙ ◙ ◙

Britt swerved Cassie's car into the dark alley next to the motor scooter rental shop at Kamari Beach. Music and the sharp chatter of cooks and waiters drifted through the open back door of the adjacent Pelican. The aroma of Greek spices wafted into the night.

Britt picked up an empty liter water bottle from one of the waste bins at the rear of the shop. She set the bottle next to the single fuel pump and tried to lift the nozzle out of its position. A short chain, looped through the handle and fixed with a padlock, stopped her. She yanked at the links a couple of times. They held fast.

"Damn." She searched around the area's rubbish and found a piece of rebar. Back at the fuel pump, she broke the chain and filled the bottle to the top.

As she twisted the cap on, the restaurant's back screen creaked open. Andreas stepped out.

"What are you doing!" he yelled.

"It's me—Britt. I need gas for my scooter. It's an emergency."

"Emergency?" Andreas wiped his hands on the white towel tied around his hips.

"No time to explain." Britt reached into her pocket and withdrew several bills. "Here's for the gas," she said, pressing fifty Euros into Andreas's palm.

Reluctantly, he accepted the cash. Britt returned to the task at hand.

"You will be all right? Is Cassie okay?"

"No," Britt replied, giving the cap an extra twist. Andreas watched her, money in hand, then retreated to his building muttering.

As soon as he had disappeared, Britt stashed the bottle in the alley. No need to take it when she'd be back this way in a few minutes.

◙ ◙ ◙ ◙

"You don't need to bring Britt into this." Cassie dabbed at the cut on her arm. A few beads of blood still swelled to the surface. Nicki lay sprawled on the floor of the terminal, barely conscious. Cassie had torn off a strip of her shirt and tied it around Nicki's head. Blood seeped through the cloth.

Collins looked up from studying an inventory list with Theo Alevras. "You don't get it, do you?" he said. "I'm too close to let anyone stop me."

"What happened to you, Bob?"

"Nothing. You just never knew me."

Cassie scanned the room for a way to escape. The small terminal had a long ticket counter and a few rows of seats. Entryway doors led to the road that had brought them here. A pair of doors, set into a bank of glass, opened to the tarmac. Other doors led, she guessed, to offices.

"I've spent two years planning for tonight's delivery," Collins said. "It will make me the go-to man for my product."

"It makes *us* the go-to men, partner," Alevras broke in.

Cassie caught the look of distrust in his eyes. "Arms smuggling is a pretty competitive market, from what I've read," she said.

Collins smirked. "Depends on what you're selling." He called over a couple of men and dispatched them to the airport entrance.

Cassie ran her gaze across the half dozen guards milling around. One lazily bobbed an AK-47 in her direction. *You plan to kill us,* Nicki had said. Cassie moved to a chair and lowered herself slowly. As the weapon tracked her movement, Cassie felt the cold, hollow of truth spread out from her diaphragm. Nicki had been right.

40

"All I need is luck and a bungee cord," Britt muttered as she stepped onto the patio and into the cool night air. She shut the French doors softly behind her. Inside her wetsuit, a book of matches wrapped in plastic stuck to her forearm like a medical patch.

As she turned to cross the small sitting area, Britt saw a black sedan pull in front of the Seaside. She stepped back into the shadows and watched two large men in suit jackets get out. One man lumbered up the sidewalk toward the entrance of the Seaside. The other stayed with the car, leaning against it. Were these the thugs who had tried to kidnap Nicki on the ferry? They fit Nicki's description.

Britt pressed herself closer to the building. Unfortunately, the man at the car faced her way, talking on his phone. Her Vespa was parked at the nearside of the lot where the stand of pistachio trees began, directly in his line of sight. *Damn!*

Sidling along the wall, Britt moved forward, her mind running through options. But time was a luxury she did not have. She had to act now. She chose the bluff.

Britt stepped on the path alongside the B&B and nonchalantly walked toward her Vespa. She had taken no more than ten steps when the light from her room snapped on behind her. With the light shining out the French doors, surely the man at the car would see her.

And he did. He stared at her, but she was backlit, and he couldn't see her face. He continued talking on the phone, watching her closely.

As Britt neared her Vespa, though, the lights of the parking lot revealed her identity. The man pushed himself off the car and shouted, "Anton! Anton!"

Britt bounded to her Vespa and ripped the two bungee cords off the back of the scooter. She could see the patio doors to her room burst open as Anton rushed out. Britt was caught between them.

But only for a moment. She sprinted across the parking area at an angle and ran down the street toward the beach. She veered to the right, a block in, for misdirection. As she rounded the corner, two shots zipped past her, and a third broke off a chunk of a stucco building.

Britt cut into the grounds of a hotel. Hiding behind a pool shed, she listened for the men. For a few moments, the only sound was faint music and laughter coming from a room across the way. Then one of the men ran past on the sidewalk, wheezing. Britt saw the other rolling down a side street in the black sedan. Heart thumping, she waited until the car passed and counted to ten.

Britt stepped from the shadows, turned, and dashed in the opposite direction for the beach, the bungee cords twisting in her hands like snakes.

▣ ▣ ▣ ▣

Susan Marcello rolled to a stop at the airport gate, leaving the headlights on bright to blind the two men smoking by the fence. She watched them confer, then one lifted his Uzi and ambled toward her, shading his eyes with his free hand.

The guard spoke sharply in Greek. No doubt ordering her to turn around.

Susan rolled down the window. "Sir! Sir!" she cried out in Arabic. "Let me pass!"

The young man threw down his cigarette. Dressed in a dark sweater and camouflage pants, he neared the driver's window. "Who are you?" he said in Greek. The side of his face took on a yellowish glow from the airport lights. His eyes were sunken in shadow. Behind him, the second guard observed the interaction and lowered his automatic at the car.

Susan let loose another string of Arabic, then shook her head as though realizing the guard could not understand her. She switched to a heavily accented English. "It is emergency. I must see Collins. Bob Collins."

The guard's face stiffened. He leaned in closer to examine Susan. "Collins? What you want with him?"

"I meet him here. I late. Trouble in town."

"Who are you?"

"I am wife of client." Susan pointed toward the plane sitting at the far end of the tarmac. "My husband cargo on plane. He buyer."

"Your husband cargo?" The guard's face screwed up in confusion. "I know nothing of this."

"I go on flight. I meet my husband."

"You meet your husband?"

Was this a fucking echo chamber? "Yes, yes. Let me through."

"He is in Cyprus?"

"YES!" *In Cyprus.* Susan slipped a hand under her leather jacket and wrapped her fingers around the gun grip. She began to count to three.

"I go with you," the guard said.

Susan put both hands back on the steering wheel, relieved she didn't have to fire a shot—a sound that could have alerted others. The guard spoke to his companion, who sauntered to the gate and opened the steel barrier. *Can you move any slower, for god's sake?*

"Okay," the guard said, slipping into the back seat, his Uzi pointed at Susan, "we go to terminal."

Susan checked her watch. Britt should be on her way.

▣ ▣ ▣ ▣

The night winds swept over the blackened sea, chopping it into a field of glittering shards that reflected the light from the waning moon. Britt bungeed the bottle of gasoline she had retrieved from the rental shop to the second aft foot strap and dragged her windsurfer into the sea. She stood for a few moments knee-deep in the cold water gathering her concentration.

The surf lapped at her legs while Britt marveled at Homer's wine-dark sea and the black sky filled with hard points of light. Once, the Minoans had stood on this very shore looking into a night such as this. The Trojans had stood on their beaches, the Greeks on theirs. Above all of them, the constellations of their destiny rotated—Orion, Cassiopeia, Perseus. Life was theirs to seize by merely stepping forward, by accepting the wonder and the risk, the gain and the loss.

"Great Goddess," Britt prayed, "please be with me now."

She oriented the windsurfer so the wind blew at her back. In a move that had become second nature, Britt placed a foot on the board and stepped onto the fiberglass platform.

The past weeks of windsurfing had sharpened Britt's confidence, as well as her skills. Her body knew the drill and had the strength to execute flawlessly. Britt slid her feet, protected by surfer shoes, into the middle foot straps. She pulled on the uphaul. The sail rose out of the water and filled with the night wind. She gripped the boom and secured her harness. In moments she was bouncing across the skin of the dark sea, her voyage underway.

She concentrated on the bend of her knees, the straightness of her back and arms. It had to be a perfect run; a spill would waste valuable time. She was behind schedule, but the strong wind promised a quick trip.

Britt moved both feet behind the mast base and blasted across the sea. Her grip on the boom stayed firm and assured. In minutes she reached the small promontory separating Kamari Beach from the airport. Cassie was on the other side. Alive? She had to be.

Britt felt Cassie's presence as she rounded the nub of land. The lights of the airstrip and the cluster of beach businesses farther north glowed in the darkness. A quick glimpse laid out the scene for Britt: Several men were loading crates from a truck into a plane parked on the south end of the runway.

Britt sailed past the southeast edge of the airport, where it nearly touched the sea. The hurricane fence stretched north with no break as far as she could tell. The corner seemed her best bet. Cold sea spray splashed her from head to foot as she waited for a wave lip to back loop. The salty air was crisp and invigorating. The perfect combination of wind, wave, and muscle propelled her across the black water.

Britt executed a perfect pivot, one that normally would have filled her with joy. But not this time: there, cutting around the southern bend, was the *Praxis* bearing straight for her.

41

Susan Marcello swung open the door of the terminal, her silent escort angled behind her. The ticket counter was deserted, as were the rows of blue chairs in the middle of the room. The large arrival and departure monitor was blank.

After a day in subtropical sun, the building was warm as the air conditioning had not been able to keep up. Susan tucked a strand of black hair behind her ear. It was almost 11:30. *Where is Britt?*

A man in a black polo shirt and designer jeans stepped through a door in the back, closing it behind him. The guard at Susan's side let loose a flurry of explanation in Greek.

"Quiet!" Susan's voice boomed through the empty terminal. "I'm from the U.S. Embassy in Athens. Who's in authority here?"

"I am." The man in the black shirt took a step toward her. "What do you want?"

"Who are you?" Susan demanded. Based on Britt's description, he must be Theo Alevras, the son of the colonel.

"I ask the questions here." He took another step toward her. "You are from the Embassy?"

"Correct. I've been told you're holding an American woman hostage here. A Cassandra Burkhardt."

"Your information is wrong. No hostages here. You go now."

Susan glanced around the lifeless and unadorned room. Not even travel posters decorated the white walls. A few flies buzzed in harmony with the ventilation system.

She quickly appraised the situation. Three immediate objectives popped to mind: buy time until Britt and Stamos arrived; find Cassie and Nicki; avoid getting shot.

Most likely the women were in one of the back rooms. Maybe the one Alevras had just exited. *Okay, time to step in it.*

"The situation is unacceptable. I demand recourse." She watched Alevras screw up his face trying to translate unfamiliar English words. *Confuse the enemy.*

Alevras looked to the guard standing at Susan's back. The man shrugged. "This man takes you back. Go now, or things get unpleasant."

"But first…" Susan turned toward the suspicious door. "Cassie! Nicki!" she shouted in a voice loud enough to fell a tree. "Are you here?"

"Help!" The cry came from the back room. A woman's voice.

Alevras froze for a moment. The cry had torn the veil from the masquerade.

The guard stepped toward Susan and raised his Uzi as Alevras yelled for back up. Susan whirled around and knocked the guard's weapon to the side, then ducked behind a row of chairs just as the backroom door swung open. The barrel of an automatic weapon protruded from the doorway. Susan reached for her gun.

She shot the guard in the shoulder, snapped around, and fired one round into the door jamb. As the weapon withdrew, she started to dash for the front door. But another guard suddenly appeared in the doorway, his Uzi cradled to shoot. Susan shot him and wheeled around. She leapt over the yellow ticket counter, crashed into the wall behind it, and slid to the tile floor, gun still in hand.

The room vibrated in silence, like the shocked moment after an earthquake. Crouching, controlling the adrenaline coursing through her blood with steady breaths, Susan listened for Britt's arrival. What the hell had happened to her? Now she was trapped. She heard an animated exchange in Greek. Receding footsteps. A rustle.

Susan lifted her head for a quick peek. A guard had plucked a grenade from his vest and was looping his finger into the pull ring.

Susan ducked back down. She grabbed a stapler from under the counter and threw it several meters away from her, hoping to draw the guard's aim there. A small click sounded. *The grenade is live.*

⊡ ⊡ ⊡ ⊡

Britt launched another 180-degree turn as the engines of the *Praxis* cut out. Only seconds from shore, she focused on her approach despite the shouts coming from the yacht's deck.

A series of whining reports rent the air and then a *plop-plop* as two holes burst through the sail. Britt heaved the mylar sheet around. She dropped it into the water when the board scraped the stony bottom and uncoupled the mast.

The *Praxis* crew was lowering a small motorboat, and several armed men were waiting to jump into it.

Britt released the bungee cords binding the bottle to the aft foot strap. She scrambled up the rocks, carrying the sail, and secured it against the fence. She tossed the bottle over the fence then glanced toward the sea. Raffa, soaked with sea spray, was perched at the prow, barking orders.

On the other side of the fence, a Cessna 208 Cargomaster sat fifty meters away. Workers had finished loading crates on the plane and lingered by the left wing looking seaward at the commotion from the motorboat. Another hundred meters away, the terminal glowed in the bright lights of the airstrip.

Britt glanced at her watch. *Damn. Five minutes late.* She had to move now, and hope Susan was already at the terminal. And hope the men from the *Praxis* would not find her within their sights. Suddenly, a pop sounded across the airfield, then several more. *Gunfire.*

⊡ ⊡ ⊡ ⊡

The guard drew back his arm to lob the grenade over the ticket counter where Susan crouched. Before he could bring his arm forward, two bursts of gunfire dropped him to the floor. The grenade rolled under a plastic chair.

Alexander Stamos ducked behind a pillar as the grenade exploded with a bang that reverberated off the walls. Stamos ignored the sting of several cuts from fragments flying through the waiting area. Behind him, the glass in the front door he had come through moments earlier shattered, and shards skidded across the front sidewalk.

"Susan!" Stamos cried. "Susan!"

"Here!" she called. She looked over the ticket counter and scanned the room.

Theo Alevras cowered against the wall, doubled over.

Cassie, hands raised, emerged from the back room, her face ashen, her eyes wide.

"Stop!" Bob Collins yelled, one hand grasping the collar of Cassie's shirt, the other holding the Beretta to her head.

◫ ◫ ◫ ◫

An explosion inside the terminal shattered a plate glass window. The men standing by the plane shouted to one another. Britt saw them gallop across the tarmac toward the terminal. Raffa and his crew had not yet landed.

Taking a deep breath, she made a running dash toward the fence, scrambled up the sail, her feet finding quick purchase on the rib-like battens, and jumped over. Britt landed in a roll and, without stopping, jumped to her feet. She grabbed the bottle of petrol and dashed to the Cessna where she stuck her head through the open doorway. Rows of crates and boxes lined the fuselage. "Cassie! Nicki!" she shouted. No one answered. The plane was deserted.

Britt unscrewed the cap from the plastic bottle of gas and doused two of the three tires. Dark rivers stained the concrete, and the biting odor of petrol permeated the air.

Steady, steady. She drew the box of matches from inside her wet suit. The first strike broke the match. The second strike lit and held. She tossed the tiny flame on the left tire. With a whooshing sound, it burst into a glorious blaze. The fire rolled across the asphalt to the second wheel and engulfed it. The intense flash of heat penetrated Britt's wetsuit.

Britt saw Raffa and two of his crew scurrying over the fence to head her off. She had only one place to go.

Britt spun around and raced toward the terminal, her black mane wet and wild. As she reached the side of the building, the plane drooped to the tarmac on its melted tires. It wasn't going anywhere. Britt knelt on the brick-hard ground behind a service vehicle to catch her breath and steady herself for the next step.

42

From a Gulfstream overhead, Mikos Zerakis looked down on the mayhem—the black smoke pouring from under the Cessna, now listing like a sinking ship. People dashing around like madmen. Zerakis prayed to the powers of the Trinity that no one had been hurt, especially his beloved Nicki. Nor those poor American girls. "Set down on the northern edge of the airstrip," he told the officer, who relayed the orders to the pilot.

Zerakis had a dozen soldiers on board, a special tactical team pried from the Army. He'd had to call the President for them, who first refused, then agreed when Zerakis threatened to share with the press not only the name of the President's mistress, but certain photographs that had fallen into his hands. Zerakis grimaced. He had traded much for the President's help, revealing information that could have been useful another time, and he had done it all based on the intelligence from the U.S. Embassy and CIS. If the life of his favorite goddaughter had not been at stake, he would never have gotten involved. Politics being what they were, if CIS and Susan Marcello's hunch about smugglers had been wrong, the President would have ruined him over this escapade. But they had been right. The evidence lay below him.

The pilot circled once, closely observing the northern end of the runway. On the next pass, he set down the aircraft, bearing the white and blue of the Greek flag. He taxied as close to the terminal as he dared. Before the wheels stopped, the door flew open, and the twelve heavily armed men scrambled out. Zerakis waited inside until the area was secure before descending the stairs.

◙ ◙ ◙ ◙

"No! No! No!" Theo Alevras screamed, staring dumbfounded through the now shattered window facing the airstrip as the plane's nose sank to the ground. He seemed oblivious to the blood streaming down the side of his face from a cut on his forehead.

A Gulfstream rolled into view. It turned toward the terminal and slowly moved across the tarmac through the black smoke coming off the Cessna's tires. The jet parked a short distance from the terminal, its door facing away from the building.

Cassie stared at the scene. "It's over, Bob," she said. "Let us go."

"We've got the *Praxis*!" Collins shouted. "Get moving, Theo!"

Alevras slowly wheeled around, his jaw slack, his eyes glazed. "We? *I* have the *Praxis*."

"She's not going with you," Susan said, her gun still pointing at Collins.

"Think again!" Collins tightened his grip on Cassie's shirt.

"Ow!" Cassie cried as her collar bit into her neck. "Let me go or kill me now!"

"My pleasure," he said.

"Stop!" Alevras cried, pointing his handgun at Collins. "You said I could have her!"

Collin sneered. "Sorry, Theo." He shot Alevras, who fell to the floor with a howl.

◙ ◙ ◙ ◙

Britt carefully crept next to the whitewashed wall, which glowed harshly in airfield lights. Slowly, she leaned her head toward the gaping window. The sight nearly made her knees buckle: Collins in a rage, holding a gun to Cassie's head.

Britt grabbed for the closest projectile in sight—a baseball-sized black rock. Gripping the stone with all fingers, she eyeballed her target and went into a quick wind up. Just as Bob flicked the automatic in Theo's direction, she released the rock and watched it sail toward its target.

The gun went off, clipping Theo in the arm. The rock hurtling toward Collins struck him in between his shoulders. He staggered, releasing his grip on Cassie's shirt, and dropped the gun.

Susan plucked the Beretta from the floor and kept her own gun pointed at Collins, then at Alevras.

"Do something! Do something!" Alevras yelled at his men. He pressed his bleeding arm with one hand, and the other, holding his gun, shook violently.

But his security force was helpless. Stamos had herded together the ones still standing and had disarmed them.

Britt ran through the broken window just as the tarmac door splintered open and Zerakis's men entered. The lead soldier, in a black beret, yelled for surrender. But the action was over.

Zerakis strutted in, calm, but wearing a worried expression.

"Good to see you, Mikos," Britt said, springing forward.

"Where is Nicki?"

"Over there," Cassie said, stepping forward. She nodded toward a door where Nicki leaned, dazed, against the jamb. "She's been roughed up."

"I fight and live," Nicki called out, raising a fist. A large knot on her forehead had been added to her cuts and bruises.

Zerakis called out to a soldier, who rushed over with a first aid kit. "You fix her," he ordered, "then she goes on my plane back to Athens."

"Mr. Zerakis?"

Mikos Zerakis turned to face a woman in a black leather jacket.

"I'm Susan Marcello from the U.S. Embassy."

"Ah, yes." Zerakis took her outstretched hand and pumped it. "We meet at last."

"This is Alexander Stamos," Susan said, motioning toward her companion. Their brief nod revealed their acquaintance.

"Come on, Cass," Britt said, taking her elbow, "let's go outside and leave this mess to the pros." She mouthed, *we'll be back* to Nicki, who nodded, then gave herself over to medical inspection, protesting she did not need it even though she seemed close to collapsing.

When they reached the door leading to the airstrip, Britt fingered Cassie's blood-soaked sleeve. "What happened here?"

"Cut myself in Bob's car." Cassie patted the wound gingerly. "It's okay. It stopped bleeding ages ago."

At first the night air hit them like a splash of water, cool and invigorating. Then came the smell of gasoline and burning rubber. The Cessna sagged pitifully at the far end of the runway.

"How are you?" Britt asked.

"I'm kind of shocky, actually," Cassie said.

"You're white as a wave tip." Britt pulled Cassie into her arms. Their foreheads touched. "It's over, sweetheart."

Cassie let out a sob and clung to Britt. After a few moments, she tilted back and inspected her. Her web of black hair held streaks of sand. Smudges of soil linked themselves across her face like camouflage paint. "Am I as filthy as you are?" she said, brushing dirt from Britt's cheek.

"No, you're beautiful as ever." Britt's eyes were teary. "I was so afraid I had lost you."

"I didn't know what had happened to you. Bob said his men would get you." Cassie clasped Britt to her chest. "Honey, you're shivering."

"I'm wet and cold, halfway in shock, and having an adrenaline crash."

"Come on," Cassie said, "I have a pullover inside and maybe we can find some blankets."

▣ ▣ ▣ ▣

"There you are!" Susan Marcello called when she saw Britt and Cassie pick their way through the terminal wreckage. She looked from woman to woman, concern in her eyes. "Do either of you need medical attention?"

"Britt's about to go into hypothermia," Cassie said.

"Let's find some blankets and get you out of here. This scene will take all night to straighten out. Alex and I can debrief you in the morning."

"Wait," Britt said. "My board's down on the beach. How do we get it back to Kamari?"

"Your board? You windsurfed here?" Cassie seemed to grasp for the first time why Britt was wearing a wetsuit. "Of course, you did." She touched the fabric.

"Yeah. A two-front attack."

"I don't believe it. And this?" she said, pointing to the disabled Cessna. "Is that your doing, too?"

"Yep."

Cassie just shook her head in disbelief and exchanged a smile with Susan.

"Don't worry about the board," Susan said. "I'll make sure you get it back."

After a quick check-in with Nicki, Britt and Cassie climbed into the backseat of Susan's car. They pressed together, fingers entwined, heat blasting from the vent.

Susan glanced at them occasionally on the dark ride back to Kamari, caught them kissing, and leaning their heads together, wrapped in blankets. Not bad for civilians, she thought. *Not bad at all.*

43

"Your place, Britt?" Susan Marcello drove down the main street of Kamari.

Britt caught Susan's eye in the mirror. "Cassie's would be better." She preferred the room with the double bed instead of hers with two singles. But then she turned to Cassie. "Or would it be traumatic for you?"

Cassie thought a moment. "No, no, it'll be okay."

Susan did not miss the hesitancy. When the three got out of the car, Susan ordered them to stay in the lobby.

She slipped down the corridor to Cassie's room, gun drawn. The door was unlocked. Susan opened it. The lights were on. The unit was empty. Other than the bed, which was in disarray and had a purse and its contents scattered about, the place was in good order. Susan opened the French doors to let in fresh air—the room smelled of fear.

"All clear," Susan reported to Britt and Cassie, who had settled on a sofa in the lounge, the airport blankets under them to protect the cushions. Britt was wearing Cassie's fleece top over her swim bra, the upper half of her wetsuit turned down at the waist.

Maria Bountourakis stood close by, hand over her mouth, as she listened to the terror at the airport. She offered a soft handshake to Susan when they were introduced. "I worry so. Sophia tells me about Bob and Theo. I cannot believe it. And now this...." She gestured at Britt and Cassie.

"These are two brave women," Susan said solemnly.

"Come on," Britt said as she stood and reached down a hand to Cassie. "Let's get cleaned up. I'm exhausted."

"Me, too," Cassie said.

"Go on," Susan said. "I have a few things to handle here."

▣ ▣ ▣ ▣

Britt stepped into the shower first, still in her wetsuit, and let the water wash the sand and salt from the exterior. With Cassie's help, she peeled off the suit, rinsed the inside, and tossed it into a corner. They shampooed each other's hair and gently washed their bodies, letting the hot water sluice off the night's terror. They kissed softly, then deeply, trying to ground themselves in the moment. They were alive.

When they emerged from the shower, they saw two white robes on the vanity. The bathroom door, which they had left open, was now shut. They draped the wetsuit over the shower door, dried themselves, and slipped into the robes. They opened the door to a transformed room. The bed had been made with fresh linens. A scented candle burned on the nightstand. Two steaming mugs sat on the desk.

Susan had shut the French doors and closed the drapes. She sat in the corner chair, jacket off, holster and gun in full view, scribbling in a small notebook. "I was just writing you a note," she said, looking up. Her smile was warm, her eyes concerned. "Feeling better?"

"Yes," Britt and Cassie said in unison.

Susan nodded toward the mugs. "Maria made hot chocolate for you with a healthy splash of Irish cream. It'll help you sleep."

"Thank you," Britt said. "For everything." Her voice grew husky. "You saved us."

"It was a team effort," Susan said, rising. "Now I should get back to the airport. Alex and I will stop by in the morning for your statements. Get some sleep."

▣ ▣ ▣ ▣

They embraced. They kissed. They inspected wounds and bruises. They said "I love you" a dozen times. Their lovemaking was subdued, fitting for lovers who knew the fragility of their lives, whose flesh could be torn, whose life-force could flow away in an unstoppable stream.

But sleep eluded them. They replayed the evening's events over and over.

"How could I have been so stupid about Bob?" Cassie cried at one point. "I dated him! I slept with him! Why didn't I see through him?"

"Don't blame yourself, sweetheart," Britt said. "He was a charmer—like so many sociopaths—and a professional criminal. He had everyone fooled, including me."

"You were jealous of him."

"Maybe."

"I'm a bit jealous of Susan," Cassie confessed. "I think she likes you."

"Yeah, right." Britt ran a finger along Cassie's jaw. "I think she's complicated."

Cassie brought Britt's hand to her chest. "Do you work for her? Are you CIA?"

"No. To both questions. I was just helping her out."

"Not that it would make any difference." Cassie sighed. "I'd love you no matter what."

"Can you believe the way Susan pampered us tonight? I believe she's smitten with you, my Aphrodite," Britt teased.

Cassie laughed for the first time that evening. "I'll be looking for the recruitment letter. After all, I may soon be out of a job."

44

"How was Nicki when you left?" Mikos Zerakis asked, signaling Britt and Cassie to sit in his Athens office the following Sunday afternoon. He took his place in his favorite chair—a Queen Anne with burgundy leather. Susan Marcello resumed her seat after standing for the women's entrance and giving them each a hug.

"Fine." Britt grinned. "The nurses hover over her like mother hens."

"Good. She deserves such attention."

"Despite having a concussion, she seems quite cheerful," Britt said.

Zerakis laughed. "She is a fighter. Now we need to find her a husband."

Britt refrained from mentioning that Nicki was getting special attention filled with romantic possibilities from a nurse named Helen. "I think a medal of bravery would be more appreciated," she suggested.

"Perhaps you are right," he said, giving Britt a knowing nod. He rose from his chair to fix drinks. "A gin and tonic?"

Britt and Cassie nodded.

"What have you found out about Bob Collins?" Cassie asked Susan. "Ugh, I hate even saying his name."

"His real name is Arthur Henley," Susan said. "He worked for one of the largest arms merchants in the Mediterranean for years before going into business for himself."

"But there was a real Bob Collins," Britt said. "What's the connection?"

"College roommates. The genuine issue was an archaeology student. Henley probably got the idea of posing as an archaeologist from him. Clever approach, using various excavations around the Mediterranean as bases of operation. They gave him the perfect excuse for hopping from one country to another, sewing up a network of arms buyers."

Zerakis handed Britt and Cassie G&Ts.

"Henley came close to succeeding, and he would have, without your intervention, Britt," Susan said. "He had a great partner in Colonel Dimitris Alevras—ruthless, with his tentacles stretching into every major Mediterranean port." She accepted a freshened scotch and soda from Zerakis.

"A man with a long reach," Zerakis said, reclaiming the Queen Anne, "but with a fool for a son. Our police press Theo just a little"—he pinched together a thumb and forefinger— "and the boy cries for his mama."

"He blurted out enough to convict them all, including the military and airport officials who were bribed," Susan said, "and he's promised to testify in court. Even against his father, who claimed he knew nothing and had been dining on octopus at his club in Heraklion that night."

"Too bad he did not choke," Zerakis said. "It would save the trouble of a trial."

"What's going to happen to Henley?" Britt asked Susan.

"He's up on several charges, including the murder of Bountourakis and illegal arms trading. In the plane at the airport, we found measuring devices used in the production of chemical weapons and precision triggers for various types of bombs."

"They were going to Cyprus?" Britt asked.

"Actually, the plane was stopping there only for fuel and some additional cargo. It was scheduled to go on to the Middle East—to this year's Number One troublemaker."

"But we stop them." Zerakis smiled. "And for that, we thank you."

"The cooperation between our embassy and the Greek government won't be forgotten," Susan said. "At least not until the next political roosters get their tail feathers in a bunch." She winked at Zerakis.

Zerakis said nothing, but wore the thin, ambivalent smile of a true politician.

45

July

Two weeks later, Nicki, her new girlfriend Helen, and Britt waited for Cassie on the terrace of a restaurant in Thera. They relaxed in the shade of a bright blue umbrella, tipped to the southwest to protect them from the punishing early afternoon sun.

"I'm glad you were able to stop over for a few days," Britt said to Nicki. "I hope you have a marvelous time in Rhodes."

"Thanks. It will be a good honeymoon, eh?" Nicki winked at Helen, who smiled back shyly.

Helen's shoulder-length brown hair had blond highlights, and her smile was quick and warm. She sipped a lemonade and watched a tour boat nudge its nose into the pier on one of the caldera's islands. "Your project is done?" she asked.

"Yes," Britt said. "Cassie has six more weeks on her project."

"You are sorry to leave?" Helen asked.

"I'll stay a few weeks more, but then I need to get back to Minneapolis to prepare for fall semester."

"Will Cassie join you?" Nicki asked.

"She's looking at options. Computer engineers are always in demand."

"What about windsurfing?" Nicki teased. "Does she give it up for Minnesota?"

"It's a detail to be worked out, although…" Britt hesitated, loath to jinx her future. "I'm hoping for a job offer in California. I have several feelers out."

"Feelers?" Helen asked.

"Inquiries. Hopefully, leading to a position with a tenure track."

A chair scraped nearby as Cassie wove her way through the crowded terrace, giving a subdued smile to the table.

"Well, here you are," Britt said, searching her face. "How did it go?"

"It's over. That's the best part. I've never had to fire anyone, but Jim was expecting it." Cassie rested her hands on the back of an empty chair. "He leaves this afternoon for the States—without Irene—and the museum programmer has now officially stepped into his position. I'd say the transfer went well, all considered."

"And Dr. Gavas?"

"He's still furious at Jim and the Kazantas clan."

"It was an ugly situation all around," Britt said. "I didn't like forcing the issue, but ethically, I couldn't stand by and pretend nothing had happened."

"Deep down, I know Jim is relieved to have come clean," Cassie said. "He's got some mending to do with his reputation, but honestly, almost any firm in Silicon Valley will snap him up in a heartbeat."

"What do you have there?" Britt asked, pointing to a bag.

Cassie held up a tote with the Fira Winery logo on it. "A gift from Sophia Delopsos for our trip. Two bottles from her private stock. It's the good stuff."

"Yummm. What a sweetheart."

"The newly restored proprietor of the winery is in high spirits these days." Cassie grinned. "The Alevras family is out of her hair, she's bringing quality back to the wine, and…" She paused dramatically. "It looks as if things are getting serious between Sophia and Dr. Gavas. He's been quite solicitous since all the trouble."

"Eros is going to run out of arrows," Britt said impishly.

"Never." Nicki grinned. "That quiver is magical."

"I'm glad things are working out for Sophia," Britt said. "She was crucial to our finding you and Cassie in time."

"Yes," Nicki said. "She is one of the heroes of the night." What she did not say, could not say, was that her godfather had a soft spot for widows. The fingers of Mikos Zerakis had been busy behind the scenes securing control of the Fira Winery for Sophia Delopsos.

"I'm going to build her a cutting-edge website," Cassie said, "to attract customers to an updated wine tasting bar."

Britt checked her phone, recovered from the Seaside maid who had been Theo Alevras's accomplice. "We should be on our way, Cass."

"Got our bags?"

"Over there, in the corner."

"So, this is goodbye?" Nicki asked, a wistful twist to her mouth.

"For now." Britt kissed Nicki's cheek. "But we're leaving you in the best hands possible. Take care of her, Helen, okay?"

Helen smiled. "With pleasure. I like to take care of my Nicki."

Britt and Cassie broke away. "Have fun!" Britt cried over her shoulder.

"And do everything we're going to do!" Cassie called. She turned to Britt with a playful smile, her blond hair holding a ring of light in the bright sun.

Nicki and Helen remained on the terrace, sipping their drinks and ordering dessert.

"You have good friends." Helen slid her chair around to be closer to Nicki.

"I'm lucky." Nicki grasped Helen's hand. "In many ways."

"No." Helen stroked the skin alongside the red scab on Nicki's forehead, the last vestige of her abduction. "Here you are not so lucky."

Nicki held Helen's hand to her cheek. "My concussion brought me to you. For that, I treasure it." Suddenly, sitting with her beloved in a restaurant embedded in a cliff, and having spent time with two extraordinary friends, Nicki knew true happiness. The gears of her life were meshing at last.

回 回 回 回

Two hours later at Athinios port, Britt and Cassie stood at the stern of the ferry to Crete where they planned to hike gorges and enjoy the fine cuisine of the island.

"At last," Cassie said, pressing Britt into the railing, "I have you alone."

Britt observed the sunny deck strewn with students leaning against backpacks and sprawled on sleeping bags. "Ahh, we're not alone, Cass."

Cassie jostled Britt's shoulder. "You know what I mean."

"Yes. It's a relief to escape the craziness. At least for a while." Britt looked up at the soaring cliffs to the north and the white-washed buildings of Thera sparkling in the sun. "Just think, Cass, thousands of years ago, Minoans could have been high above us on the mountainside harvesting their grain, putting it in baskets to take home and to turn into loaves of bread."

"Now this." Cassie swept her arm toward Thera. "The scar in Mother Earth has been transformed. Shops and restaurants and hotels—and people's homes—engineered into a rock face. Life goes on."

"We've had our moment of glory and lived." Britt leaned into Cassie. "Our story won't be taught in classrooms three thousand years from now, but I have you. Alive. That's all that matters."

"Alive because you came after me on a windsurfer. You're as wily as Odysseus."

"God forbid I'm anything like that unfaithful scoundrel."

"Ha!" Cassie cried. "Who's flying back to America in two weeks, leaving me alone?"

"My dear Penelope," Britt said, "come to Minnesota when your job's done here." She covered Cassie's hand on the railing. "We'll figure out the rest."

"We seem to be good at that—reading the waves and riding them."

"And jumping back on when we fall off." Britt smiled. "Or maybe I should say when *I* fall off. You never do."

"Unless you're in the vicinity distracting me."

Britt laughed and snuggled closer to Cassie.

"Here's another possibility," Cassie said. "Join me and my parents in California over Labor Day weekend. My mom's dying to meet the woman who windsurfed to my rescue…and into my heart."

"Meet your parents? Cassie Burkhardt," Britt said, "you never cease to surprise me."

Cassie peered into those dark eyes that had captivated her from the beginning. "My perpetual wave," she said, pulling Britt into her arms.

They kissed long and deep, as the salty breeze swirled around them, and the chatter of excited voyagers and the sharp cries of circling gulls faded into the background.

Breaking away, they grinned and leaned against the railing until the ship cleared the crater. Once in the open waters, they moved to the forward deck, where they could see their route, invisible on the dark waters of the Mediterranean to all but them.

Acknowledgements

A big thank you to Beta readers Linda North, Kitty Johnson, and Tess Imholt. Their suggestions were invaluable. Cheyenne Blue's meticulous editing and witty commentary made revising a pleasure. The Carefree Writers' Circle provided a perceptive sounding board. Proofreaders Sherron Smith, Sara Fleming, Kelly Flanagan, and Heather Peters deserve a special round of applause.

Special kudos to Sara Yager for the stunning cover. It inspired me to rewrite the novel to be worthy of her artistry. The lovely interior design is her doing as well.

Most of all I want to thank my wife Nancy Manahan, a.k.a. the goddess Meticula, for her support at every phase of this project. She cheerfully discussed my concerns about character and plot development with scrupulous insight. Our sessions of read-out-loud line editing not only polished the prose and lifted the novel to a higher level, they embodied our fun and productive partnership.

Finally, a special call-out to friends Rita Clifford and Sara Jane Elliot, whose love of Greece and its cuisine (*more Retsina anyone?*) continues to be a shared pleasure.